The Dragon Slayer's Daughter

Robinne Weiss

Book 2 of the Dragon Slayer series

Published by Sandfly Books

ISBN-13: 978-0-473-43258-4

Cover Illustration: Brendon Wright

This book is also available in electronic formats.

Discover my other books and stories on my website:
https://robinneweiss.com

To my dragon-hearted friends.

One

Dad didn't use the term dragon slayer much. He preferred to call himself kaipatu tarākona. He thought it sounded better in te reo Māori. He said Māori had been managing dragons in New Zealand for centuries before Pakeha, Europeans, came. He told me his people—our people— were brave warriors. His nickname for me was Māia— courage.

I certainly felt courageous when we returned to school that bright summery day. My friends and classmates, Nathan, Ella, Oliver and I had found Nathan's dad, rescued him, and gotten rid of the evil headmaster, Professor Drachenmorder, and the soulless Sir Christopher. We'd met and worked with dragons, spending almost two weeks with them. And when Sir Leandro told us he needed our help to change the Alexandra School of Heroic Arts from a dragon slaying school to a dragon *saving* school, we all felt like heroes.

It wasn't until late that night, back in the dorm room, that the feeling wore off. By the time Ella flicked on the light, I had already punched a hole in the wall by my bed.

"It's. Not. Fair!" With each word I delivered a punch. "Why. Not. Mine!"

"Tui! What are you doing? Stop it!" Ella grabbed my arm as I swung it again.

1

"Get off me!" I shoved her hard and punched the wall again. "It's. Not. Fair!"

Though we were both thirteen, Ella was a head taller than me. I was still a wiry kid, but she had filled out and was practically adult-sized. She might have been able to pin me down and stop me, but I think I scared her at that moment. Looking back, I scared myself. Ella backed off and blinked at me, then dashed out the door.

I kept punching the wall. "It's. Not. Fair! Why. Not. Mine!"

I was surprised when a firm hand grabbed my wrist and held it, stopping it in mid-swing. I tried to pull away. I might have growled.

"Tui." Professor West's steady voice made me look up.

I blinked at him through my tears. "It's not fair!"

"Tui, you need to stop. We need to take care of your hand."

I looked at my torn and bloody knuckles and suddenly felt the pain. I saw the hole in the wall and Ella's worried face. The fight went out of me, and it was all I could do to put one foot in front of the other as West led me out of the room.

"Professor?" Ella stood with her arms wrapped protectively around herself.

He stopped. "Ella, give me a minute or two to deal with Tui's injuries, and then will you please come to the dining room? And bring Nathan and Oliver with you. You have my permission to go wake them. Try not to disturb any of the other boys."

Ella nodded, and Professor West guided me down the steps into the darkened atrium.

We crossed the dining room in the night-time emergency lighting, and the professor lowered me onto a chair, then turned on the kitchen lights. Light spilled out of the serving window and pooled where I sat. He brought a first aid kit from the kitchen and pulled a chair over to face me.

"Let's see the hand." I held it out for him. It was shaking. Blood welled from every knuckle and dripped to the floor.

Professor West talked as he cleaned and bandaged each finger. "My father went on his last mission with another dragon slayer. When things went badly, they activated their locator beacons. Can you hold that in place right there?" I pressed my left hand over the wad of gauze on my knuckles while Professor West rummaged in the first aid kit for bandages. "When Search and Rescue got there, my father was already dead. Okay, you can let go." He dabbed at the blood on my hand and then opened a bandage, wrapping it around my index finger. "His partner survived."

I sniffed, and Professor West pulled a tissue from his pocket and handed it to me. He opened another bandage and smoothed it around my middle finger.

"Two days later I kicked a hole in my bedroom door. Mum tried to stop me." He opened a third bandage. "She yelled at me, and pulled at my arm, but by then I was taller than her. I kept kicking the door." He wrapped my pinkie. "Finally she slapped me." He chuckled. "I was so startled by it, I stopped kicking."

With a strip of gauze, he wrapped the knuckles on the back of my hand, tucking the end under my palm. Then he held my hand in both of his, and part of me marvelled at how naturally he used his prosthetic right hand. "Some people live and some die, and there's no fairness in it. But please, if you're angry, come talk to me. I understand how you feel. I felt the same thing, and I got through it. Punching holes in the wall doesn't help."

I finally met his eyes. The last of my anger fizzled, and a fresh wave of tears poured down my cheeks, but I managed a weak smile. "Thanks for not slapping me."

Professor West smiled.

The door to the dining room opened, and Ella entered, with Oliver and Nathan following. They slowed as they neared me. Professor West waved them over, and I quickly swiped the tears from my face and sat up straight, covering my bandaged hand with the other.

"Why did you tell them to come?" I muttered.

"You four need to talk." He stood. "Pull up some chairs."

My friends formed a small circle and sat. Oliver clutched his stuffed cat Pooky, looking even younger than his eight years. Ella gazed at me sadly, and Nathan wouldn't meet my eyes. Professor West stepped behind my chair and rested a hand on my shoulder. I shrugged him off.

Oliver pushed a lock of his dark hair out of his eyes and blinked in the light. "What's going on? Tui, what happened to you?"

West held up his hand. "You kids have all been through a lot the past couple of weeks. The past six months," he added, and I knew he meant the loss of our parents. We wouldn't have been at the Alexandra School of Heroic Arts if we hadn't lost a parent to dragons—we were supposed to be training to take their places as dragon slayers. West continued. "Tui has been through more than the rest of you, of course, with both her parents having been dragon slayers. It's understandable what she's feeling—"

"I'm fine," I said. "I'm not feeling anything."

Ella snorted. "*It's not fair? Why not mine?* You're angry because Nathan got his dad back and you didn't." She shrugged. "Of course you are. So am I. So is every other kid in the school. It was on everyone's faces when Sir Leandro explained what happened."

Oliver examined his feet.

4

Nathan frowned and lowered his head until his messy ginger curls hid his eyes. "I'm sorry."

"I'm fine. I'm not mad. I'm glad Nathan got his dad back." I swallowed hard. Ella was right, but I wasn't about to admit it, and I resented her ability to read my—everyone's—emotions. I was Tui Rahui. A warrior. I didn't need any touchy-feely rubbish.

"I don't blame you for being upset, Tui," Oliver said, still looking at the floor. "It's true. We do all feel the same." He cast a worried look at Nathan.

Nathan grimaced. "I'm sorry."

I'm sorry. I'm sorry. It wasn't good enough. It didn't bring my parents back. I felt the rage rising again, and I wanted to punch Nathan like I'd punched the wall.

"It's not your fault, Nathan," Ella said.

"No. It's not." Professor West laid a heavy hand on my shoulder, like he knew what I was about to do. "Nathan is not responsible for your parents' deaths. But Ella is right. Every student will be thinking, 'Why couldn't it have been *my* dad rescued?' Every student will be jealous of Nathan. Some will blame him for what happened to their own parents."

My anger simmered for a moment, then drained away again as I watched Nathan. He had shrunk into himself. He blinked furiously and studied his slippered feet. How would I have felt if every kid in the school hated me because my parents *weren't* dead?

"I ... I'm sorry." He took a deep breath, then continued. "Thank you all for helping to rescue my dad. Without you ... without you he would have been killed. Tui, what you said to me on the top of Mount Crosscut—that we'd find my dad, and then make sure no other kid had to lose a parent to dragon slaying again—that's what I intend to do." He looked up at me, and though there were tears in his eyes, there was also a challenge. A warrior's challenge.

"Nathan's difficulties, our difficulties, have only just begun," Professor West said. "The question is, will you allow your pain to turn against you, or will you direct it into something positive? Will you allow jealousy to tear your friendship apart, or will you embrace what life has dealt you?"

Another warrior's challenge. I blinked back tears. I glanced down at my hands, one clenched in a fist, one bandaged to immobility. I breathed in, looked up, and unclenched my fist. I reached out to Nathan. "Let's do it." We grasped hands, and I turned to Ella. She reached out and put her hand over mine and Nathan's. Oliver grinned as I met his eyes. He joined in. I met their eyes, one by one. Warriors. All of them.

Two

I felt awful in the morning. My hand throbbed, and I had a headache. I growled at Ella when she shook me awake. "Leave me alone!"

"It's breakfast time. And Sir Leandro wants to meet with us at nine."

Sir Leandro, acting headmaster until Nathan's dad took over in the new year. I couldn't exactly ignore a meeting with him. Besides, it must be important if he was pulling us from end-of-year exams for it. Eyes still closed, I flipped the covers down, willing myself to get up.

Ella hovered by my bedside. "God, your hand looks awful!"

I sighed and opened my eyes, holding the aching hand up. Even bandaged, I could see it had swollen and turned black and blue overnight. No wonder it hurt. Some warrior I was—beaten by a wall. I swore, and then hauled myself out of bed.

Five minutes later, Ella and I slid into seats across from Oliver and Nathan in the dining hall. Nathan barely looked at me. "Hi."

"Whoa! Look at your hand!" Oliver exclaimed. I scowled at him, but he grinned back, and I struggled to maintain my scowl. "Think of all the awesome stories you can make up about that injury!"

Nathan glanced up enough to see my hand and winced, but then a smile crept to his lips. "You *did* fight Sir Christopher and Drachenmorder and a bunch of wildlife smugglers two days ago. You could make up a great fight story about your hand."

"We don't need to embellish that fight. It was crazy enough all on its own." I shuddered at the memory and ran my finger over the cut left by Sir Christopher's sword on my neck.

Nathan finally met my gaze. "Are you okay?" He had bags under his eyes, and his face was set in a grimace. He looked as bad as I felt, and my flash of anger at his question fizzled.

I took a deep breath. "Yeah. I'm okay."

We were silent for a while as we ate. The dining hall buzzed with the other students' chatter. Then Nathan observed quietly, "Notice how no one is sitting next to us this morning?"

"Yeah, and they're all trying to watch us without seeming to stare," Oliver added.

Ella barked a laugh. "It's because they're terrified of us."

"Why would they be afraid?" I asked.

Ella rolled her eyes at me. "Think about it, Tui. We vanish from school, and return along with the news Drachenmorder and Sir Christopher are dead, Nathan's dad is alive *and* will be the new headmaster, and the school is going to start training us to *save* the dragons, not slay them?"

"But Sir Leandro didn't say anything about our role in all that when he met with the students yesterday."

"Tui, we all look like we've been in a war." Nathan raised his bandaged hand, where he'd been bitten by a baby dragon we had rescued. He waved it toward Oliver's face, black and blue where he'd been punched, and Ella's arm covered in scratches. "The other students aren't stupid. They know we had something to do with it."

"Speaking of which …" Ella made a slight motion with her head, and I followed the movement to see Hunter Godfry stalking our way.

I groaned. "I don't think I can deal with Hunter today." If Hunter had only been the school bully, it wouldn't have been too bad, but he was also Drachenmorder's nephew. When Drachenmorder wanted to find out what we'd been up to with our secret group, the Dragon Defence League, he'd encouraged Hunter to beat up our friend Josh until Josh dobbed us in.

Nathan frowned. "We rescue my dad, and his uncle ends up dead."

"Something tells me this isn't going to go well," Oliver said.

As Hunter neared Nathan and Oliver's side of the table, the four of us stood. The room fell silent.

Hunter stopped a step away from Nathan, narrowed his eyes, and then punched Nathan in the face.

The watching students gasped, and I leapt onto the table with a roar, scrambling to get to Hunter and tear him to pieces.

"Hunter Godfry!" Miss Brumby's voice boomed across the room. Everyone froze as the cook strode from the kitchen holding a large wooden spoon like a club. She waved the spoon at Hunter. "Kitchen. Now. I want every inch of that floor spotless, and then you'll go to the headmaster's office."

Hunter sneered. "And what if I don't?"

Miss Brumby waved her spoon and opened her eyes wide. "Then I'll think up an even more unpleasant punishment." Miss Brumby wasn't quite as tall as Hunter, but no one in their right mind would stand against the fury rolling off her. Hunter smirked at Nathan, clutching his nose, and then followed Miss Brumby into the kitchen.

I jumped off the table and clenched my fists, feeling the injured one throb. "Next time I want to punch a wall, I'm going to punch him instead."

"Are you okay, Nathan?" Ella hurried around the table.

Nathan nodded. "I think so," he mumbled through his hand.

"Is it bleeding?" I asked.

He nodded again.

I growled and turned toward the kitchen. I nearly ran into Miss Brumby. "Don't go making it worse by hitting him back, Tui." Had I been that obvious? She wagged a finger at me. "I'll happily make you scrub the floor alongside him." Then she held an ice pack out to Nathan. "Here. Put that on your nose. It'll help. And here's a paper towel for the blood."

Miss Brumby marched back into the kitchen. Nathan sank into his chair, the ice pack pressed against his face.

"Well, that was exciting," Oliver said.

Ella frowned and looked around the room. The other students had gone back to their breakfasts, and were again studiously pretending to ignore us. "Have you noticed Joshua's gone?"

I glanced up sharply. "Is he?" I scanned the room. I hadn't given a thought to Josh for weeks. "You don't think Drachenmorder … did something to him for being part of the Dragon Defence League?"

Ella shrugged. "I don't know. We'll have to ask Sir Leandro."

Ella, Oliver and I sat again and picked at our food, no longer interested in eating. After a few minutes, Nathan lifted the ice pack and wiped his nose.

"I think it's stopped bleeding. Doesn't hurt too much anymore, either."

"Well then, let's get to the meeting with Sir Leandro." I stood, and the others followed.

We stepped out onto the porch of the Lodge as an unfamiliar dark blue sedan drove up and stopped, raising a cloud of dust that wafted slowly away on the breeze. A woman stepped out of the car, notebook and pen in her hand.

"Excuse me." She flashed us a smile. "Is this the Alexandra School of Heroic Arts?"

I flicked a glance at the others. The school was supposed to be secret, like the dragons we studied.

Nathan shrugged, as if to say, *well, she knows about it*. He turned to the woman. "Yes."

"Can we help you?" Ella asked, sounding distinctly like she didn't want to help this woman. I didn't blame her. Something about this lady rubbed me the wrong way, even though she'd only said half a dozen words.

The woman smiled. "Then you four must be students." When we said nothing, she continued, her smile a little strained now. She held out a hand to Nathan. "I'm Katie, from *The Press*."

We darted wide-eyed glances at one another.

"The school isn't open to the public," I said.

"I'm here to ask a few questions. Everyone's so curious about what goes on here."

Ella raised her eyebrows. "Everyone, huh?"

"I'll go get Sir Leandro," Oliver said. He ran for the staff chalets. The rest of us crossed our arms and stood our ground, effectively pinning Katie against her car. Her eyes darted back and forth, as though looking for an escape. Then she pasted a professional smile back onto her face.

"Who is Sir Leandro?" Her pen was poised above her notebook.

"He's …" I glanced at Nathan.

11

"He's the headmaster," Nathan said.

Katie's pen scribbled and her eyebrows rose. "And you kids call the headmaster *Sir*? I thought that was only for knights."

None of us answered. She cleared her throat.

"So. This seems like a very nice place." She cast her eyes over the main building we called the Lodge, and then up the drive at the little chalets that housed the staff. "Very ... ski-lodge-like. Is this where you students live? There must be room for, what, forty students there?" She gestured to the Lodge.

I suppressed a smile as none of us rose to her bait. We simply stood, staring at her and waiting for Sir Leandro.

"What sort of *heroic* things do they teach you here?"

Silence. I could tell we had unnerved her. Her breathing was shallow, and she licked her lips. Then she took a deep breath, leaned in and hissed, "I hear there are dragons living up here in the mountains. Real, live dragons. And this school has something to do with them. Is it true?"

I struggled not to react. I could feel Ella and Nathan tense next to me. No one but trained dragon slayers were supposed to know the animals existed. I worried Katie could read the truth in our eyes. Then movement distracted me.

"Here comes Sir Leandro," I said. I smiled a little as I watched him stride toward us, Oliver jogging at his heels. Like most of the school staff, Sir Leandro was a retired dragon slayer, taken off active duty due to injuries. Sir Leandro had lost an eye and an ear, and one side of his face was a mass of scars that pulled his mouth into a half-grimace. He was terrifying the first time you saw him, before you learned to read the sense of humour and compassion in his good eye.

Katie straightened up and her eyes went wide for a moment before she regained her composure. As Sir Leandro neared, she plastered a smile on her face and clutched her notebook to her chest.

"You must be the headmaster," she said, holding out a hand.

Sir Leandro shook her hand. "And you are?"

"Katie Garner, *Press* reporter. I was just speaking to some of your students here."

"Oh?" Sir Leandro's gaze flicked briefly to us.

"They're not particularly talkative, though."

Sir Leandro's good eye crinkled. "No. I expect they're not."

Oliver stifled a giggle.

"We've heard some very interesting rumours about the Alexandra School of Heroic Arts, and I was wondering if I could ask you a few questions."

"You can *ask* whatever you'd like." The suggestion that Sir Leandro might not answer the questions was clear from his tone.

"Um. Okay. Do you have an office where we could sit and talk?"

"Whatever questions you have, you can ask them right here." Then Sir Leandro looked at us. "Thank you. I assume you were on your way to the meeting. Archie will be joining us. Tell him I'll be a few minutes late."

We nodded and quickly headed toward the staff chalets. Once out of earshot, I asked, "How did a reporter hear about dragons? And the school?"

Nathan grimaced. "I hope we didn't have anything to do with it."

I hadn't considered the possibility, but we'd flown all over the place on the green dragon Foggy Bottom during our hunt for Nathan's dad. Could someone have seen us?

"We were careful," Ella said. "I can't believe we gave them away."

"We're not the only ones who know about dragons, either," Oliver reasoned.

I sighed. "It was bound to happen sooner or later."

"Yeah, but if it's happening soon, we can't sit around and wait for it," Ella said. "Not unless we want to see all the dragons slaughtered by every bloke who thinks killing a dragon will make him a hero."

We reached the chalet to find the door propped open to the summer morning. I glanced at Sir Magnus' desk in the reception area, but it was empty. A heavy thud and a curse came from the headmaster's office. We stepped into the chalet and peeked around the corner.

"Oh! Kids." Sir Magnus, the school's secretary, accountant and all-around handyman stood on top of a ladder, frowning down at a mounted dragon head lying on the floor, one of its spines broken off. "You didn't hear me swear just now, did you?"

"We heard nothing," Oliver said with an innocent look.

"Cleaning out Drachenmorder's things?" Nathan asked.

Sir Magnus nodded. "Not sure where I'm going with all this stuff. But Sir Leandro and your dad don't want it in here." No surprise. Who would want mounted dragon heads—Drachenmorder's hunting trophies? They made me shudder, knowing those dragons were once thinking, feeling, talking creatures.

"We were supposed to meet with them this morning," I said.

"Yes, of course. In the kitchen. Go on through."

We thanked Sir Magnus and pushed our way into the kitchen.

Nathan was wrapped in his dad's hug by the time I stepped through the door. I clenched my fists as a spike of rage shot through me. Nathan hugged him back, but then extracted himself with a shrug and a red face. I took a breath and forced my fingers to uncurl.

"Have a seat." Sir Archie waved at the chairs around the dining table. "Magnus says Leandro stepped out a minute ago."

"Yeah," Oliver began. "There's a reporter here."

Sir Archie's eyebrows rose. Nathan nodded. "She's heard about dragons and about the school."

I pulled out a chair and sat. "We need to do something. If she publishes a story about dragons …"

Sir Archie sighed and joined me and the others at the table. "Well. This changes things." He looked around at us. "As you all know, I've been working with Storm Cloud to convince the dragons to work with me to end dragon slaying and reveal dragons to the public."

"But Storm Cloud said if people knew about dragons, they'd either panic and try to hunt them all down, or want to control them," Ella argued.

Sir Archie nodded. "Exactly. And that's why we want to reveal them ourselves—so we can protect the dragons with legislation before their existence becomes public, and control the publicity around them to minimise public panic."

Sir Leandro entered and we broke off the conversation to ask about the reporter.

"She's gone. For now."

"What did you tell her?" I asked.

He chuckled. "Very little. She drove off in a huff. The problem is, she knows enough already to make trouble."

"What are we going to do, Sir Leandro?" Ella asked.

Sir Leandro grimaced. "Please don't call me that. Just Leandro is fine."

"You can drop the Sir from my name, too," Sir Archie added. "No more dragon slayer titles."

"So, what are we going to do?" Ella repeated.

Leandro and Archie looked at one another and smiled. "That's exactly why we called this meeting," Leandro said.

"What? You knew a reporter was going to come snooping around this morning?" Oliver asked.

Archie sighed. "No. That was a surprise. But it doesn't change what we wanted to talk to you about. It only makes it more urgent. We'd like you to stay on at school after the other students leave for the holidays tomorrow. We need your help."

We all sat up straighter.

"I've been talking to Storm Cloud for years about ending dragon slaying and revealing dragons to the public. It's never gone beyond Storm Cloud and me, despite my best efforts to engage with the Draconic Council. But you four? Within days of meeting Storm Cloud, you convinced not only him, but the entire Draconic Council to work with you, to seek me out and rescue me. And in the process you revealed their vulnerability to them."

"What do you mean?" Nathan asked.

"As long as dragons are secret, they're at risk. As long as there are no human laws or codes of conduct around dragons, any unscrupulous person who happens to know about them can exploit them without fear."

"You mean hunting and wildlife smuggling?" Ella asked. We'd seen plenty of both in the past few weeks. Drachenmorder's illegal trophy hunting had been bad enough, but then we found out a wildlife smuggler, Ling Chang, was stealing dragon eggs for the international pet trade.

"Exactly. You can bet Storm Cloud and the other dragons are sitting in their lairs right now brooding about that. We need to strike while the iron is hot. We—you—

need to go back to the dragons and work out an agreement with them."

"An agreement to go public, and be protected by human law?" I asked.

"You want *us* to do that?" Oliver's eyes were wide.

"Over the summer?" I asked.

"When you couldn't do it in … ten years?" Nathan asked.

Ella's eyes narrowed. "Is this going to involve camping?"

I smiled, and as I looked around at my friends' faces my smile grew into a full-body laugh. We were being sent back into the mountains. Back to the dragons. The warrior in me swelled. "I'm in."

"Me too!" Oliver piped up.

Nathan grinned and nodded.

We all raised our eyebrows at Ella. She sighed. "Yes, I'm in."

Three

It was weird being at school after all the other students had left. The Lodge felt cavernous. My footsteps echoed in the empty dining hall when I went down for breakfast. Miss Brumby was the only one there. The smell of eggs and bacon wafted from the kitchen.

"Good morning, Tui," Miss Brumby called. "I thought you kids might like to eat with the staff, instead of sitting all by yourselves in here. The others have gone to the headmaster's chalet."

"Thank you, Miss Brumby. Do you need help carrying anything over there?"

Miss Brumby smiled. "No. Magnus has already taken it all over. I'm cooking up a little something for myself now."

I hurried out of the dining hall. When I reached the front door, I paused. A gusty wind drove rain across the drive between me and the chalets. I considered going back upstairs for my raincoat. Then I shrugged. It wasn't that heavy; I wouldn't get too wet if I ran.

Squinting against the rain, I sprinted down the steps and pounded up the drive.

Suddenly, a scaly leg the size of a tree trunk blocked my way. I yelped in surprise as I nearly ran into it.

A rumbling laugh rolled like thunder through my chest. "Scared you, did I?"

I looked up. "Storm Cloud!"

"Tui. Nice to see you again." The enormous green dragon lowered his head and huffed in my face. The warm blast made steam rise from my wet clothes.

"What are you doing here?" I stepped a little closer to Storm Cloud, letting his body block the worst of the rain.

"I came to check on little Archie and invite him to a Draconic Council meeting next week. Is he here?"

"Yes. I was just going to join him and the others for breakfast." We walked together to the headmaster's chalet. When we arrived, I turned to Storm Cloud and smiled. "I'd invite you in, but ..."

The dragon chuckled. "I don't think I could even get my head through the door."

"I'll be out in a minute with Archie," I said as I mounted the steps.

Archie wasn't the only one who came to the porch with me a moment later. Everyone wanted to say hello.

"Archie!" Storm Cloud's voice boomed as Archie stepped out the door.

"Greetings, your Majestic Green—"

"Oh, cut it out. You know I hate those stupid titles." There was amusement in his voice, and Archie smiled. Storm Cloud lowered his head and sniffed at Archie. "You smell well."

"Yes, I'm well, thanks to you and these kids." He waved his hand at us.

"Hi Storm Cloud," Oliver said, stepping up and patting the dragon's leg. Storm Cloud twitched a little at the touch.

Nathan and Ella greeted him too, but neither patted Storm Cloud.

"What are you doing here?" Nathan asked.

"I came to check on young Archie and make sure you all got back safely. I've also come on behalf of the

19

Draconic Council. In light of recent events, we've called a meeting for next week. We intend to discuss a number of matters, including the future of this school."

I grimaced. "By 'the future of this school', do you mean you're going to discuss whether to burn it to the ground?"

"Yes."

Well, at least he came right to the point.

Archie spoke up. "You should know, Storm Cloud, that with Drachenmorder gone, Leandro is now acting headmaster. Provided the board approves, I will take over as headmaster in the new year. The school will be changing."

"All the more reason you should be at the Council meeting. There is a growing feeling among the dragons that the school needs to go. I alone won't be able to convince them to spare you."

Archie sighed. "I'm supposed to be meeting with the board all next week. We've called an emergency meeting, and they've all cleared their schedules."

"So change your meeting. Tell the board they won't have a school to govern if you don't attend the Draconic Council meeting." Storm Cloud's voice took on the edge it had had the first time we met him—an edge more than a little menacing, coming from a thirty-metre-long dragon.

"If the dragons threaten the school, how am I going to convince the board to change the nature of the school to dragon conservation? You're making a good case for the need for dragon slayers."

"And how am I to convince the Draconic Council you are genuinely changing, that you're trustworthy, if you won't show up to a meeting?" Storm Cloud huffed and a gout of flame shot from his nostrils. We all took a step back.

"We'll go," Nathan said. Ella's eyebrows shot up, but Oliver nodded.

"That was the plan, wasn't it?" I added. " preparing to spend our summer negotiating dragons."

"But you're not fully prepared yet," Professor West said.

Oliver shrugged. "It didn't stop us last time."

Nathan nodded. "Yeah, we're a whole lot better prepared than when we left school to rescue you, Dad. At least we won't have to run out the door in the middle of the night."

"And," I added, "With that reporter out there, we need to do this quickly. We can't postpone Archie's meeting with the board, and we can't postpone a meeting with the Draconic Council. We *have* to go."

Archie opened his mouth, as if to protest. Then he shut it again. He met each of our gazes, assessing us, no doubt. I stood straighter and set my jaw. Archie sighed. "What do you think, Storm Cloud? Will the Council accept the children's word on behalf of the school?"

Storm Cloud's eyes narrowed. Now it was his turn to assess us. I crossed my arms and glared at him. "Humph! I suppose they'll have to."

Oliver grinned. "Yes!"

"So, when's the meeting?" Nathan asked. "And where?"

"And how will we get there?" Ella added.

"Thursday night. Prospector Peak. I'll come get you. Arriving with me will help your credibility."

"Can you guarantee their safety?" Archie asked.

"No more than I can guarantee yours, Archie. But as long as they keep their wits about them, they should be fine."

With less than a week to prepare, there was no time to waste. We knew the Draconic Council meetings were held in Draconic, and our skills in that language were still rough. We spent every minute either practising Draconic or planning our strategy for the meeting. By Wednesday, as we sat at the big table in the library with our Draconic-English dictionaries, we were at each other's throats.

"*Zhe vilknit blinch drunig,*" Ella said.

I frowned. "What?"

"Speak in Draconic. It's the only way we'll learn. *Zhe vilknit blinch drunig.*"

"I don't understand. What are you saying?"

"Ask me in Draconic. *Zhe vilknit blinch drunig.*" Ella scowled.

I gritted my teeth. "Just. Tell. Me. What. You. Are. Saying."

Nathan jumped in before it came to blows. "I think Ella is saying *the weather is pleasant today.*"

Oliver grimaced. "But it should be *blinchne* because weather is feminine."

Ella turned her scowl to Oliver.

I clenched my fists. "Why are you practising talking about the weather? There are more important things we need to learn to say."

Ella huffed. "We need to be able to be polite, to hold a conversation. We can't simply go in, blurt out our plan, and leave. Honestly! Don't you take this seriously?"

"I *am* taking it seriously. But when I still don't think I have the vocabulary to talk about the issues we're meeting to discuss, I think it's a waste of my time to practise chatting about the weather."

"Well, I think it's important to be able to carry on a proper conversation."

"Good on you, then!" I shoved back my chair and stood.

The door flew open.

"Well, then. This looks like a good time for a break," Magnus called as he strode into the room. He had a cheery smile on his face that told me he knew we were all on edge.

I crossed my arms. "What sort of break?"

"I've been authorised to take you four to the movies in Alexandra this afternoon."

"But we have work to do!" Ella cried. "We're not ready for the meeting tomorrow."

"And fighting about whether *blinchne* is masculine or feminine isn't helping you get ready." Magnus gave us all a stern look. "Miss Brumby says you didn't even show up for lunch."

"Is it past lunch?" Oliver asked.

"See? You're working too hard. I'm taking you to the movies, and that's that."

We looked at each other and shrugged. He was right. We needed a break.

"It might involve ice cream afterwards, too." Magnus winked.

"All right! Ice cream. What're we waiting for?" Oliver jumped up and started gathering up the books and papers we had strewn across the table.

Ella sighed. "I still think we should work more on our Draconic."

"If you want to practise, you could order your ice cream in Draconic," Oliver said with a grin.

Ella stuck her tongue out at him.

Magnus raised a finger. "No Draconic in public. You all know that."

As we followed Magnus out the door, Nathan said, "Is there even a word for ice cream in Draconic?"

"Not likely," Ella said.

I snorted. "If there is, it's something weird like, *sweet frozen udder liquid.*"

Four

Thursday evening, the four of us waited for Storm Cloud on a small rise above the school. Technically, Storm Cloud was supposed to return us to school after the meeting, but we had come prepared to camp for the night, just in case the meeting ran long and Storm Cloud couldn't get us back before dawn. Each of us had a pack with some food, water, and a change of clothes. We hadn't bothered with tents.

"We'll just spend the night with Storm Cloud if we have to," Oliver suggested, his eyes sparkling.

"As long as I don't have to eat rabbit, like last time we stayed with him," Ella agreed.

I frowned. "We should be prepared for anything. We should take tents."

"I checked the weather forecast," Nathan said. "Even if we have to spend the night out, I don't think we'll need tents. It's supposed to be fine, and not too cold. I'd rather go light."

I shrugged. He was probably right. We'd spent a night out without tents before. And anyway, most of the night would be taken up by the meeting. If we had to sleep out, we'd be sleeping during the day. A snooze in the sunshine actually sounded pretty nice.

Ella yawned. "I hope I can stay awake for the meeting."

"If it's as exciting as the last one, you'll have no problem," Oliver said. "Look! Here he comes."

Spiralling down in the darkening sky was the unmistakable form of a dragon.

"That's not Storm Cloud," I said with a frown as the dragon neared.

"You're right," Nathan agreed. "It's too small."

The dragon spiralled closer.

"It's Foggy Bottom!" Oliver grinned. Foggy Bottom was one of the two dragons who had come with us on our quest to rescue Archie.

As Foggy Bottom made her final descent, we scattered off the top of the hill to give her room.

"I thought Storm Cloud was supposed to pick us up," Nathan said once the dragon had landed.

Foggy Bottom snorted. "Not even a hello? How about, 'Hi Foggy Bottom, nice to see you'?"

Nathan blushed. "Hi Foggy Bottom. It *is* nice to see you."

Foggy Bottom snorted, and Nathan stepped backward as a puff of smoke shot out of her nostrils. She raised her head. "Well, are you ready to go?"

We clambered onto the dragon's back, and she lifted heavily into the air.

"So, why did you come for us and not Storm Cloud?" Nathan asked as we got underway.

"Storm Cloud is dealing with a … a situation."

"What sort of situation?" I asked.

Foggy Bottom huffed. "Nothing you need to worry about. A couple of dragons who don't want the Council to negotiate with humans. They showed up at Storm Cloud's lair earlier today, and the conversation got a little heated."

I could imagine what that was like. Heated wasn't a figurative description when it came to dragons. The Draconic Council meeting we attended while searching for Archie had ended in flames.

Foggy Bottom continued. "He lost track of time and was so out of sorts when I arrived at his lair, I volunteered to come get you."

"Thanks," Oliver said.

The rest of the flight passed in silence. Talking on dragonback is difficult—rushing wind makes it hard to hear and, for most of us, holding on and not freaking out took all of our concentration. When we reached Prospector Peak and slid off Foggy Bottom's back, Ella was pale. "Next time, we come on horseback."

"I thought it was awesome!" Oliver said. "We should go everywhere on dragons. I especially liked it when she swooped down to catch those ducks on the wing!"

Ella shuddered. I shook my head. "You are completely insane, Oliver."

It looked like all the other dragons were on the peak by the time we landed. Storm Cloud's enormous form stood out, but I also saw a pair of blue dragons and several other suspiciously dragon-shaped humps in the darkness. As we got our bearings, a small form flitted around our heads. I smiled. Here was our second companion from Archie's rescue.

"Nathan! Tui! Ella! Oliver!" The little dragon's scales glinted in the moonlight.

"Rata! How are you?" Nathan asked.

Rata settled on Nathan's shoulder. "I'm great. How's Archie? Has he recovered?"

"Yeah, he's fine. He's—"

"Ahem!" Storm Cloud gave Rata and Nathan a fierce look, his tail lashing. "If you're done with your chitchat, we'll call this meeting to order."

I leaned close to hear Rata whisper, "Watch out for old Stormy today. He's in a mood."

"Thank you all for coming," Storm Cloud said. "Special thanks to Nathan, Tui, Ella and Oliver for joining us." We nodded to Storm Cloud, and then at each of the dragons as he introduced them all. "From the southern blue dragons, we have Bluette and Bluebottle. Representing the Fiordland fringed dragons, we have Night Stalker and Dawn. From the gold fairies, we have Rata and Kowhai. Of course, Foggy Bottom and I represent the green dragons. And Jade and Flint represent the scree dragons this evening. You've all met one another, except Flint." He indicated a smallish scree dragon I'd mistaken for a rock.

"Greetings, Flint." We nodded in his direction. He stood and seemed to flow like a rockslide toward us. I gritted my teeth and submitted to his sniffing greeting. At least the other dragons didn't feel a need to sniff us like they had last time.

"Flint replaces Rocky on the Council."

"What happened to Rocky?" Oliver asked.

Storm Cloud's tail thrashed. He snorted, and a gout of flame puffed from his nostrils.

I jabbed Oliver with my elbow. "What were you thinking?" I hissed.

"I was just asking. I thought I was being polite," he whispered back.

"Rocky visited me earlier today, along with two other scree dragons, Gneiss and Greywacke. They are unhappy with the Council's decision to meet with representatives from the School of Heroic Arts. They believe we should incinerate you, rather than negotiate with you."

I swallowed and shared a frightened glance with my friends. Did the scree dragons know where the school was?

"I didn't agree with him," Storm Cloud continued. I heard Ella's sigh of relief. "We had ... words. In the end, I removed him from the Council. And I removed him from my lair." The dragon's laugh, punctuated by a blast of fire, made my scalp prickle. "He and his companions will be licking their wounds for some time."

27

Storm Cloud never let us forget we were dealing with dragons. I cast my eyes around, noting the best escape route, should we need it, and the closest shelter from flame and claw.

"I told you he's in a mood," Rata whispered.

"At least he didn't agree with Rocky," Nathan replied.

"The purpose of this meeting," Storm Cloud continued, "is to discuss the ramifications of the rescue of Archie McMannis, and what we learned in the process."

Nathan spoke up. "If I may …" He was right to be nervous, but Archie had made it clear we needed to start the meeting off properly if we were to gain the dragons' respect and support.

Storm Cloud turned to Nathan. "Yes?"

Nathan stepped forward. "I'd like to start the meeting with a thank you from all of us, and from my father. Without you, we never would have found him. Without your help, none of us would have survived. We would especially like to thank Storm Cloud for your leadership in coordinating the dragons' help." He bowed his head slightly in Storm Cloud's direction—a sign of respect among dragons. "We would also particularly like to thank Foggy Bottom and Rata for putting yourselves in danger to help us." He bowed toward Foggy Bottom with a smile on his face. Rata was still perched on his shoulder, and she gave him an affectionate nip on the ear.

"Nathan, your thanks is duly acknowledged, but we hope your thanks goes beyond words."

"It does." Nathan took full advantage of the chance to explain more. "The reason Dad couldn't be here is that he's currently meeting with the school's governing board. His goal—our goal—is to change the school's focus from dragon slaying to dragon conservation. We want to train up a whole group of people committed to helping you, to preserving your lives and cultures."

"And what sort of influence does young Archie have with the board? And at the school? He has never been affiliated with it."

Oliver piped up with a grin. "He's going to be our new headmaster!"

"And the remaining staff at the school are behind him," I added. I wasn't sure this was entirely true. Professor Marshall, the grumpy horsemaster, could potentially cause trouble, but I doubted he would act on his own.

"Why should we need your help?" Jade asked. "We've done fine without you for a long time."

"Yeah, why don't you simply abandon the school and leave us alone?" Flint added.

Rata flitted off Nathan's shoulder to land on a large rock at the centre of the circle of dragons. "For you scree dragons, it might work … for now. It's not a good long-term solution, though. We can't hide forever, even if we wanted to. Once our presence is generally known, we're going to need allies among the humans."

Jade snorted. "Real dragons don't need human help. Maybe you pathetic miniature dragons do, but—"

"Just because we're small doesn't mean we're not real dragons. Yes, it means we're more vulnerable to human predation, but we're not the only ones at risk."

Foggy Bottom spoke up. "It's true. Searching for Archie, we uncovered the presence of wildlife smugglers who are targeting dragons of all sizes. They're well-outfitted with tranquilliser guns and modern weaponry, and they're fully capable of capturing an adult New Zealand green. We're all at risk."

"But allying ourselves with dragon slayers?" Night Stalker asked.

"They've been our sworn enemies for hundreds of years," Bluette said. "What makes you think they're going to help us now?"

"Why should we agree to anything with people who've been persecuting us for ages?" Bluebottle asked. "Not to mention how they almost wiped out the seals we eat."

"And don't forget those climbers who come poking around everywhere, invading our homes," Flint added. "No doubt they'll want to keep doing that."

Ella, who had been watching and listening with a frown on her face, stepped forward and put her hands on her hips. "When did dragons become a bunch of whingers? I thought you were supposed to be fierce."

I cringed. Ella had proven she could hold her own against dragons, but I wondered if she'd gone too far, calling them whingers. "Did you think humans were going to simply lie down and take it when you burned villages and ate people and livestock? Should we have just said, 'Well, dragons are predators; we should let ourselves be eaten'? If you live by the claw, you should expect to die by the sword."

"Are you supporting dragon slaying, then?" Dawn asked, rising up from her crouch and snaking her head toward Ella.

"No. None of us supports dragon slaying." Ella waved her hand toward Nathan, Oliver and me. "That's why we're here. It's time for us all—dragons and humans—to stop acting like animals. We're better than that. We're intelligent and able to negotiate. We don't need to kill each other to address our differences." She frowned and looked pointedly at Flint. "At least, I thought so. Now I'm not so sure. *We've* come to this meeting in good faith. If *you* haven't, then we can simply leave and let you fend for yourselves. We know how well *that's* gone in recent times. And if you think you can stay hidden forever, think again. What do you plan to do when the public finds out about you, and it's more than just the wildlife smugglers up here with guns?"

The dragons shuffled uncomfortably. I darted a glance at the nearest boulder, calculating how quickly we could take cover behind it.

Storm Cloud cleared his throat. "Ella has a point. We're here because the current state of affairs cannot continue. We're here because Archie and his friends have reached out to us in good faith. Though we have been foes, the relationship between dragons and dragon slayers has always been one of honour and respect. How can we keep that respect if we respond to this overture with violence?"

I dared to breathe again. If Storm Cloud was still speaking up for us, we would be okay. I hated to admit it, but whiny Ella knew how to play on the dragons' emotions. I almost laughed as I considered it. Ella was an awful lot like a dragon herself—a bit self-centred and keen on comfort, with an explosive temper. No wonder Storm Cloud had called her a *blarghstra*—the Draconic term for a bossy, overbearing female.

"So, what sort of agreement would you like to negotiate?" Foggy Bottom's question snapped me out of my thoughts. This was my part. We'd each practised the important bits of our negotiations so we wouldn't misspeak anything in Draconic.

I stepped forward. "Before we discuss the details, let me outline our goals. These negotiations, and the agreements we come to within this group will have implications around the world. Our ultimate goals are the protection of dragons worldwide and the complete elimination of dragon slaying." Murmurs broke out among the dragons, and I paused for a moment to let them die out before continuing. "First, though, we must start locally. We want New Zealand to become a model for how dragons and humans can work together for mutual benefit. First, we aim to create a dragon conservation corps. We will re-train former dragon slayers and train new recruits from within the dragon slaying community to be part of this corps. The dragon conservationists will work alongside dragons to ensure dragon populations are healthy and robust, and dragon habitat is protected. Second, we plan to establish a binding treaty between the New Zealand government and dragons ensuring protection for both humans and dragons. Third, we want to reveal the existence of dragons to the public—" I was cut off by rumbles of dissent and snorts of fire. I raised my voice over the ruckus. "We want to reveal the existence of dragons in a controlled manner, only after legal protections are in place. We believe public support is critical for dragon conservation efforts, as it has been for the protection of many other species worldwide. With good public support, the public becomes a watchdog, helping to detect and prosecute any who defy the conservation laws and treaties."

"That's preposterous!" Flint stepped forward and glared at me. "Dragons have always been kept secret from the public. If humans all knew about us, they'd come swarming around, either to kill us or to gawk."

"That's why we want to have the legal protections in place before we go public," Storm Cloud explained. "Archie and I have spoken of this often, and he has convinced me of the need to break the secrecy surrounding our existence."

"And you think some words on paper are going to protect us from the likes of Drachenmorder?" Bluebottle snorted. "Yeah, right."

Emboldened by Storm Cloud's support, I spoke up. "A hundred years ago, the New Zealand fur seal was nearly extinct—hunted, as you pointed out, Bluebottle, by humans. Less than forty years ago, laws were passed to protect the seals. Now there are hundreds of thousands of them, and their population is growing every year. Laws work."

32

"And I still find seals killed by humans," Bluebottle retorted. "In spite of your silly laws."

Ella gave an exasperated sigh. "Of course there are people who don't obey the law. The point is, most people do obey. And if there is a law against it, people can be punished for breaking it. Don't you dragons—"

Ella's words were cut short as Foggy Bottom suddenly leapt toward us spouting flame. Ella screamed and dropped to the ground. Nathan, Oliver and I dived away from the oncoming dragon.

As I hit the ground and rolled, I saw Foggy Bottom land practically on top of Ella. What was she doing? I thought Foggy Bottom was on our side. I reached the boulder I'd been eyeing earlier and turned back. It took me a moment to make sense of what I saw. Foggy Bottom was standing over Ella, her wings outstretched. Her flames lit a smaller dragon barrelling toward her. Was that Flint? No, not coming from outside the circle of the meeting. Movement behind Foggy Bottom caught my eye, and I focused on it in time to see another dragon leap onto Storm Cloud's back. The Council meeting was being attacked.

By scree dragons.

Flint and Jade looked around wildly, like they didn't know who to support—the Council or the attacking dragons. Flame and growls filled the air. I couldn't tell how many dragons were attacking, or where they were coming from. I suddenly realised my boulder wasn't offering me any protection—a dragon could be creeping up on me from behind. I turned and squinted into the darkness.

A yelp drew my attention. Oliver and Nathan were in flames, rolling away from a blast from an attacking dragon. No. No. No! This wasn't supposed to happen. We had been *invited* to this meeting. Why were we being attacked? Couldn't Storm Cloud control the dragons? I clenched my fists. I had to do something. But I had no weapons at all; we'd purposely left behind anything that could be construed as threatening.

The dragon was advancing on Nathan and Oliver again. Nathan had managed to extinguish his burning clothes, and was scrabbling on hands and knees to Oliver, who screamed in terror as he tried desperately to beat out the flames on his pant legs. Neither of them saw the approaching dragon.

Flames lit the night, and I found an arsenal of weapons at my feet. I picked up a particularly jagged rock and hurled it at the dragon bearing down on Nathan and Oliver. It missed, and the dragon kept moving. With shaking hands, I grabbed another rock and lobbed it. It struck the ground in front of the dragon, and the animal jumped back in surprise. Determined not to miss this time, I snatched up another rock and started running toward the dragon as I threw it. Direct hit, right on the snout. I scooped up another rock. Yes! Another hit. The dragon snarled and turned toward me. I skidded to a halt. Now what? Not daring to look away from the dragon, I bent and scrabbled around with my hands for another rock. I came up with nothing.

The dragon advanced. It hissed, as though laughing at me. I couldn't blame it. What did I think I was going to do barehanded against a ten-metre-long dragon armed with fire, teeth and claws? I stepped backward, trying not to show how terrified I was. Think! What could I do? Ella would have turned on her *blarghstra* act and insulted the dragon until it backed down. I couldn't seem to remember any Draconic at the moment. My brain felt frozen. My limbs moved of their own accord, and I staggered away from the oncoming beast. I stepped on a loose rock, and it rolled. I sprawled onto my bottom, and the dragon lunged.

Then a rock came winging out of the darkness, pegging the dragon on the head. I scrambled to my feet, picking up the rock that had tripped me and hurling it at the dragon. It bounced off its shoulder. Another rock came flying from the right, and I saw Nathan advancing, picking up rocks as he came.

The dragon swung its head toward Nathan and blasted him with fire. Nathan jumped and rolled deftly out of the way, exactly as we'd been taught to do in our dragon slayer training.

But watching that dragon try to torch my friends lit a fire inside me. Anger flared and swallowed my fear entirely. I grabbed the biggest rock I could and heaved it like a shot put at the dragon. I didn't even wait to see if it hit; I snatched up another rock and started toward the animal with a snarl. I fired angry words with each rock I threw, not giving the dragon a moment to react.

"You! Vile! Beast! That's! My! Friend!"

None of the rocks did much damage individually, but the constant barrage made the dragon stagger back. I advanced slowly, pushing the dragon back a few more steps. I didn't know how long I could keep up the hail of rocks. At some point, I'd run out of ammunition within easy reach.

Then something heavy shoved me from behind and pushed me forward onto my knees. Terror returned for a moment, until I saw what had knocked me down.

Storm Cloud thudded to the ground between me and the scree dragon. One swipe of his front claws and the scree dragon went tumbling down the hill. His tail thrashed and whacked me on the side, knocking me face-first onto the rock in my hands. I tasted blood. I swiped my hand across my mouth and it came away dark.

"Tui!"

I looked up to see Ella atop Foggy Bottom. She was waving me over. I staggered to my feet and ran between burning tussocks to climb onto the dragon.

"What about Oliver and Nathan?" I asked. "They were burned."

"We're picking them up now," Foggy Bottom assured me. She half ran, half flew to the lee of a large rock. Nathan and Oliver lay beside it. Oliver was sobbing, and Nathan's eyes were shut in a grimace. Ella and I slid off Foggy Bottom's back and crouched over the boys.

"Oliver? Nathan?" I tried to keep my voice steady, but wasn't sure I managed.

"Can you get up?" Ella asked. Her voice definitely shook.

Nathan silently nodded and sat up, wincing.

"I don't know," Oliver said. "It hurts!"

Seeing the ever-cheerful Oliver in tears lit that fire inside my chest again. I wanted to jump up and run after the dragon who had done this. I wanted to scream insults at it before running it through with a sword. Instead I swallowed hard and looked at Ella. "You and Nathan go back to school. Tell Leandro we need help."

"Why don't you set off the locator beacon?" Ella asked.

I shook my head. "No point. They can't fly the helicopter up here at night anyway. And they know where we are. I'll stay here with Oliver. Leave me your water bottles—I'll try to cool his burns as best I can through the night."

Nathan was clearly in too much pain to process what was going on. Ella grabbed our packs, which we had left in a pile where we'd landed. She tossed all four beside me. "Take everything. We'll be fine."

Then she helped Nathan onto Foggy Bottom's back, and they were off.

I jumped as claws suddenly gripped my shoulder.

"Sorry," Rata chirped. "Didn't mean to scare you. I'm here to keep watch. I'll let you know if anything's coming." The tiny dragon flitted to the top of the rock beside us.

"Thanks, Rata." I hated the way my voice shook. At least Rata was a friend. I pulled out a water bottle and fumbled with the cap. It wouldn't open. My hands were shaking too much. My whole body was shaking. *Come on. Hold it together, Tui. You're a warrior, remember?* I closed my eyes and took two deep breaths, willing my body to stillness. I still felt quivery inside when I opened my eyes again, but at least I was able to open the bottle. I couldn't see much in the dim light, but I poured the water where Oliver's clothes were most burnt. He hissed and cried out when the water first hit his skin, but then he seemed to relax a little. Maybe the water was helping. I tossed the empty bottle aside and pulled out a second. After the third bottle, I stopped. We would need something to drink.

"Hang in there, Oliver. You're going to be okay." His eyes were closed, and he made no indication he'd heard me. I blinked back tears. Was this how my parents had died? Burnt and in pain? I started shaking again, but this time it was anger. Dragons did this. Dragons were responsible for my parents' death, Oliver's dad's death, Ella's dad's death ... why should we risk ourselves to help them? All they'd ever done was kill people.

I jumped again as Rata flitted back to my shoulder.

"They're gone."

"Who?" I'd completely forgotten about the fight raging around me.

"The scree dragons who attacked us." Rata hopped to the ground beside Oliver. She gently nuzzled his hand. He didn't open his eyes, but he smiled.

"Hi Rata," he whispered. "Are you okay?"

"I'm fine. I'm staying with you and Tui tonight."

Oliver smiled again. "Thanks."

37

Rata thrashed her tail, and it was then I noticed half of it was gone.

"Rata! Your tail!"

"I'm fine." Rata gave me a warning look, and then hopped to my shoulder. "I'm trying to stay positive for Oliver. He doesn't need to know about my injuries," she whispered.

"What happened?" I mouthed back.

"Gneiss. His first target was you. I bit him on the snout, but wasn't fast enough to get away."

"He bit your tail off?"

"It'll grow back. Eventually." Rata sighed. She was particular about her appearance. Even once the bloody stump healed, she would feel the mar in her looks.

And she'd lost her tail protecting me. The seething anger inside my chest turned to a heavy weight that seemed to crush everything else in me.

"Thank you," I said.

"We dragons look after our own."

"I'm a dragon?"

Rata chuckled. "You're certainly dragon-hearted." Then she sighed and looked at Oliver. "I wish you kids *were* dragons, for your own protection. But, no. You're not a dragon." She turned her eye back to me. "You're a friend. Dragons look after their friends." She leaned her head against mine.

The heavy weight rose into my throat and I blinked hard.

The ground shook, and Storm Cloud was beside us. He looked down at Oliver and growled, smoke curling out of his nostrils. "Those scree dragons will pay for this." He huffed again and turned to me. "We have disbanded the meeting. We weren't going to get anywhere after that attack. I'll be meeting with each Council member individually over the next couple of days." He looked back at Oliver. "How will we get him back to school?"

38

"Foggy Bottom has taken Nathan and Ella back. I'll stay here with Oliver overnight, and the Dragon Slayer Search and Rescue helicopter should be able to pick us up in the morning."

"And I'm staying with them here," Rata added.

"Good. I'll keep watch from the top, in case the scree dragons return. I'll have to leave in time to get back to my lair before dawn, but it still gives you some time to rest without worrying."

"Thanks." Storm Cloud turned, and I saw the dark streaks where blood had dripped down his hide. He'd been attacked, too. Attacked for working with me and my friends. I tried to swallow my remaining anger.

Rata flitted back to Oliver's side. "Tui, he's shivering."

Shivering? Of course he was. I'd soaked him, and he was lying on the ground. What had I been thinking? I pulled out a sleeping mat and laid it on the ground next to Oliver. I spread one sleeping bag on top of the mat, for extra protection from the cold ground. Now, how was I going to get him on top of it? I hated to touch him—I didn't even know where the worst of the burns were. I thought for a moment, and then said, "Oliver. I'm going to try to warm you up. I want to get a sleeping mat under your body to get you off the ground. You don't need to do anything, but I'm going to roll you onto your side, slip the mat under you, then roll you back onto your back, okay?"

Oliver gave a weak nod. He whimpered as I rolled him over and back as gently as I could. When I had him on top of the mat, I threw a second sleeping bag over him. There was no way I was going to try to get him into a bag.

I was relieved when Oliver's shivering stopped a few minutes later.

"Do you have another sleeping bag?" Rata asked. For a moment, I thought she wanted one, and then I realised *I* was shivering now. Whether it was from cold or shock, I didn't know, but I was thankful Ella had left me all the gear. I laid out a second mat next to Oliver's and crawled into a sleeping bag. Rata settled herself, sphinx-like, on top of my stomach. "Sleep. I'll keep an eye on Oliver and wake you if he needs you."

I closed my eyes with a sigh.

Five

"What happened to your face?"

"What do you mean, *my* face? You've got no eyebrows!" I hugged Nathan, and then Ella. They'd run up the hill as soon as the helicopter had touched down at school.

"At least I don't look like a casualty of war." Nathan smiled.

"Give her a break, Nathan. You looked every bit as bad when we got back last night. She hasn't even had a chance to shower."

"How's Oliver?"

Professor West came up behind me. "He's going to be fine. He's at the hospital in Queenstown. His mum's with him. She said she'd let us know the details once they'd done a full assessment of his burns."

"Is—" West raised a hand, cutting off Nathan's question.

"How about we let Tui shower and have some breakfast first."

I nodded. Now that I was back at school and I wasn't trying to keep Oliver and myself alive on a remote hillside, exhaustion crashed over me. Tears, too, were threatening to leak from my eyes. I didn't understand why, and I certainly didn't want anyone to see them.

"Take the day to rest. All of you. We'll meet to assess the situation tomorrow. Archie will be back then, and he'll want to hear everything."

I nodded and trudged to the Lodge without speaking.

Ella was sitting on her bed in our dorm room when I came out of the shower. "Are you okay?"

"Just bruises and scratches, really." I shrugged. "Looks worse than it feels."

"No. I mean, are you *okay*? Nathan and I left you out there alone with Oliver last night, and—"

"I'm *fine*." How many more times was I going to have to say that? I ran a comb through my wet hair.

"Well, you're not acting fine."

"I'm tired and I'm hungry and, until five minutes ago, I was covered in blood. Of course I'm not acting fine."

I tossed the comb onto my bed, barged out of the room, and descended to the dining hall in search of breakfast.

I was glad to find the dining hall empty. I could hear Miss Brumby washing dishes in the kitchen, and I went to the serving window, where a plate of scrambled eggs, bacon and toast sat steaming beside a glass of orange juice.

Miss Brumby's face popped out from behind a rack of pots. "That's for you, love. Oh! You're a sight. How's that wee dag?"

I knew she meant Oliver. "He's in hospital. Sounds like he'll be fine, though."

"Oh, good. You eat all of that, you hear?" She pointed a soapy finger at the plate. "Protein is important for healing."

I smiled. "Thanks, Miss Brumby."

I ate in silence, replaying the events of the night in my head and wondering how Oliver was getting on. I took my dishes to the kitchen when I finished, and then headed out of the dining hall feeling a bit more human than I had before. I was still tired but, clean and fed, I felt a little bad about how I'd barked at Ella earlier.

I stepped into the atrium and found Nathan and Ella sprawled in armchairs. They sat up straight as I came in.

Nathan's eyes searched mine. "How are you feeling?"

I bit down on my angry retort and shrugged. "Better, now I'm clean and have had breakfast. Tired."

"Yeah, me too. We didn't get much sleep last night, either."

"So, there's nothing happening today?"

"That's what Leandro says." Ella propped her feet up onto a coffee table. "He says we should rest."

"And we're just going to sit around?" I thought I'd scream if I didn't do something. "The Council meeting was a fiasco, we were attacked by dragons, and Oliver is in the hospital. *And* that reporter's probably still out there gathering information about dragons. We need to regroup and plan what's next. We can't wait a day."

Nathan grinned at Ella. "See! I told you she'd say that." He clapped his hands together. "Right. So let's get to it."

I sat down on the couch opposite Nathan. "We've got to get back out there as soon as possible. Send the message to those scree dragons that we're not going away."

Ella frowned. "Do you think Archie and Leandro will let us?"

"You've got a point, Ella," Nathan said.

I laughed. "Will it stop us if they don't approve?"

Ella sighed and shook her head. "I don't want to go out there unprepared again, like we did when we rescued Archie—no food, no shelter, no nothing."

"If we make a new plan *with* them, they'll be more likely to approve," Nathan suggested.

I stood. "Then let's go make a plan."

Nathan smiled and rose. "And whatever they say, we argue with them until they send us back to the dragons."

I frowned. "I hope Oliver will be able to come with us."

"Maybe they'll have news of him," Ella said.

We headed out of the Lodge to the staff chalets.

Magnus was at his desk in reception. I saw his eyes take in my battered face. He opened his mouth and I knew what he was going to say. I scowled at him, and he closed his mouth again.

"Any news about Oliver?" Nathan asked.

Magnus shook his head. "I haven't heard anything, but Leandro may have."

"Is he here?"

"No. He's next door, in his office."

"Not in the headmaster's office?" I asked.

"I believe that's Archie's now," Magnus replied with a wink at Nathan.

I felt like I'd been gone for a week, not one night.

We said goodbye to Magnus and marched over to Leandro's chalet. He was standing at the window, talking on the phone. He waved us in when he saw us.

"Excellent. I'll let everyone know. Thanks for ringing." Leandro hung up and turned to us as we stepped in the door. "Perfect timing. That was Oliver's mum."

"What's the news?"

"Is he going to be okay?" We all talked at once.

Leandro smiled. "He's going to be fine. Most of his burns were relatively minor. A few small spots of deeper burns on his legs, but nothing that won't heal in time. He's at home now, and resting comfortably."

"Is he coming back?" I asked.

"His mother doesn't want him to."

"What?"

"He has to come back," Nathan said.

"We're a team," Ella added.

Leandro laughed. "Apparently that's what Oliver said. And then he threatened to run away if his mum didn't let him return."

"So …?"

"They had quite a lengthy discussion."

"And …?" I could tell Leandro was enjoying dragging out his answer.

"Apparently Oliver has a stubborn streak. At least, that's what his mum said."

"And …?"

Leandro smiled. "And he'll be back tomorrow."

"Yes!" My grin split my lip again and I winced.

"In the meantime, we should talk about what your next steps should be."

"That's why we're here," Nathan said. "To plan how we're going to approach the dragons again."

Leandro chuckled. "You think we're going to send you back out there, eh? After you've been attacked?"

I shrugged. "Apparently we have a stubborn streak."

Leandro sighed, but his good eye twinkled. "We'll talk about it. Come out back. Dan's on the porch."

"Dan?" I asked.

Leandro laughed. "Professor West. It'll be first names from now on at the school. No titles, no formality."

45

We all nodded. It would take some getting used to, but I didn't mind. It was like being admitted to the adult world.

"Is my dad back yet?" Nathan asked.

"No. But Archie's put Dan and me in charge of helping you with your mission. He's got a school to run when he returns."

Leandro led us through to the kitchen, where he offered us something to drink. "Sorry, I've only got tea, coffee or water," he said as he poured himself a coffee. We all declined and headed out the back door.

Professor West—Dan—looked up from his laptop and smiled at us as we stepped onto the porch. "I thought you'd be sleeping, Tui." His smile fell away. "You had a long night last night."

I shrugged. "I slept some." I didn't need a reminder of how I'd been terrified for Oliver all night. I'd fallen asleep quickly, but had woken in a panic half a dozen times when he cried out.

Dan invited us to sit at the picnic table with him. Leandro joined us and took a sip of his coffee before speaking. He addressed Dan first. "Oliver's home. He'll be back here tomorrow."

Dan seemed relieved, and Leandro continued. "So, we need to regroup after yesterday's fiasco."

"I don't think it was entirely a fiasco," Ella said, her brow furrowed.

"What?" My eyebrows shot up. "How can you say that when Oliver spent half the day in the hospital and Nathan and I look like we've been in a war?"

"Yeah, we were attacked by dragons," Nathan agreed.

Ella raised a hand. "I know, but didn't you see? All the dragons on the Council fought against the ones attacking us. Even Flint and Jade. They fought against their own kind."

"They didn't seem terribly convinced by our arguments before that, though," I said. "Maybe they only fought against the others because they were being attacked."

"No. I could see it in the way they stood. Even before the attack, they were coming round to the idea of working together." I opened my mouth to argue, and she held up a hand again. "I know. They spoke against it. But they were only asking the questions they needed to. They were only making sure we'd thought everything through."

It wasn't how I'd remembered their words. I frowned.

"Nathan, what do you think?" Leandro asked.

"I don't know. It didn't really seem to me like the whole Council agreed with us. And I was busy trying to stay alive. I didn't see what Flint and Jade did after we were attacked."

A whir of wings and flash of gold startled us all. Rata came winging around the side of the chalet and landed on Nathan's shoulder.

"Hi guys! Am I late to the meeting?" She peered at Nathan. "Your eyebrows are gone." Nathan laughed. Then she turned toward me. "And you look like roadkill."

"Thanks Rata. And you look like you lost a fight with a pair of pruning shears."

"What?" Nathan pulled his head back to get a better view of Rata.

"Her tail!" Ella exclaimed.

Rata sighed. "It looks terrible doesn't it. And when it grows back in, the scales won't match."

"It'll grow back?" Dan leaned forward, peering more closely at the stub of Rata's tail.

"Of course." Rata ruffled her scales and straightened up. "Please stop staring. How would you like it if someone stared at your stumps?"

Dan smiled and sat back. He waved his false arm. "You're welcome to stare all you want. But, I'm sorry. I know, when it's new it's hard to have people gawking at you. I've had a lot longer to get used to the stares."

"Rata, what are you doing here?" Nathan asked.

"The Council sent me. I'm the new Draconic Council representative at the school." She turned to Leandro. "We didn't consult with you on that one, I know. But we assumed you'd agree to the idea of a resident dragon."

Leandro glanced at Dan, then replied, "We'll have to double check with Archie when he returns. I assume it will be fine."

"Good, because Storm Cloud said if you refused me, he would come and sit on the roof of Archie's office until he agreed." She giggled. No question he would do it. And his weight would crush the building.

"So you're going to live here?" I asked.

"Yeah. Think of me as a new staff member." Rata puffed herself up and I couldn't help laughing.

Dan raised his eyebrows. "And do you expect a whole staff chalet for yourself?"

Rata laughed. "Don't be ridiculous. I can't open doors."

"Where *do* gold fairy dragons live?" Nathan asked.

Rata sobered a little. "Hardly anywhere anymore." She gazed into the distance and was silent.

"Do you live in caves like other dragons?" Ella asked.

"Before stoats and possums were brought to New Zealand, most gold fairy dragons nested in tree holes. We're much more adapted to forest living than mountain living." She shrugged. "Cliffs are safer nesting spots these days—some of us scrape out spots in the midst of seabird colonies on the coast, others prefer more inland sites."

"And your home?" I was almost afraid to ask. Rata had lost all the sparkle I was used to seeing in her.

"Mount Somers." She seemed to perk up a bit. "Lots of nice snug holes in those rhyolite cliffs, and forest down below to hunt in. And," she added with glee, "trampers dropping all sorts of interesting things. You should see the shiny stuff I've got in my lair."

I imagined a hole stuffed with muesli bar wrappers, lost carabiners, bottle caps and bits of aluminium foil. All arranged artfully, no doubt, and in a fashion complimenting the little dragon's own glittering scales. I couldn't help but smile.

"Can she stay in the dorm with us?" Nathan asked.

Leandro and Dan shared a look, then both said, "No."

Rata agreed. "I'm not living anywhere I can't get in and out on my own."

Nathan's shoulders slumped.

"I'm sure Magnus can build you something cosy," Leandro assured her. "So, what does the Draconic Council intend for you to do here?"

"Represent dragons."

"Yes. That's obvious, but in what way?"

"Well, after the attack on the Council meeting, Storm Cloud thought it best to conduct our negotiations more discreetly. I'm here to represent the Council in those negotiations."

"Storm Cloud sent you to do that?" I was surprised. Rata wasn't known for wise decisions, and her attention span was fleeting.

Rata shrugged. "Kowhai and I are the only ones small enough to stay here discreetly. He asked Kowhai first." Rata's head and tail drooped a bit. "But she's got eggs in the nest, so I came instead."

My smile was mirrored by the others'. "We're glad you've come, Rata."

Rata's arrival was perfect, but we didn't get very far in our discussions. First, she asked about Oliver, and then Leandro asked for her account of the meeting and attack.

49

Then Rata begged for something to drink, and spilled her glass of water across the table and into Ella's lap.

As Leandro mopped up the water with a tea towel, a car came labouring up the drive.

"That's probably Archie," Dan said. "We should go out to meet him. He's been worried about you, in spite of my assurances you were all fine."

I saw the look on Nathan's face and frowned. No doubt Archie's worry had mostly been for Nathan. No one was going to worry about me. Why did that make me want to punch something? I crossed my arms and followed the others around to the headmaster's chalet.

Rata flitted back to me and landed on my shoulder. "You look like someone farted. What's wrong, Dragonheart?"

I smiled. At least she didn't ask if I was okay. But I didn't want to talk about it. What good would that do? It couldn't bring my parents back.

"What does it mean to be dragon-hearted?" I asked instead.

Rata considered my question for a moment. Her head bobbed gently as I walked. "A dragon is never far from anger."

I barked a laugh. "*You're* not. I've never seen you mad. Not like Storm Cloud."

Now it was Rata's turn to laugh. "What good would it do for little me to blow up like Storm Cloud? Doesn't mean anger doesn't simmer below the surface."

"What are you angry about?"

Rata raised an eye ridge at me and didn't answer.

"Stupid question."

"The important question at the moment is what are *you* angry about?"

I shrugged. "Nothing."

"Uh-huh."

Six

Rata and I caught up with the others as Archie stepped out of the car in front of his office. The passenger door opened too, and a woman stepped out. She wore dressy trousers and a blouse, but with hiking boots. Her greying hair stood in spikes on top of her head. She might have been my mum's age, or maybe a little older, if Mum had still been alive.

Archie gave Nathan a bear hug. My chest tightened, and I caught myself frowning at them. A moment later, Archie hugged Ella, and then Rata fluttered off my shoulder as he hugged me. Tears threatened to leak out of my eyes.

"I'm so glad you've all returned safely. I understand Oliver will be back tomorrow?" I nodded. Rata settled back onto my shoulder as Archie stepped away. "Good to see you, too, Rata."

Archie turned to the woman, who stepped around the car with wide eyes. I felt my cheeks flush. She was staring at me.

Then I remembered the dragon on my shoulder.

"Everyone, this is Roz Piper." Archie ushered Roz forward. She tore her eyes from Rata and smiled at us all. "Roz is interviewing for a new position here—maths and English teacher."

51

"Maths and English? We didn't have to do those subjects before." Nathan's frown was wiped out by a warning look from Archie.

Ella shrugged. "Well, we knew the curriculum would be changing." Then she leaned to me and whispered, "It'd be great to have a female teacher, wouldn't it?"

I nodded. The dragon slayer profession had been entirely male until recently. My mum had been one of the first female dragon slayers, and aside from Miss Brumby, Ella and I were the only females at the school.

Leandro stepped forward and introduced himself, shaking Roz's hand.

Dan did the same, and then Archie took over again.

"These three are students. They, along with one other, serve as our negotiating team with the dragons."

Roz frowned, and her eyes took in my battered face and Nathan's missing eyebrows. "You send children to negotiate with dragons?"

Nathan stepped forward. "We have … experience … with dragons." He glanced at me and Ella and we grinned at each other. "I'm Nathan. I'm Archie's son." He shook Roz's hand.

Ella introduced herself, and then all eyes turned to me.

"I'm Tui." As I reached out to shake Roz's hand, I realised she was no taller than I. She met my eyes and held them as we shook hands. Then her eyes flicked to the dragon.

"And I'm Rata." Rata bobbed her head toward Roz, sniffing loudly to catch her scent. "Representative of the Draconic Council."

"I thought dragons were … larger," Roz ventured.

Rata laughed, and I couldn't help smiling. "Rata is a gold fairy dragon. Other dragons are bigger."

"A lot bigger," Nathan agreed.

Roz nodded. "Size isn't everything."

"That's what I say," Rata agreed.

"Well," Archie said, bringing everyone's attention back to him. "Roz will have a formal interview with the faculty this afternoon, but I thought we could all have lunch together, so she can learn a little more about the students and the school."

We walked in a loose group to the Lodge and filed into the dining hall.

"Oooh! What's that smell?" Rata asked, still riding on my shoulder.

"Miss Brumby's chicken noodle soup," I replied, nodding appreciatively. My split lip bothered me. Soup would be easy to eat, and Miss Brumby's chicken noodle soup was excellent.

Everything was set out for us already, but Miss Brumby came to the serving window to greet us. She had a smile for everyone and reached over the counter to shake Roz's hand. She turned her eyes to me last.

"Oh! And who is this?" She leaned over the counter again, but didn't extend her hand. Instead, she brought her face close to Rata's and *sniffed*, as Rata did the same to her. The perfect Draconic greeting. My eyes must have widened in surprise, because Miss Brumby harrumphed as she straightened up. "You don't work at this school unless you know a bit about dragons." I blinked at her, my mind spinning, and all but missed Rata introducing herself. By the time I tore my mind away from wondering how the cook knew how to properly greet a dragon, the two were chatting comfortably about Rata's dietary needs.

I shook my head to clear it and broke into their conversation. "Whatever you do, don't let her near bread."

Miss Brumby raised her eyebrows. Rata sighed. "I suppose you're right. I think I'm gluten intolerant."

"Bread makes her fart." Nathan waved a hand in front of his nose as though warding off a bad smell.

"Well, we could try some gluten-free bread and see if you can handle that," Miss Brumby suggested.

Rata's eyes widened. "There's gluten-free bread?"

Miss Brumby smiled. "I'll see what I can do for you." I could practically see the wheels turning in her brain. Feeding a gluten-intolerant dragon was a challenge Miss Brumby clearly looked forward to.

I filled my tray with food for both Rata and me, and then headed toward the table where the staff, Roz and my friends had gathered. I sat and set Rata's bowl of soup on the table next to me, along with a mandarin the dragon assured me she could eat. Rata hopped lightly to the table and dunked her head straight into her soup. She slurped the broth in noisy gulps, and then lifted her head and licked the drips off her lips.

"Delicious!"

We all laughed.

"Just don't eat the noodles," I warned her. "They've got gluten in them."

"But they look so yum. Maybe I could try one?"

Ella and Nathan joined me in an emphatic, "No!"

Roz raised an eyebrow. "It sounds like you all had quite an adventure—Archie told me about how you rescued him. But you didn't get your current injuries rescuing Archie, did you?"

"No. We got these from a Draconic Council meeting last night," I replied.

"Hmm." She shook her head and frowned. Then she turned to Archie with an apologetic smile. "I still don't quite agree with you on sending children to negotiate with dragons."

Archie laughed. "Good."

Leandro seconded him. "We need staff who'll help keep us in line." He shrugged. "We want to change, but sometimes we fall back on dragon slayer thinking."

Nathan straightened in his chair. "Wait. Are you saying you agree with her?"

"Well … let's just say I understand her concerns." Archie shrugged.

"It's not generally acceptable to put kids in danger," Leandro agreed.

I scowled. "You're not going to keep us from dragons, are you?" After all we'd been through. After we'd rescued Archie himself. After we'd accepted the responsibility of negotiating with the dragons, now they might take it away? My fists clenched under the table.

"Dad, you gave us a job," Nathan said. He frowned. Even Ella didn't look happy about the prospect of being pulled from dragon negotiation.

Rata raised her head and hopped to the centre of the table, right in front of Archie. "Do you really think a full dragon slayer could have done better than these kids?"

"It's not about how good a job they can do. It's about their safety."

Rata snorted. "You weren't there last night. You have no idea. A dragon slayer would have been dead. You've been trained for confrontation. You've been trained to speak first with your sword. A dragon slayer could not have taken a sword to the meeting, and I'd be hard-pressed to believe he would have done better than these four. Nathan's words were courteous, but strong. Tui's explanation was forthright, her defence of your plans clear and compelling. Ella's timely interventions were nothing less than inspired. And Oliver?" Rata laughed. "Even dragons can't resist Oliver's charm."

"Yes. I know they're a good negotiating team, but safety—"

Rata snorted her contempt in a gout of flame that made Archie lean away. "When the scree dragons attacked, not only did these children fight like dragons, the entire Council fought with them. Do you hear that,

Archie? The dragons fought *with* them *against* other dragons. No dragon slayer, not even you, could have inspired that level of support." She launched herself from the table to perch on Nathan's shoulder. "As the Draconic Council's representative here, I declare we will deal with no one but these four." She huffed smoke from her nostrils and puffed up her scales.

Nobody spoke for a minute. I stifled a smile. Archie glanced at Nathan. Nathan shrugged and grinned.

Dan lost it first, breaking out in a belly laugh. "Well, she told you, didn't she, Archie?"

Archie sighed and scrubbed his face with his hands. It failed to hide the smile threatening to break out on his face. "This isn't the time or place for this conversation." He turned to Roz. "I think we have an interview to do. Shall we go to my office?"

Roz nodded, and all three staff members rose with her and headed out the door.

As soon as the door closed behind the adults, we burst out laughing.

"You are such a *blarghstra*," Ella said.

"Takes one to know one," Rata retorted.

When we'd gotten control of our laughter, Nathan asked the question on the tip of my tongue. "So is it true? Or were you just giving my dad a hard time?"

"Is what true?"

"That we did better than a dragon slayer would have."

Rata snorted. "Of course it's true."

Seven

Oliver must have begged his mum to drive him back to school first thing the next morning, because he was there by morning tea time. Rata had left before it was light to fly back and report to Storm Cloud that her residence at the school had been accepted, and to get further orders from him. Nathan, Ella and I were on the back lawn, tossing a Frisbee back and forth and listening for the sound of an approaching car. I think we all felt Oliver's absence. Knowing he was supposed to return soon, none of us could focus enough to plan our next steps. Besides, we wanted Oliver there to help us plan. We ran to the Lodge at the first sound of a straining engine climbing the hill.

We were standing by the drive waiting when Oliver's mum pulled up. The maroon station wagon had barely come to a halt when Oliver sprang out and raced to hug each of us. When he reached me, he frowned. "You look worse than I do."

I rolled my eyes. "Thanks, mate." Then I hugged him again, tears pricking my eyes. "I'm glad to see you up and running around. Does it hurt?"

He stepped back and shrugged, his smile fading. "Yeah, but they gave me painkillers that help. As long as I remember to take them, it's not too bad."

Oliver's mum stood behind him—a tiny woman, with the same sparkling eyes as Oliver. She stepped forward and hugged me, too. She smelled vaguely of cinnamon. "You must be Tui. Thank you so much for looking after Oliver. You saved his life."

I blushed and pulled away from her. "I don't know about that, Mrs. Ng. Mostly I kept him company."

"No, the doctors told me he was lucky to have you there. His burns weren't too deep, but because they cover most of his legs he was at risk of shock, which might have killed him if he'd been out there alone with no one to care for him. You saved his life." She gently touched my face. "All while you were injured, too. Poor dear."

"Mum! Mum!" Oliver pulled on his mum's sleeve. "You should come up and see the dorm, and I bet Miss Brumby's got cookies. It's morning tea time, isn't it?"

Nathan and Ella followed Oliver and his mum inside. I watched them go, a familiar lump in my throat. Seeing Oliver with his mum was every bit as bad as watching Nathan with his dad. They each had a parent. Ella had a parent. Who did I have? My Auntie Mel had dealt with all the details after my mum died, but she was happy to send me off to the convenient but mysterious Alexandra School of Heroic Arts where my brother had gone a few years before when dad had passed away. Auntie Mel was nice, but overwhelmed with her own kids, and I hardly knew her. I squeezed my eyes shut. "Not fair," I whispered to myself.

My hands were balled into fists. I uncurled my fingers, took a deep breath, opened my eyes, and followed the others inside.

I joined the others for morning tea, but left as soon as I'd eaten a cookie. My stomach was too knotted; I couldn't sit across the table from Oliver and his mum, watching her dote on him. Thankfully, she didn't stay long. I was hopping from stone to stone along the creek behind the Lodge when I heard her drive away. I made my way back to the Lodge.

"Tui. There you are," said Ella as I stepped through the front door. "Archie wants to meet with us before lunch. We're headed to his office now." She frowned. "Are you okay?"

"I'm fine." I gritted my teeth. When would people stop asking me that?

We left the Lodge and fell into step together. Oliver limped a little, but his burns hadn't dampened his spirit.

"Mum got a new kitten! It's all black, like Pooky, but smaller. Pooky's not too happy about it. The kitten chases Pooky's tail."

I knew Oliver's cat's name was Pooky, but I hadn't known he was a black cat. We had all laughed at the cat's name when Oliver first mentioned it, but now I thought I understood. "Oliver, you named your cat Pooky when you were little, didn't you?"

"Yeah, I was four when I got him."

"Were you trying to name him Spooky? Because he's a black cat?"

Oliver laughed. "I had trouble with the letter s."

"What's the new kitten's name?" Nathan asked.

"Māo."

"Māo?" Ella cocked her head.

Oliver shrugged. "It's Chinese for cat. I don't know why Mum named the cat Cat. Kinda dumb."

"Yeah, unlike Pooky." I grinned and wrapped an arm around Oliver's shoulder. "Good to have you back." I hadn't realised how worried I'd been about Oliver, but now he was back and joking around with us, I felt lighter somehow.

59

"What does Archie want with us?" I asked.

Nathan shrugged. "Not sure, but we've got to figure out our next steps soon. Maybe he's got information that will help."

We climbed the steps to Archie's chalet and walked in without knocking. Archie called out as we entered. "Come on in."

Filing into his office, I appreciated the change in decor from Drachenmorder's days. The mounted dragon heads were gone, replaced with framed botanical sketches and photos of Nathan—kayaking, playing rugby, digging in the sand at the beach. My chest tightened, but then I caught Nathan's blush as he, too, took in the photos. I might envy Nathan his dad, but I certainly didn't envy his position as the headmaster's son.

Archie waved us into chairs arrayed around a small round table in the corner.

"I thought you four should have an update on my meeting with the board." Archie sat down with us, a stack of papers in his hand.

"Did it go okay?" Nathan asked.

Archie grimaced. "At first, no. You've got to understand, the board is made up of retired dragon slayers. I had some serious work convincing them the school needs to change. First I had to convince them the profession needs to change." He sighed. "But I got there in the end. The last day was good. They had finally warmed to the idea, and we were able to come to some agreements."

"So tell us," Ella encouraged.

"I won't bore you with all the financial and structural details, but the school will be changing. A lot. As of the beginning of the year, its new name will be the Alexandra Institute."

"Well, that's boring," Oliver blurted out.

Ella wrinkled her nose. "Sounds like a mental institution."

I frowned. "Why does the school's name need to change anyway? It's the Alexandra School of Heroic Arts—is saving dragons less heroic than killing them?"

"It's a matter of distancing ourselves from not only the practise of dragon slaying, but the language of dragon slaying, too. The term heroic arts has always referred to combat. We don't want to imply anything of the sort with our name."

"But, *Alexandra Institute*?" Nathan asked. "It doesn't say anything about what the school is or does."

"Precisely. Remember, while our ultimate goal is to lift the secrecy about dragons, we're not there yet. We can't exactly name the place the School of Dragon Conservation."

We nodded. I supposed he was right.

"Besides, the Alexandra Institute is not only a school. With the name change come some major mission changes as well. The Alexandra Institute will have three main divisions: conservation, education, and training. The conservation division will focus on policy matters related to dragons—formal agreements, legislation and whatnot. The education division will operate an official secondary school focusing on preparing students for a career in conservation."

"When you say *official*, do you mean we have to do NCEA exams and everything?" Ella's voice was suspicious.

"That means we have to do maths, doesn't it?" Nathan asked.

Archie chuckled. "Yes, it means both those things. We want to prepare students for the modern world. Conservation is a career, unlike dragon slaying, which is a …"

"Life sentence?" Ella suggested.

61

"That's a fair way to characterise it," Archie admitted.

"And the training division?" I asked.

"It will focus on re-training dragon slayers for conservation and equipping conservation staff for working with dragons."

"You mean teaching them Draconic language?" Oliver asked.

"Yes. And cultural studies, history of dragon/human relations, dragon biology and ecology—all those things they wouldn't have gotten in their regular university coursework."

"That's a lot. How is the staff going to manage all of it?" Ella asked.

"We'll be hiring more staff as the year progresses and each division develops."

"Will each division be separate, with different staff?" The words *institute* and *division* conjured images of big buildings and lots of people bustling about on official business. It didn't feel like the small mountain school I'd attended for the past six months.

Archie laughed. "I know it all sounds grandiose, and maybe someday it will be. For the foreseeable future, I think most staff will work in more than one division. The board was looking to the future. Part of what sold them on the idea was the thought of being the only facility of its kind in the world. Eventually they want to be able to attract global attention—students from overseas, rich donors, research funds."

"So it's all about money? I thought this was about saving dragons." I found myself frowning.

Archie raised a placating hand. "It *is* about saving dragons. The board focuses on money because that's their job. If they didn't, there would be no funds for the work we do. They figure out how to raise money so we don't have to—so we can focus on the real mission of the Institute."

I crossed my arms and sat back in my chair. "I suppose."

Oliver piped up. "So, what does it mean for us?"

"Yes. It's a sticky question. You are students of the Alexandra School of Heroic Arts, and as such, are invited to enrol as students of the Alexandra Institute. We've also asked you to act as our negotiating team with the dragons, which would make you employees in the conservation division of the Institute."

"You mean we get a salary?" Oliver grinned at the idea.

Archie gave us all a stern look. "First, let me tell you the board was not happy about the idea of four kids in their first six months of training negotiating with dragons. It may not even be legal. The law says employees under the age of fifteen can't work in any area where they're likely to be harmed. Given three of the four of you came back from the Council meeting looking like casualties of war, I don't think we can meet that requirement."

We all sat up. My own indignation showed on everyone's face.

"No way!" I said. "You heard what Rata said. The dragons won't talk to anyone but us."

"You could argue it wasn't *likely* we'd get hurt at the meeting," Oliver said. "No one expected dragons to attack a Draconic Council meeting."

Never mind every one of my injuries was from Storm Cloud—a *friendly* dragon.

"Come on, Dad. We were being trained as dragon slayers. This is a whole lot less dangerous than that."

Archie raised his hand. "I know. But the school is already under investigation because of Drachenmorder's illegal activities. We've been operating in secret for over a

63

hundred years. Now we're going to be operating openly and legitimately. We've got to obey the law."

"But—"

"Which means," Archie continued, "we'll have to make sure you have proper safety gear next time you go out."

"Woo hoo!"

"Yes!"

Nathan, Ella, Oliver and I hi-fived, grinning and laughing. Then Ella's face grew serious and she turned back to Archie. "How much are you paying? The world's only dragon negotiation team doesn't work for minimum wage, you know."

I didn't really care about the details of our contracts. I don't think Ella did, either. Anyway, because of our ages, the contracts weren't really ours to negotiate. Archie told us the basics of our responsibilities, which we already knew, and our pay and benefits. It was then up to our guardians to deal with all the details. I hung back after the meeting, waiting until the others had gone before broaching the subject with Archie.

"Um … about the contract … my Auntie Mel? She's my legal guardian, but …"

Archie nodded. "She knows nothing about dragons. Yes. We can't exactly send her the details of your contract." He furrowed his brow. "Your brother Anaru is eighteen, isn't he?"

I nodded. "Can he do it?"

"I think we might be able to arrange for him to act on your behalf in this. Let me see what I can do."

Eight

I caught up with the others on the porch of the Lodge. As I was mounting the steps, a sound caught my attention.

"Guys. Be quiet."

The others turned. A car was coming up the drive. We waited for it to turn in the gate, but it slowed and stopped before we could see it.

I raised my eyebrows. The school didn't get visitors. And why would a car stop just outside the gate?

"Up the creek bed," Oliver said. We nodded and clattered off the porch, circling around the building and across the back lawn. The creek tumbling down the hill behind the Lodge crossed the drive about a hundred metres before the gate. There was plenty of shrubbery along the stream bank from which we could spy on whoever had driven up.

We neared the drive in silence, stepping carefully on rocks in the middle of the stream. The dark culvert under the drive loomed in front of us. When we reached it, we peered over the top, through sparse grasses growing on the edge of the drive.

"Back again to snoop around, huh?" I whispered. Katie Garner's blue car sat ticking as it cooled at the side of the drive.

"Where is she?" Ella asked. The car was empty.

A rustle from above silenced us. A rock shifted, and pebbles skittered down the bank. A female voice swore.

Nathan's eyes were wide. "She's following the stream," he mouthed.

"Let's get ahead of her," Ella suggested.

"And do what?" I asked.

Oliver grinned. "I have an idea." He motioned us downstream, and we followed as quickly and quietly as we could. Katie was obviously trying to push her way through the brush on the bank. Wanting to stay hidden, no doubt. But it meant she was making noise and moving slowly, and we had no difficulty getting ahead of her.

When we'd gained some distance, Oliver stopped and turned. "You know, I've heard there are wild pigs up here." A smile spread across his face. "Dangerous animals, pigs. I'd hate to have one chasing me." He looked pointedly at Ella, Nathan and me. "Or *three* chasing me."

"But she's from the city. Even if we pretend to be pigs, will she know to be scared?" asked Nathan.

Oliver's smile broadened to a grin. "She will if I come out screaming."

I stifled a laugh. We all looked up as we heard Katie approaching. "It's worth a try, I suppose."

Nathan grinned and snorted like a pig. Ella rolled her eyes, but nodded agreement.

Oliver went first, pushing his way up the bank. The rest of us followed, silently at first, and then, at Oliver's signal, we started shaking bushes and making grunting noises. We kept out of sight, but Oliver pushed ahead of us, screaming as he went.

"Ah! Ah! Get back! Get back!"

We grunted louder and thrashed through the bushes. We knew when Oliver reached Katie, because we heard her yelp.

"Pigs!" Oliver shouted. "Wild pigs! Big ones! With tusks! Run!"

"Pigs?" I couldn't tell if Katie was scared or incredulous.

"Yes! Pigs! Wild boars! Run!"

I cringed. She'd never fall for this. But the noise ahead of us increased, and I heard Oliver urging her on. We surged ahead, making even more noise.

The sound of Oliver and Katie's flight diminished as they burst from the bushes. "Go on! To your car!"

"What about you?" asked Katie. Panic made her voice rise, and I shared a disbelieving look with Ella.

"I know a safe place I can hide. Go!" Oliver yelled.

We continued our grunting ruckus until we heard a car door slam. We emerged from the bushes as Katie turned her car around and sped away, throwing gravel behind her.

Nathan shook his head, his mouth hanging open. "I can't believe that worked."

I burst out laughing.

Oliver returned to us holding his side and laughing so hard he couldn't speak.

"That was the dumbest idea." Ella shook her head, then giggled.

"Do you think she's really gone?" I looked down the hill. A cloud of dust followed Katie's car as it sped away from the school.

"For now, but you know she'll be back," Nathan said. "We should go tell Leandro."

In Leandro's office a few minutes later, we were all pacing. Dan had joined us, too.

"How *did* that reporter find out about us?" Nathan asked.

Leandro shrugged. "Who knows? I want to know *what* she knows."

I snorted. "She knows enough to cause trouble, and if she keeps sneaking around here, she's eventually going to see or hear something."

Dan's eyes narrowed. "But she'd be a fool to publish anything until she had *proof.* You don't publicly claim a mythical animal exists unless you can prove it. Not if you want to keep your job."

"So we need to keep her from getting proof," Nathan said.

"How do we do that?" Oliver asked.

"We also have to get the dragons on board as soon as possible, and then get the legislation through." Ella looked like she wanted to run out and start immediately.

I felt the same. "Yeah. If we can do it before she publishes her story, then it won't matter what she knows."

"Can we call another Draconic Council meeting?" Nathan asked.

"And be attacked again?" Leandro raised his eyebrows.

"Well it looks to me like we have a concrete reason to press the Draconic Council for an agreement as soon as possible," I said. "It's worth risking another attack to go talk to Storm Cloud."

Nathan nodded and glanced at Ella, Oliver and me. "Could we be ready to go this afternoon? Maybe wait for Rata to get back, in case she has news, and then leave?"

"How will we get to his lair?" Ella asked. "I'm *not* climbing Mount Crosscut again."

"Helicopter?" Oliver suggested with a grin.

We all looked at the adults.

"I suppose it would do no good to refuse, would it?" Dan asked with a smile.

We packed our bags for a four-day stay with Storm Cloud.

"If it's not enough time, he can fly us back here to pick up supplies," Nathan suggested.

Then there was nothing to do but wait for Rata.

Miss Brumby had arranged a barbecue lunch on the front deck of the Lodge as a celebration of Oliver's return. All the staff showed up for it, even Professor Marshall (whom I simply couldn't think of as Jack, despite the school's policy on names). To Miss Brumby's disapproval, Archie brought out a selection of Drachenmorder's leftover fizzy drinks.

"Here, I try to provide students and staff with a healthy diet, and you go ruining it."

Archie shrugged and winked at us.

Although we all had serious things on our minds, the staff kept the mood light-hearted. Leandro had us all in stitches with stories of his childhood in Peru; I could imagine him as a child, a lot like Oliver. Then Magnus related the story of his final dragon slaying mission, when he was nearly killed and gained the limp that ended his dragon slaying days.

"About fifteen years ago, I was called out to deal with a southern blue dragon that was terrorising trampers on the South Coast Track down in Southland."

"Terrorising, as in eating them?" Oliver asked.

"Well, it only managed to actually eat two, but half a dozen others were injured."

"And eight trampers going missing or being attacked by a dragon didn't hit the news?" I asked.

"People's memories of a traumatic event are remarkably suggestible. If you tell them they were bitten by a shark, they believe it was a shark. Most people are happy to think they haven't been attacked by a creature that's not supposed to exist."

"So what happened when you went down there?" Nathan asked.

"As you know, southern blues live in sea caves along the coast. I had no trouble finding this one—she was big—not a whisker under twenty metres long. And mean, too. I had only just realised I was near her lair when she swooped out from behind a rocky outcrop, all flame and fury."

"What did you do?" Oliver was on the edge of his seat.

"Nothing." Magnus smiled. He had clearly told this story before and knew exactly how to time it to get the most from his audience.

"What?"

"First rule of dragon slaying is to show no fear. So I stood and watched her come at me, jaws agape and flame roaring. Fifty, twenty, ten, five metres—the hairs on my arms were being singed off. At the very last moment, I stepped deftly to the left—the dragon's right. Remember that, son." He pointed at Oliver. "We don't teach it at school, but most dragons are left-handed, and they don't steer as well to the right. Well, this dragon had been so sure of getting me she ploughed right on past. When she realised her jaws were empty, she roared in frustration and came round for another pass at me."

"And did you step to the left again?" He had sucked me into the story, too.

"No, you can only pull that trick once. Do that move, and any dragon worth its name will know you're a dragon slayer. Puts them on their guard. By the time she turned again, I had my sword and shield out. She wasn't fool enough to come at an armed dragon slayer, so she landed just out of sword reach to parley."

"What happened then?"

"Well, she landed in front of me, and said, 'Well, well, well … Magnus MacDiermont. Fancy meeting you here.'"

"She knew your name?" I exclaimed, but Magnus ignored my interruption.

"'That's *Sir* Magnus to you, vile worm!' I said. 'You've taken enough trampers now. It's time for you to move on.' She laughed at that. 'Or you'll do what? Prick me with your shiny toothpick? I'll turn you to toast before you even get near me.' Then it was my turn to laugh. You see, I knew it was the breeding season for southern blues, and I reckoned this one had gone on a rampage because she was guarding eggs."

Ella frowned. "How would that help you kill her? Wouldn't it only make her more vicious?"

"Yes, it makes them vicious, but it also makes them vulnerable. You see, when a dragon is incubating eggs, she plucks off a patch of scales over her fire stomach." Magnus patted a spot on his chest, below his ribs. "It keeps her eggs warmer, but it also means she has a chink in her armour until the eggs hatch and those scales grow back. Of course, you've got to get right in close to hit the spot, and I knew this one wasn't going to give me that chance. So I tried something new—never been done before. Dragon slayers have always used shields to protect themselves from dragon fire. And they work fine, as long as all you want is protection from fire and claw. But with a shield, you can't simultaneously protect yourself and strike, and I knew that's what I had to do to beat this dragon."

"So, what did you do?"

"You know the shelters firefighters use if they're overwhelmed by a bush fire?"

"Um …" We kids looked dumbly at each other.

Magnus sighed. "Well, they're like little tents or cocoons that insulate the firefighter from the heat. Shiny

71

silver on the outside, and thin enough for a sword to pierce. I reckoned it would be the perfect tool. So I said to the dragon, 'Ah! You're probably right. What good is my sword against your scaly hide? Perhaps we can negotiate?' She wasn't interested in negotiation until I pulled out the fire shelter. Dragons can't resist a shiny object, you know. 'Oooooh! Pretty!' she said as I unpacked the shelter.

"'You like that?' I said. 'Well, you can have it, if you can burn me.' I dived into the shelter and readied my sword. The dragon didn't waste a moment—she breathed a gout of flame over me. I laughed and told her she needed to try harder. I heard her step closer. Another flame, and I jeered at her again. Three times she breathed on me in the shelter, coming closer each time, before she was close enough. By then, I can tell you, it was getting mighty hot in there. I didn't know if I'd survive the next blast, but it was too late to change my mind. When I heard her inhale in preparation for roasting me at point blank range, I thrust my sword upward."

"How did you hit the right spot when you couldn't see her?" Ella asked, eyes wide.

"I didn't."

We all gasped.

"I missed, and the sword did nothing except irritate the dragon and destroy my fire shelter. But with a big hole in the shelter, I could see now. Before the dragon had a chance to react, I stabbed again, driving the sword home this time."

"You killed her?" There was more than a little outrage in my voice. Magnus gave me a look that said, *of course I killed her.*

"Eventually, she died, but a wounded dragon is more dangerous than a room full of tigers. And I was tangled in my fire shelter, so all I could do was roll away as she grabbed at me with her talons." He grimaced. "Not exactly my finest moment, I have to say. She caught me by my right leg and shook me. I heard the crack as my leg broke, and I thought I was done for."

Nathan winced. "How did you get away?"

"She was badly injured. She tried to lift off to take me back to her lair, but managed only a few metres before crash landing. Broke my arm when she dropped me, but by then she was dead."

Oliver was practically falling off his chair at this point. "So you were out in the middle of nowhere with a broken leg and a broken arm?"

Magnus laughed. "I managed to drag myself up to the track, where a tramper found me. Leg never healed quite right, so I was taken off active duty."

It made the injuries we had suffered at the Council meeting seem like nothing. I looked around at the other former dragon slayers on staff. Dan, with his missing leg and arm. Leandro with his scarred and disfigured face, his dead eye and missing ear. Even Archie had ropy burn scars down his arms. Only Marshall was unscathed. Or maybe not. He always wore long sleeves. Were there hidden injuries underneath? I certainly wasn't going to ask. All those injuries and deaths in the name of dragon slaying. It had to stop.

Nine

Rata returned late in the afternoon. We had been keeping a lookout for her on the porch, impatient to be gone. Dan wouldn't let us go until we'd talked with her, and since he was our pilot, we didn't have much choice but to wait. Miss Brumby had just enticed us indoors for a snack when Rata zipped into the dining hall.

"Oooh! Food! I'm starving!" she exclaimed before any of us could say a word. Miss Brumby appeared with a special plate for the dragon—a gluten-free slice of bread smothered in butter surrounded by an artful arrangement of fruit, vegetables, and …

"Are those grasshoppers?" I asked.

Rata settled herself on the table in front of the plate. "Yeah. I mentioned to Miss Brumby I'm particularly fond of insects."

"Awesome!" Oliver leaned in to peer at the bugs.

"Ick!" Ella wrinkled her nose.

As Rata began to eat, we told her about the reporter's second visit and the renewed urgency to our work.

"So, Dan's flying us up to Storm Cloud's lair this afternoon," I said.

"No he's not," Rata replied. She took another bite of bread.

"What do you mean?" Nathan asked.

"Stwmp Cwhd mwgh whmp—"

Ella rolled her eyes. "Chew and swallow first."

Rata made a great show of chomping her food and swallowing it. "No point in going to Storm Cloud's lair. The Council is behind us."

"But the meeting—" Ella began.

"—was enough to convince them. But they won't agree to anything until we have more support. We can't have rogue dragons spoiling our plans. We've got to spread the word—travel around, meet with dragons, present our plans. He says it's the only way to bring all the dragons on board."

"When you say *we've* got to spread the word, do you mean, the four of us?" Ella asked.

"And me, and Foggy Bottom."

"And by *around*, where do you mean?" A ghost of a smile broke out on Nathan's face.

"All over New Zealand."

Now we all grinned.

"But do we have time?" I asked. "What if that reporter gets her proof and publishes a story about dragons?"

Rata raised her head and eyed me. "The Council won't agree to anything until we've done this."

Ella raised her hands. "What's the point of a council if they can't make decisions?"

"This decision has the potential to either save or destroy dragons entirely, and which way it goes depends in large part on how dragons behave. If we blindside them with this, they won't take it well. Do you want dragonkind in revolt, running rampant over towns and cities?" Rata shuddered.

"There would be slaughter on both sides," Nathan said, his eyes wide.

Rata nodded. "And the end result would be the end of dragons."

We sat in silence for a moment.

"So, when do we leave?" Oliver asked.

"Tomorrow. Foggy Bottom will pick you up as soon as it's dark."

After dinner my brother rang. It was the first time I'd talked to him since Mum's funeral.

"Little Sis, how's it going? Hey, I spoke to Archie McMannis today."

"About the job he's offered me."

"Yeah." He paused for a moment. "Look, Tui. I don't think you should do this."

"Why not?"

"You've got a chance to get your life back. Forget dragons. Be a regular kid. Why would you do this?"

"Because they need our help."

"What, the dragons? They killed Mum and Dad, Tui."

"I know that, but—"

"There's plenty of money, you know, from Mum and Dad's life insurance policies. Is that what you're worried about? You don't need to work."

"It's not that." I thought of Rata and Storm Cloud and Foggy Bottom. Anaru had been trained as a dragon slayer, graduating shortly before I arrived at the school, but he'd never actually met a dragon. How could I explain dragons weren't simply ravening beasts? I fell back on the only explanation I thought he might understand. "Anaru, the dragons are taniwha."

Anaru snorted. "And there have always been taniwha slayers."

"But not all taniwha are bad."

"That doesn't mean we don't need to protect ourselves from the ones that are."

"But we don't need to do it by killing them."

"Well, they're certainly willing to kill us. Both our parents, Tui. *Both* of them. I don't want my little sister going out there to find them before she's even fully trained."

He wanted me angry. Well, I was, but not at the dragons who killed our parents. "Anaru. I've already *been* out there. I've met dragons. I've slept in their lairs. I've fought alongside them against people who wanted to kill us. They're not beasts to be slaughtered. They're … they're like people. Individuals. Friends. Rata calls me Dragonheart."

"Rata?"

"A dragon. A friend."

Anaru was silent for so long I wondered if he'd hung up. Finally he sighed.

"Look, I'll sign the papers. Whatever. It's your decision. But Tui?"

"What." It took all my self-control not to growl at him.

"Take care of yourself, eh? You're the only family I've got."

We had a day to prepare. The idea was for us to meet with dragons individually and in small groups and basically present the same arguments we'd presented at the Council meeting.

"Not only do we want them to understand the plan, but we want them to meet you. We want them to see dragons and humans working together for something we agree on. We need to prove to them that not all humans are monsters," Rata explained.

I snorted. "That's exactly what we've got to convince people of, too. That not all dragons are monsters."

Rata nodded. "It's not necessarily going to be easy."

"Not in either case," Ella agreed.

Leandro and Dan had organised flash new equipment for us—tents, climbing gear, a lightweight cooker with all the pots and dishes we needed, and even the solar shower Ella wanted. We had new safety gear, too. Every one of us carried a personal locator beacon.

"In case you're separated. Or in case one is destroyed. Archie insisted on that," Leandro said.

We also had fire protection. Fire-resistant hoods covering head, neck, and shoulders. Coats, custom-made to our sizes, in fire-resistant material. And fire shelters, like Magnus had used on his last mission.

"The gear's not light, but it'll protect you."

"What will we do for food?" Nathan asked. "We can't carry weeks' worth of food with us."

"And I will *not* eat rabbits," Ella declared.

I chuckled. I hadn't minded eating rabbit at Storm Cloud's lair when we were searching for Archie, but after three days of little besides unsalted, half-burnt rabbit, even I looked forward to something else.

Leandro grimaced, and for a moment I thought he was going to say we *would* have to eat rabbit all summer. "Since you are employees of the Alexandra Institute, I can give you an Institute cash card."

Oliver's eyes widened and he grinned. Leandro gave us all a stern look.

"It is not for you to use for just anything. You'll need to keep your receipts, and you'll need to be able to justify every purchase. Magnus will be keeping an eye on how much you spend, and we will know if you're taking advantage of it."

"Aw. No movies?" Oliver gazed at Leandro with puppy eyes.

"No movies." Leandro was trying not to smile now. "No bungy jumping, helicopter rides, or jet boats either. It's for food and other necessary supplies *only*."

Oliver gave a dramatic sigh. Ella rolled her eyes. "Let me carry it. I'll make sure it only gets used for important stuff."

"Yeah, like *combs*?" Nathan teased. He was referring to our quest to rescue Archie. Ella had insisted on buying a comb with some of the money we'd taken from Foggy Bottom's lair to buy food.

"Exactly," she retorted.

At lunchtime we were walking to the Lodge from Leandro's office when we heard a vehicle coming up the drive. It rounded the bend, and I recognised Katie Garner's blue car.

"It's the reporter!" Oliver turned to look back at the rest of us, and sucked in a breath. "Rata!"

Rata was sitting on my shoulder, in full view of the oncoming car.

In a heartbeat, Nathan snatched the dragon and stuffed her under his shirt. "Be quiet! And quit squirming," he warned as Rata gave a squawk. The lump under Nathan's shirt flattened a little and went still. Nathan shuffled around so he was behind us as Katie Garner slowed her car to a halt in front of us.

She rolled down her window and coughed in the dust. "Oh. It's you again." She didn't sound happy to see us.

"I thought we told you the Alexandra Institute isn't open to the public," Ella said.

"The Alexandra Institute? Isn't it the School of Heroic Arts?" Katie waved a hand. "Never mind. Leandro

said I should come back if I had more questions and—"
She smiled. "I have more questions."

I was certain Leandro hadn't invited her back. And
anyway, now it was Archie she needed to talk to, not
Leandro. "I'm afraid Leandro is no longer headmaster.
But I can get the new headmaster for you."

"Oh, no need. I'll just wander over there to his office
and introduce myself." She waved her hand vaguely in the
direction of the chalets.

Wander, huh? And poke her nose into places she
shouldn't.

"I'm sorry. We can't let you do that," Nathan said.

Katie snorted. "Oh? Are you kids in charge, then?"

I sauntered to the front of her car. "No, but we *can*
keep you from *wandering*." I sat down on her bonnet.

"Get off my car! You have no right to stop me. Your
headmaster invited me here."

Oliver laughed. "Unlikely."

"You mean the *former* headmaster?" Ella waved a
hand, dismissing the detail. "And assuming he *did* invite
you here, why shouldn't we go get him?"

Katie huffed. "Well, I'm sure he doesn't want to be
disturbed by a bunch of students."

Nathan laughed. "Yes, I'm sure he'd rather be
disturbed by a nosy reporter than his own son."

"Of course he ... his *son*?" Katie's demeanour
changed and my heart sank. With a dragon under his shirt,
Nathan was the last person we wanted Katie's attention
focused on.

I tried to deflect her attention. Sliding off the bonnet,
I stood and waved back down the drive. "You're
trespassing on private property. You need to leave."

Katie's eyes flicked to me momentarily, but she'd
found her prey. She smiled at Nathan and her voice went
sweet. "So, you're the headmaster's son. I imagine you

know all the secrets of the school, don't you." She winked at him, and Ella snorted a laugh.

"Give it up, lady. He's not going to tell you anything."

"No one is going to tell you anything," Oliver added.

Katie pressed her lips together in a thin line and scowled at Ella and Oliver. Then she pushed open her door and stepped out of the car. "Well, then, I'll simply find things out for myself." She took a step forward, but Ella quickly stepped in front of her. Katie sidestepped left, but found her way blocked by Oliver. When she turned to the right, Nathan planted his feet in her way, his arms wrapped protectively around his middle.

Katie shuffled back and forth for a moment. "Get out of my way!"

"Go away," Ella said.

Katie jumped back into her car, and before I had a chance to move, lurched forward, knocking me to the ground. As I scrambled to my feet, she backed up, turned, and then stepped on the gas to swerve around us.

She didn't get far. With a rumble of its engine, the Institute's tractor rolled out from behind the stables and parked across the drive in front of Katie's car. As Leandro hopped out of the cab, Dan parked the Institute's ute to her left, and Archie pulled his own car up on her right. Dan strode over to me with a frown.

I waved him away. "I'm fine. Not hurt."

Leandro stepped up to Katie, fuming behind the wheel. "Didn't I tell you I'd call the police if you showed up here again?"

"You can't keep me out!"

Leandro raised his eyebrows. "Oh? This is private property. I most certainly *can* keep you out."

"I know you're hiding something here!"

"And I know you purposely knocked down a child with your car. Do you want to explain to the police why you did that?"

Katie glanced my way. "She's not hurt."

"But the CCTV cameras caught it all on film."

"I know you're hiding dragons! You can't deny it."

Leandro frowned. "Now I'm a little worried. You've run down a child with your car and you claim there are dragons, here, at a school for conservation. Are you sure you're feeling well?"

Katie growled in frustration. "I will find out what you're hiding here. I'll find proof, and then we'll see who's not feeling well." She gunned the car, reversing down the drive until it widened enough for her to turn around. Then she sped off in a cloud of dust.

We stood for a moment, watching her go, and then everyone wanted to know how I was.

"I'm fine," I assured them. "Not even a bruise. It was just a bit of a shock."

"How are we going to keep her away until we've talked to the dragons?" Ella asked.

Archie raised a hand. "Leave that to us. We'll delay her as best we can. You four—"

"Five!" chirped Rata, crawling out from under Nathan's shirt.

Archie smiled. "You *five* focus on meeting with the dragons."

Leandro nodded, his face grave. "But make it as quick as you can. I don't know how long we'll be able to hold her off."

Ten

Late that night, we stood on a rise above the school, our packs stuffed and propped against one another on the ground, waiting for Foggy Bottom. Archie waited with us. Rata stalked the tussocks, snapping up moths and beetles, which crunched loudly between her teeth in the still silence.

"Rata, that's disgusting," Ella said. "Can you at least chew more quietly?"

"Probably not," Rata replied, lifting her head and biting down on a large black beetle. "Blech!" She spat out the crushed insect. "Ew! What was that thing? Disgusting! Tastes like *skobni*."

"Serves you right," Ella grumbled.

"*Skobni*? What's that?" Nathan asked.

Archie raised an eyebrow. "I'm not sure you kids should know that word."

"What's it mean?" I smiled at the prospect of a naughty word.

"Never mind," Archie said.

Oliver grinned. "Aw, come on. We promise we won't use it. Just tell us what it means."

"Besides, if you don't tell us now, we'll ask Rata later," I added.

Archie sighed. "Well, it's not like you don't hear worse in English. Rata? Would you like to explain?"

Rata fluttered to Nathan's shoulder. "*Skobni* is, essentially, poo. But it specifically refers to poo still in an animal's lower intestine. Dragons avoid eating this because, well, it tastes like *skobni*."

Oliver giggled.

"You don't ever want to use that word when referring to a dragon," Archie warned.

"Why not?" I asked, though I could guess. My brother used to call me 'a little sh—' whenever I got into his things. If I'd been a dragon, I might have torched him for it.

Rata laughed. "There's nothing more disgusting to a dragon than *skobni*. If the intestines of a prey animal are broken during the kill, *skobni* can contaminate the entire animal. Makes the whole thing taste bad. So when you call someone *skobni*, you're not only saying they're disgusting, but they make everything around themselves disgusting, too. You're saying they're something that should be tossed aside, left to rot."

"I can see how you wouldn't want to call a dragon that … especially not a big dragon," Nathan agreed.

Still, I tucked the word into my head. It rolled nicely off the tongue, and I thought it might be a valuable addition to my vocabulary.

"Here she comes." Oliver pointed. Foggy Bottom's massive shape loomed in the darkness, gliding in for a landing. We scrabbled out of her way and she touched down—lightly for such an enormous animal—but with a crunching of stones under her feet.

She greeted all of us, but was particularly attentive to Oliver. She peered closely at him, her huge head so low her head spikes brushed the ground. She sniffed. "Good to see you are better, my little friend. Still, you smell like pain and burnt flesh."

Oliver grimaced and shrugged. "They say it'll heal. I've got medicine for the pain."

Foggy Bottom then turned her attention to me. "Your face is more colourful than Rata's scales."

I laughed. "No offence to Rata, but I think I'd rather it weren't."

"But you are well?"

"I'm fine. Just bruises."

Foggy Bottom sighed. "Let's hope for nothing worse on this trip."

Ella darted a worried glance at all of us, but said nothing. We all knew it wouldn't be easy.

"Are you ready?" Foggy Bottom asked.

We shouldered our packs. I boosted Oliver onto the dragon's back, and then Ella. I looked back to see Archie give Nathan a hug, and I gritted my teeth. Nathan broke away and gave me a foothold on his hands so I could clamber up, and then I reached down to haul him up behind me.

Rata flitted to my shoulder.

"Rata!" Foggy Bottom's voice was menacing.

"Foggy Bottom, I would love to fly myself. But you know I can't keep up with you over such a long journey. If you want me to actually be there for your discussions with the other dragons, I'm going to have to ride."

Foggy Bottom snorted her displeasure, but bunched herself up for takeoff. Ella and Oliver, in front of me, waved to Archie, and then Ella yelped as Foggy Bottom took off.

Rata's claws tightened painfully on my shoulder. "Wee heee!"

Foggy Bottom rumbled. I wondered how long it would be before she and Rata came to blows.

Our first stop was Black Cone, a peak northwest of Te

Anau, in the Murchison Mountains.

"Who are we meeting there?" I asked Rata. It was impossible to talk to the others with the wind whistling in our ears, but with Rata on my shoulder, we could manage a little conversation.

"There are a few coming to meet us. Black Cone is home to two scree dragons—"

"Scree dragons?"

"Neither of these dragons were part of the attack on the Council meeting." Rata paused for a moment. My grip tightened on Foggy Bottom's back spikes. "Anyway, Serpentine and Boulder will be there, and we're hoping three local Fiordland fringed dragons will come up to meet us, too. Evening Sun, Starlight, and Moonshine all live in the area."

"Do we know how friendly they are?"

Rata snorted. "How friendly was Storm Cloud when you first met him?"

I thought back to our first meeting, when we were snatched off the side of Mount Crosscut by scaly claws, then threatened by our snarling captor, even after we explained who we were. "He tried to eat us."

"Yeah. That's about right."

"Are you saying these dragons are going to attack us?"

"Not necessarily. They know we're coming. I expect they'll let us have our say."

"And then eat us?"

Rata made a noncommittal grunt. "Not necessarily."

Hardly comforting. I rode in silence the rest of the way. I glanced down once, only to feel my stomach lurch at the sight of the ground so far below us in the moonlight. Enough of that. I looked up at the stars, glittering in the clear sky. It made my head spin, and I felt myself sway on Foggy Bottom's back, so I stared at Oliver's back and clutched Foggy Bottom's spikes. Maybe we should have rigged up some sort of harness system so if one of us fell, it wouldn't be to our deaths.

The flight only took two hours, and we'd prepared, wearing warm, windproof jackets, but even so, my fingers were numb by the time Foggy Bottom began the spiralling descent to Black Cone. Rata leapt off to flutter down on her own. I dared a look down. Black Cone was exactly that—so black it seemed to suck away the moonlight illuminating the tussocks further down the slope. The few pockets of snow remaining near the peak glowed like beacons. Foggy Bottom brought us down amidst a jumble of angular rock at the top of a long scree slope. I eyed the scree warily, wondering if the two dragons, Serpentine and Boulder were hidden within the stones. We all slid off, and I made a point of dropping down Foggy Bottom's right flank, positioning her between me and the scree. Ella came off on the right, too, but Nathan and Oliver slid down her left. I leaned toward Ella, who steadied herself on Foggy Bottom's side. She looked as dizzy and cold as I felt.

"Rata says we're meeting two scree dragons here, and maybe three Fiordland fringed."

"Scree dragons?" Ella kept her exclamation to a whisper, but I heard the worry in it. "That scree slope—" Ella's own scream cut her off as she backed into a scree dragon's muzzle.

The dragon jerked back, its eyes going wide. Then it slowly backed away from Ella. "I swear, I didn't touch her. I simply wanted to—"

"Don't. Ever. Do. That. Again!" Ella took a step forward, forcing the much larger dragon back. "You hear me? Never! You scared the … the *skobni* out of me."

Oliver giggled. He and Nathan had come running at Ella's scream.

"Ella, relax." Nathan's voice was calm, but I could tell he was fighting his own laugh. "I think she was simply greeting you. Getting your scent."

"Well, she could have announced herself, instead of sneaking up on me."

"Greetings, Serpentine," interrupted Foggy Bottom with an impatient flick of her tail. "Have the others arrived?"

"Ah. Yeah." Serpentine seemed to be having trouble collecting her wits after Ella's outburst. "Everyone except Evening Sun."

A deep voice to my right made me start. "She said something about men and missing eggs." It was a male Fiordland fringed dragon. Even in the dark, his bright orange neck fringe was impressive.

Foggy Bottom's eyes narrowed, and Nathan, Oliver, Ella and I shared a glance. I knew they were all thinking the same thing I was—men and missing eggs could only mean Ling Chang. She was the wildlife smuggler who had kidnapped Archie to try to force him to help her capture and breed dragons for the pet trade. So she was still operating in Fiordland, even after we'd had her crew arrested.

"Well, you'll need to take tonight's information to her," Foggy Bottom said.

Rata fluttered in and landed on a boulder. On second glance, I realised it was Boulder the dragon she'd landed on. The scree dragon gave a shake and a growl. Rata giggled as she flitted off. "Let's get this party started, then."

We made our formal introductions, and the dragons leaned in to sniff us all. I smiled when Serpentine sniffed Ella. She kept as far back from the girl as possible. Ella glared and stood her ground. I hoped Ella's behaviour wouldn't make the dragons think less of our proposal.

Despite the fact my fingers were still cold, I was sweating as we launched into our presentation. I thought back to the attack on the Council meeting—all ten of the Council members had fought alongside us against three attacking dragons, and Oliver had still ended up in hospital. We were seriously outnumbered here, if these four dragons decided to turn on us. None of us had thought to put on our fireproof gear before climbing onto Foggy Bottom's back.

We presented our case, exactly as we'd done at the Council meeting. Boulder scoffed when I mentioned our ultimate goal was the protection of dragons worldwide. I swallowed and carried on with my speech. When I got to the part about revealing the existence of dragons, I braced myself. This is where it had all gone to custard before.

"You want to *what*?" Serpentine raised her head and narrowed her eyes. Smoke curled from her nostrils. "We're safe only because we're hidden."

"I'm not telling any *glavnig metzi flenka* where my lair is," Boulder growled.

"Boulder!" Foggy Bottom's voice boomed with threat. "There is no need for that sort of language." I furrowed my brow. *Glavnig metzi flenka*? Literally translated, it meant weak dirt-eater. Foggy Bottom's reaction made me think it had a stronger meaning. It was an insult, for sure. An insult aimed at humans. Ella obviously knew the meaning. Her eyes narrowed, and she folded her arms across her chest. She opened her mouth, but I was afraid of what might come out.

"Stop!" I held up a hand. "No one is going to tell anyone where individual dragon lairs are. The idea is simply to make the public aware dragons exist, and to protect dragons and their habitat through legal means. Right now, there is no way to punish people who harm dragons, because there are no laws against it."

"Because no one—well, almost no one—knows you exist," Nathan added. "My dad has been working for years to make this happen. He nearly gave his life, willingly, to make it happen. If we weren't interested in helping you, we could go right now to the media, tell them dragons exist, and let folks loose on you all."

The dragons shuffled uncomfortably and said nothing. Nathan continued. "If we didn't respect you and your right to have a say in your own futures, we could carry out our plan without you—treat you like any other endangered native animal, relocate you to predator-free offshore islands, put you in captive breeding programmes." One of the Fiordland fringed dragons growled. "But we're not doing that. We are working with the Draconic Council, as a team, to ensure dragons have a say in the plan. We don't want to do something *for* you; we want to do something *with* you."

No one spoke. Gravel crunched under shifting feet. From far off in the valley below, a morepork's call came. *More pork! More pork! More pork!*

Starlight finally broke the silence. "So, what do you want from us?" I let out my breath. Ella uncrossed her arms, and Nathan and Oliver relaxed their stances.

"We want your support. Your agreement to abide by whatever decisions the Draconic Council makes regarding this plan," Nathan replied.

"And we want your assurance you won't join any opposition group," Foggy Bottom added.

"Opposition?" Moonshine asked.

"A few days ago, a meeting of the Draconic Council was attacked." Foggy Bottom turned to Boulder and Serpentine. "By scree dragons."

"Ha! Can you blame them?" Boulder said. Foggy Bottom narrowed her eyes at him. "I mean, er …"

"The Draconic Council was set up specifically to avoid situations in which dragons aired their grievances

90

with violence. An attack on the Council is an attack on all dragons."

"Yes, but when the Council is ... conspiring with the enemy ..." Serpentine said.

"They are not our enemies."

"Yeah, that's what Storm Cloud's been saying. He's gone soft, that one. Too old." Boulder's voice was hard. "Maybe it's time for him to be kicked off the Council."

I was beginning to wish we'd remembered to put on our fireproof clothing. Foggy Bottom's tail thrashed. "Storm Cloud is the only dragon to have shown real leadership on this issue. You know as well as I do we can't keep dragons hidden forever. Sooner or later, it will get out we're here. People will come swarming around, killing and capturing dragons. Fancy being in a zoo? Behind bars for the rest of your life?"

"Ha! Scree dragons are good at hiding."

"Not that good. We need to take control of the situation before it is beyond our control."

"So, let's torch them, like we used to." Boulder stretched his neck toward Oliver. Oliver jumped back. If I'd been a dragon, I'd have torched Boulder—I could feel the fire rising in my chest. Instead, I strode over to stand between Boulder and Oliver.

"You will torch no one! You have the opportunity to direct the future of all dragonkind. Will you fall back on the violence that brought you to this point in the first place? What has torching people gotten you, except persecution by dragon slayers?"

"Lunch?" Boulder licked his lips and snorted smoke. I tried desperately to quell the shaking in my knees as my anger turned to terror.

"Boulder, give it up." Serpentine shoved Boulder away from me and Oliver. "Quit being *skobni*." Boulder snarled, but Serpentine ignored him. Addressing us, she said, "I don't like the idea of dragons going public. But I

91

hear what you're saying. It will happen, sooner or later, and we'll be in a better position if we control the process. I will support the Council, whatever it decides to do."

"Thank you," Nathan replied.

"I'll support you, too," Moonshine said.

Starlight nodded. "Me too."

Serpentine nipped Boulder on the flank. He flinched, and then sighed. "Fine. I don't agree with you, but I won't oppose you."

My shaking finally subsided. Suddenly I was exhausted. We said goodbye to the dragons, and they all vanished downhill, into the dark.

"Now what?" Rata asked. I'd almost forgotten she was there.

Nathan pulled out his phone and checked the time. "Almost four in the morning."

"The sun will be up soon. We should camp here; we can't make it to the next stop before daylight," Foggy Bottom said.

"Maybe not right here," Oliver suggested, glancing around at the jagged rocks.

We hiked downhill until we reached a field of tussocks. It wasn't particularly level, but we pitched our tents anyway—one for Nathan and Oliver, and another for Ella and me.

"Oh! Can I sleep with you?" Rata asked.

"I thought you didn't like to be anywhere you can't get out on your own," I replied.

"I can always burn my way out of a tent."

"You are *not* burning a hole in our tent," Ella said.

"How about we leave the door open, just a little."

We crawled into our sleeping bags. Rata curled up at our feet. I was asleep in an instant.

Eleven

The sun was high by the time I woke the next day. Ella was still sound asleep. I unzipped the tent flap and peered out. Oliver sat on the slope in front of me, and Foggy Bottom was sprawled in the shade of a rock nearby, snoring softly.

"Shh!" Oliver put his finger to his lips, then pointed. A few metres away were two big birds with blue chests, red beaks and olive-green backs.

My eyes widened. "Are those ..."

"Takahē!" Oliver's excited whisper was accompanied by a grin. I slipped out of the tent and tiptoed to where Oliver sat. The birds took no notice of me, but pulled at the tussock leaves, muttering back and forth to one another.

"They're so tame," I whispered.

Oliver nodded and handed me a topo map. "Look where we are. Top right corner."

I unfolded the map. In the top right corner I found the Murchison Mountains and Black Cone. And there, across the whole area, in red letters: SPECIAL (TAKAHĒ) AREA RESTRICTED ACCESS ENTRY BY PERMIT ONLY. "We're in the takahē reserve?"

Oliver grinned and nodded. "This is awesome! No one gets to come in here."

"It's why there are so many dragons in the area." I jumped at the sound of Rata's voice; I hadn't seen her. "The restricted area protects more than takahē." She alighted on a rock nearby and cocked her head at the birds. "I'll bet they make a tasty morsel for a scree dragon."

"But takahē are endangered," Oliver protested.

Rata snorted. "So are scree dragons."

"Huh. What do you do when one endangered species eats another?" I mused.

I heard the zip of a tent flap, and Ella crawled out, yawning. She rubbed her eyes, blinked, and then sucked in a breath. "Takahē?" I grinned and pointed to the map.

"Ah, here comes Nathan," Oliver said. "Now we can make some breakfast."

Nathan was climbing the hill with our billy, full of water.

"Mmm. Porridge. I'm starving," Ella said.

The pair of takahē ignored us, foraging their way down the slope away from us as we made and ate our breakfast.

"Where's our next stop?" Ella asked.

"Mount Ward." Oliver tapped the map.

"How long do you think it will take us to get there?" I asked. "An hour or two?" I looked over at the sleeping dragon. "She must be exhausted, carrying us all the way here last night."

Rata agreed. "She'll probably sleep most of the day."

"Well, we won't leave here until dusk, anyway," Nathan said. "There'll be trampers all over the place outside the takahē reserve."

Oliver checked the time on his phone. "It's only noon. That gives us all afternoon to explore!"

Ella frowned, but Nathan, Rata and I agreed exploring would be fun.

"So, if you're not coming with us, what are you going to do all afternoon?" I asked Ella.

She shrugged. "I think I'll go down to the stream and wash up."

Oliver rolled his eyes. "Right, 'cause it's so much more fun than exploring."

"Suit yourself," I said. I can't say I was disappointed to leave her behind. She'd only complain the whole way if she came with us.

"Since you'll be here, you can make lunch—or would it be dinner—for us," Oliver suggested with an impish grin.

Ella scowled. "In your dreams, mate."

"We need to be back in time to talk to Foggy Bottom before we leave, anyway. She's part of our team, too, not just our transportation. We'll all help cook." Nathan didn't like it when we argued. He'd gotten good at smoothing things out between us all.

"Let's go then!" Oliver started off down the hill. Nathan and I followed. Rata zipped ahead, turning somersaults in the air.

We scampered down to the stream and spent the afternoon clambering around the rocks, working our way downstream as we went. The forest was dark and wet. Birds called from the treetops, and leaves rustled gently underfoot. It was a welcome change from the dry tussocklands around the school. By unspoken agreement, we didn't discuss dragons at all, focusing instead on simply having fun.

I hadn't realised how far we'd gone until we had to slog back in the downpour.

"I can't believe we forgot our raincoats," Nathan said.

"I didn't even think about it," I said. "It was so sunny when we left camp."

"We *are* in Fiordland." Oliver still grinned, even though rivulets coursed down his cheeks from his rain-plastered hair. "It's not so bad." He launched into an off-key rendition of Singin' in the Rain.

"Oy! Enough!" I appreciated Oliver's upbeat nature most of the time, but not enough to listen to him sing show tunes.

Oliver giggled, and his singing subsided to a hum. After a minute, I growled at him. He flashed me a grin, but fell silent.

It was still hosing down when we trudged up the slope toward our camp. Foggy Bottom was awake. Ella stood beside her in full rain gear, hands on her hips, a frown on her face.

"Where have you guys been? We need to be moving on soon. You still need to pack up your stuff—"

"Don't get your knickers in a twist," I barked. "It won't be dark for hours." I noticed Ella had packed up our tent, and all my things were piled in a heap. In the rain.

"Ella! My stuff!" I hustled to the pile and started shoving things into the dry bag in my pack. I didn't worry about packing neatly; I simply wanted my gear out of the rain. "I can't believe you left my stuff like this. My sleeping bag is soaked!" I threw a glare at Ella.

She shrugged, giving me an innocent look. "You weren't here. When it looked like rain, I packed up the tent so I wouldn't have to put it away wet."

"You could at least have put my stuff away so it wouldn't get soaked."

"Your things are not my responsibility. Maybe you should have thought about that before you ran off to play all afternoon."

"Maybe you could have been more considerate about my gear. I'm going to have to sleep in a wet bag now." I cinched the top of my pack shut and clipped the flap over it.

Rata flitted to a nearby rock and chuckled. "Good thing you two don't breathe fire."

Both of us glowered at Rata. "This is serious. I'm going to end up with hypothermia because I have a wet sleeping bag."

"Well it wouldn't be wet if you hadn't left me to do all the work."

"Left you? We invited you to come with us. You're the one who chose to stay behind."

"Enough!" Foggy Bottom's voice rumbled. "There's a cave nearby. Let's get you all out of the rain. I'll do a little foraging while you make a meal and dry out as best you can."

Nathan and Oliver had already packed up. Working together, no doubt. It had taken almost no time at all. Why couldn't Ella have waited? I bit my tongue before I said anything.

We swung onto Foggy Bottom's back and ducked our heads against the stinging rain as she launched herself in a running heave off the mountainside. We didn't soar long before she wheeled over a small lake and into the valley below. The forest closed in beneath us, and I wondered if we'd have to jump off; Foggy Bottom couldn't land through the forest canopy. Then she banked and circled a tiny clearing, dropping lower and lower. She landed awkwardly and we slid off her back.

"The cave is that way," she said, nodding her head toward the stream. "I can't squeeze in there very well. Meet me back here when it's dark."

Rata zipped out of the trees. "Follow me. I think you're gonna like this."

We slipped and stumbled down the slope toward the stream. I was thankful for the trees; they gave me something to hold onto so I wouldn't land on my bottom.

Oliver, ahead of me, hopped down a ledge. "But there's no water." When I joined him, I understood. We were clearly at the bottom of the valley, where the stream should have been. But the forest was unbroken, and there wasn't so much as a trickle of water visible.

"Wait until we get to the cave. You'll see." Rata's eyes sparkled.

We clambered over mossy rocks and under downed trees. It was hard going, at the bottom of the valley. I kept my eyes on my feet so I wouldn't slip between rocks and break an ankle.

Oliver sucked in a breath. "Awesome!" His voice echoed.

I looked up. A cavern yawned in front of us.

"The stream must have come out of the cave once," Nathan said. "But where's the water now?"

"Underground," Rata said. "I scoped the place out this morning while you guys were asleep. The cave is huge. Goes on for kilometres. I didn't explore the whole thing."

In the cave entrance, we shrugged off our packs. It was good to be out of the rain, but I didn't think anything would actually dry in the cave. The place was decidedly wet. We fished out our torches and stepped in to explore.

"I don't think we should go far," Ella frowned as she peered into the darkness. "If the cave is as deep as Rata says, we could get lost."

"If you're so worried about our safety, maybe you could have kept my sleeping bag dry," I snapped.

"Ella's right, you know," Nathan agreed. "We're not at all prepared for caving."

"But we've got to go in a *little* way," Oliver urged. "How could you come here and *not* explore?"

"Yeah, go on. You've got to see it," Rata said.

"Aren't you coming with us?" Nathan furrowed his brows.

98

"I'll stay here and see about Tui's wet sleeping bag." In response to my questioning look, she added, "Spread it over a rock, and I'll give it a little blow drying."

I hesitated. Rata using her fire to dry my sleeping bag could end badly. But the thing wasn't going to dry any other way, and the idea of a wet, cold sleeping bag was not appealing. I pulled the bag out.

"Great. Let's go!" Oliver grinned. I forgot about my sleeping bag and followed Oliver further into the cave, Nathan and Ella close on my heels. Stalactites hung, dripping, from the ceiling, and lumpy stalagmites rose from the floor. The green light filtering through the trees at the entrance faded as we penetrated deeper.

"Do you think there are glow worms?" Oliver asked.

"Turn off your light. Let's see."

Four torches clicked off. As my eyes adjusted to the dark, the ceiling and walls lit up like the night sky, with vast constellations of glow worms.

"That. Is. Awesome!" Oliver whispered. We stood in silence for a few minutes, the only sound the dripping of the stalactites.

"How many do you think there are?" Nathan asked.

"Must be tens of thousands," I replied.

"One hundred and seventy-six thousand, three hundred and twenty-four, to be exact," came a rumbling voice at my left shoulder.

I jumped. Ella shrieked. Someone tripped and hit the floor with a wet slap, then scrambled to their feet. A moment later, four torches were directed at a female Fiordland fringed dragon. The dragon squinted into the light.

"Not in my face. Shine those things somewhere else."

We all turned our lights to the floor.

"What are you doing here?" Nathan asked.

99

The dragon's eye ridge rose. "I could ask you the same. This is *my* lair, after all." A low growl rumbled from her throat.

Ella sucked in a breath. We all froze for a moment. The deadly possible consequences of our mistake flashed through my mind. Why hadn't Rata told us this was another dragon's lair?

"That explains how you knew the number of glow worms. Did you really count them all?" Oliver smiled at the dragon. I thought if his dad had had half as much sheer cheekiness as Oliver, he must have been an incredible dragon slayer. The dragon peered down at Oliver.

"As a matter of fact, I did."

"Wow! How long did it take you?"

"About a week. Now—"

"Cool! How did you keep track of the ones you'd already counted?"

"Look, *I'm* asking the questions here. You're in *my* lair." The dragon snorted smoke and we all took a step back.

"We only came in for shelter from the rain." *And because Rata didn't bother telling us this cave was occupied*, I thought.

"We're from the Alexandra S—" Nathan caught himself. "From the Alexandra Institute, with two representatives of the Draconic Council. We're travelling the country gathering support for a dragon conservation plan."

"Oh, are you?" The dragon snaked its head closer, and Nathan took another step back. "And where are these members of the Draconic Council you're travelling with? I see only four—" she sniffed, "—unwashed human children here."

"It's not me," Ella said. "I washed in the stream this morning. It's these guys who stink." The dragon turned its attention to Ella, who shrank back and stammered, "We

… we've come with Foggy Bottom and Rata. Foggy Bottom dropped us off in a clearing nearby before going off to forage. Rata is at the mouth of the cave. We were actually leaving soon."

The dragon snorted again. "I don't think so."

My palms were sweaty. Ella's torch beam quivered. *Skobni*. I knew that word would come in handy.

The dragon looked us over and nodded. "You're certainly not leaving until I've given you a proper tour."

We all darted glances at each other.

"This part of the cave is nothing compared with further in. There's a waterfall back here. It's worth the trip to see it." The dragon turned and shambled further into the cave. None of us moved. A moment later, the dragon turned. "Well, are you coming?"

Oliver grinned. Ella seemed unconvinced, but Nathan and I smiled, too.

"I'm Nathan." He pointed his flashlight at each of us in turn and told the dragon our names. "And you are?"

"Sorry, I forgot to properly introduce myself. I am Evening Sun. Call me Eve."

Twelve

As Eve guided us deep into the cave, we shared questions and news. We told her about the dragon conservation plan. She explained why she didn't make it to our meeting.

"I was incubating two eggs until yesterday."

I grimaced, knowing where this story was headed.

"Two men entered the cave while I was out foraging around dusk. I smelled them when I returned, but I didn't worry too much at first. This cavern is known as Aurora cave. Humans sometimes come here. My eggs were well-hidden, and the visitors never spend too long here. They rarely even enter the side chamber I use; they're always headed to the waterfall, and my chamber is snug and dry, away from the stream."

"But these weren't cavers," I said. "They didn't come to see the waterfall."

Eve snorted. "No. By the time I discovered my eggs were missing, it was full dark and the men were long gone. I tracked them toward Lake Te Anau. Caught up with them as they were loading my eggs into their boat, hidden on the shore. When they saw me, they panicked. Obviously didn't know Fiordland fringed dragons are flightless. They argued for a moment about what to do. Convinced I'd sink their boat in the middle of the lake, they tossed the eggs out and raced away." She chuckled. "I didn't manage to sink the boat, but I did take a bite of the outboard motor. They were in for a long paddle back to Te Anau."

"And you got your eggs back," Ella said.

Eve sighed. "Not quite. They both cracked when they hit the shore."

"Oh no!"

"It was fine. One hadn't been fertile. It never would have hatched. That was clear after it cracked."

"But the other?"

"It was on the verge of hatching, anyway. The crack simply sped up the process." She chuckled again. "If they hadn't tossed out the eggs, those men might have gotten quite a surprise on their way across the lake."

Oliver giggled. "So your baby? The one who hatched?"

"Is beautiful and healthy."

"Can we see her?" I asked, unable to resist the thought of a baby dragon.

"Him," Eve corrected. "Yes, I suppose you may see him. But first, let's enjoy the waterfall."

The sound had been growing for several minutes. We had been following the stream, and now our flashlights revealed an impressive waterfall spilling from a hole in the wall of the cavern. Water surged out, split by a large rock in the centre, and splashed onto jumbled boulders on the floor of the cavern. It wasn't the biggest waterfall I'd ever seen, but to find it here, hundreds of metres underground, was …

"Awesome!" Oliver breathed.

After admiring the waterfall, we backtracked and entered a side chamber. Eve was right; it was dry and cosy, at least compared to the main tunnel running with water.

We cast our lights around the chamber.

"No gold?" asked Oliver. The chamber was bare and unadorned—indistinguishable from the rest of the cave.

Eve snorted. "With regular human visitors here, I can't take any chances. But the lair isn't without its beauty. Turn off your lights."

We did so, and revealed a ceiling dense with glow worms.

"Nice," I said. "Did you do that?"

"There were glow worms here before I moved in, but I've shifted some myself. And I feed them, so they've multiplied on their own, too, over the years."

"How do you feed them?" Nathan asked.

"I bring in a bit of maggot-riddled carrion every couple of weeks. The flies emerge and are attracted to the lights. The glow worms seem to like them."

I was glad the lights were off so Eve couldn't see my nose wrinkling at the idea of maggoty carrion.

"Now, would you like to see my son?"

"Yes, please." We flicked on our lights. Eve shuffled to the back of the chamber and grunted as she nosed into a small alcove. A little squeak and then loud shrieking echoed around the chamber.

I winced. Ella covered her ears. I remembered the baby southern blue dragons Ling Chang had imprisoned along with us—they had chirped when they were hungry, but they hadn't had this piercing shriek. I was thankful I wasn't a dragon mother.

Eve chuckled. "Little bubba's hungry." She opened her mouth wide and gave a deep hacking noise. Her whole neck convulsed.

"Ew!" Ella vocalised what I was thinking.

Eve regurgitated food for her baby, like a bird. The little dragon poked its head out of the alcove and into its mother's gaping maw.

"Sounds like Rata," Oliver said with a giggle. He was right, the slurping and smacking of the baby dragon's feeding sounded exactly like Rata eating a bowl of soup.

"They seriously need to work on their table manners," I whispered back to Oliver.

When the baby had eaten its fill, Eve licked drips of half-digested goo off his face and neck, and then nudged him out of the alcove toward us.

"What's his name?" Ella asked, crouching down as the terrier-sized dragon toddled across the floor.

"He hasn't got one yet. It's customary to wait until the baby is two months old before naming. It gives time for the child's personality to develop and for a meaningful name to be chosen."

"Fiordland fringed dragons name their babies after the sun and moon cycles, don't they?"

Eve raised her eye ridge at Ella. "Impressive. Yes."

Oliver laughed. "Then this one should be named Nighttime Landing, since that's what hatched him."

"Hmmm … not a bad idea," Eve mused.

Nighttime Landing was a dull copper colour. He didn't have the full neck flap of the adult Fiordland fringed dragon, but sported what looked like a small orange collar. He was unsteady on his feet, but obviously curious, and keen to investigate the four unusual creatures in his lair. He reached Nathan, who crouched and stuck his hand out toward the dragon. It hissed, and the little collar around its neck flipped out. Nathan jerked his hand back, and then laughed. He slowly extended his hand again, and Nighttime Landing took a step closer, swaying his head from side to side as if trying to get a better view of Nathan.

I held my breath as Nighttime Landing stretched out to sniff Nathan's hand. Nathan grinned and wiggled his fingers, as if to tickle the dragon's chin. Like a snake, the dragon struck, delivering a sound nip to Nathan's index finger.

Nathan cried out and pulled his hand to his side. Nighttime Landing shrieked and scurried back to his mother. Everyone else laughed.

"Hey, that hurt!" Nathan looked indignantly at us.

I tried to curb my laughter. "Are you okay?"

Nathan examined his hand. "Yeah. It was only a nip. Hardly broke the skin."

"Here sweetie." Ella tried to entice the dragon back out by making squeaking noises. It worked, and now the dragon tottered toward Ella's hand.

"I wouldn't do that if I were you," Nathan warned.

Ella ignored him and presented Nighttime Landing with her closed fist. "You have to give him something he can't bite." The dragon nudged her hand and she slowly uncurled it to scratch his neck. The dragon gave a little growl and Ella froze. The dragon growled again and pushed its neck against Ella's hand as if to say, *don't stop*. She smiled and resumed her scratching.

Once Nighttime Landing had discovered we were all good for scratches, he clambered between us all, begging attention from each of us in turn. Eventually he fell asleep draped across Nathan's lap.

"We should go," Nathan said reluctantly.

"Thanks for letting us see him," Ella said.

We stood, and Nathan tucked the sleeping dragon back into the alcove.

"Why *did* you let us see him?" I asked. "Why didn't you just kill us when you found us here? Not that I wanted you to," I added quickly. "I'm glad you didn't."

Eve chuckled. "I knew who you must be. I could smell Foggy Bottom's scent on you. Moonshine already come and told me about last night's meeting. I know what you're trying to do, and if your plan can stop the men who steal dragon babies, I support you."

"Thanks." What more was there to say?

"Now, let's get you on your way. It must be nearly dusk out there. You'll be travelling at night, no doubt."

Eve led us back to the mouth of the cavern. She was right. The light was fading. But the rain had stopped, and I was glad we wouldn't be flying in it.

"Where's Rata?" Oliver asked. I scanned the entrance, wondering what could have happened to her.

"You don't think she went looking for us in the cave, do you?" Ella asked. "Maybe she got lost."

My eyes lit on my sleeping bag. It had fallen off the rock where I'd spread it out. I stepped over to pick it up. I noticed several scorch marks, but it felt much drier than it had before. I picked it up to stuff it back into its sack.

Out rolled Rata. "What? Hey! I was asleep!" She picked herself off the ground and shook to settle her scales. Then she saw Eve, and her eyes widened in surprise.

"While you were napping, Rata, we were meeting Evening Sun, *who lives in this cave*. Why didn't you tell us the cave was occupied? We could have been killed, walking into a dragon's lair unannounced and uninvited."

"I didn't know. I told you, I didn't go far into the cave when I explored it earlier. I …" The little dragon slumped and hung her head. "Sorry." Then she perked up. "But you didn't die."

"No thanks to you." I shoved my sleeping bag into its stuff sack, noticing more singe marks as I did. I knew I should thank Rata for drying it for me, but that familiar lump stuck in my throat again. I was furious with Ella for letting my stuff get soaked. And with Rata for sending us unprepared into a dragon's lair. I fumed over the fact Rata was unaware we'd spent hours inside the cave because she was asleep in my sleeping bag, which she'd burnt with her stupid fire. "Shouldn't we be going? We said we'd meet Foggy Bottom in the clearing at dusk."

"You should. And I should get back to my son," Eve said. "Travel safely, and good luck."

We said goodbye, and Eve disappeared into the darkness.

"But we haven't had anything to eat yet," Oliver said. "I'm starving."

"It'll have to be quick," Nathan said.

"Sandwiches, then. I think the bread is in my bag." Oliver rummaged in his pack and produced a squashed loaf. Nathan found a block of cheese, and Ella hauled out a bag of carrots.

As dinners went, it was lame, but I didn't care. I nursed my bad mood, eating in silence, answering the others' questions with grunts. Nathan asked Rata what she knew about our itinerary. Rata explained that Storm Cloud and Foggy Bottom had mapped out a route that would take us down the eastern ranges of the Southern Alps. We would fly across to Stewart Island, then head back north along the West Coast, all the way to Kahurangi National Park.

"Then we're off to the North Island. Not as many stops there—more people, fewer dragons than on the South Island. Aorangi Forest Park, Whanganui National Park, and Te Urewera are the main stops. If we can manage it, we'll make a brief stop in Waimangu—North Island fire lizards live in the hot pools there, but they're not really a priority."

"Why not?" Nathan asked. "They're dragons, too."

"Yeah, in a fashion." Rata shrugged. "They've always kept to themselves, even more so than scree dragons. They've refused to join the Draconic Council. They won't leave their hot pools. They don't even talk to each other much. I can't imagine they'll care what we do—they won't support our plan, and they won't oppose it. They simply won't care."

"But we're going to talk to them anyway?" Nathan's brow was furrowed.

"Storm Cloud says we need to give them the chance to be involved. Says we can't leave them out simply because they've never been interested in working with others in the past."

"He's probably right," Ella conceded. "What we're doing will affect all dragons. It wouldn't be fair if we didn't give them the opportunity to be involved."

Rata chuckled. "I don't think Storm Cloud was as worried about fairness as he was about future uprising."

"Yeah, but if you say they don't care ..." Oliver shrugged.

"They don't care now. But the truth is, they're the dragons most likely to suffer from public knowledge of dragons."

"Why's that?"

"They live closer to humans than any other dragons. Many of the hot pools they inhabit are already popular tourist destinations. It's easy for people to get there. Easy for people to cause trouble if they know the dragons are there."

"And people are going to freak out when they find out dragons are living so close to them," Ella added.

We ate in silence, digesting the scope of our plan, along with our sandwiches.

Nathan finished his sandwich and dusted the crumbs off his shirt. "We should get moving. Next stop, Mount Ward?"

"To visit Lightning, Storm Cloud's cousin," Rata added.

"And three scree dragons?"

"I think we should suit up in our fireproof gear, don't you?" Ella suggested.

"A good idea," Rata said.

Twenty minutes later, we were soaring over the treetops on Foggy Bottom's back, headed to Mount Ward.

Thirteen

Mount Ward reminded me of Mount Crosscut—Storm Cloud's home. I was thankful we didn't have to climb it, like we did Mount Crosscut. The peak was bare rock, with a broad ridge leading up to it. That part would have been an easy stroll. But below the peak a jumble of glacial ice and steep slopes would have made the climb nearly impossible for us. A line of peaks stretched south from Mount Ward like the spikes on a dragon's back. Foggy Bottom had mentioned this area was popular with climbers; I could see why. You could climb a different route every day for a year and not even begin to explore the area. I turned to Oliver, behind me, and grinned at him. My bad mood had evaporated during the flight. Oliver grinned back. I knew he was dreaming of climbing those peaks. Both of us had a lot of practise to do before we were ready for them.

Foggy Bottom glided in along the ridge, landing on a mostly flat expanse of scree. We slid off her back and scanned the area.

"When were we supposed to meet them here?" I asked, seeing nothing but rock.

"About now," Foggy Bottom replied.

"Is that 'about now' in human time, or 'about now' in dragon time?" Ella asked. Archie had told us about dragon time—according to him, dragons were notoriously late for meetings. Since we had always been brought to meetings by a dragon, I hadn't noticed dragons were late. I suppose we had been late, too.

Foggy Bottom shrugged. "Does it matter? They're not here yet. We'll wait."

Ella shivered. "I'm cold. Do you think we have time to make some hot chocolate?"

I was carrying the camp stove and wasn't inclined to do anything for Ella at the moment. "I don't want to pull out the stove. It's in the bottom of my pack."

"It's not *hot* chocolate, but I have a chocolate bar. I could share it out if you want," Oliver suggested.

"Chocolate sounds g—"

The scree around us exploded. I'm sure the others screamed, but I didn't hear them over my own yell. I ducked and rolled as a gout of flame surged toward my face. A boot kicked me in the side, and I looked to see Nathan next to me, his eyes wide. "Scree dragons," I growled.

"To me!" Foggy Bottom bellowed. She roared and shot flame at a scree dragon swooping low over the ground toward her. I was surprised by the sight of the scree dragon aloft on its stubby wings, and momentarily thought of my auntie's chickens flapping heavily across the yard. Then panic set in and I rose, dragging Nathan with me.

Oliver and Ella stumbled toward Foggy Bottom from the other direction. Oliver's face was a mask of terror. Out of the corner of my eye, I saw a dragon closing in on them. My panic turned to rage. I stopped and picked up a rock, and hurled it at the dragon. It missed, and that made me angrier. I picked up another and hurled it, hitting the dragon's side with a satisfying thud. It turned toward me and I flicked on my torch, aiming the beam for its eyes.

The dragon blinked and growled in the sudden light. It ducked its head, but I kept the beam focused on its eyes, hoping to keep it disoriented and blinded long enough for Oliver and Ella to find cover.

"Tui! Come on!" Nathan urged me over. The dragon took a step toward me, still trying to dodge my torch beam.

"Come on, you *glavnig skobni*," I taunted. "Come and get me."

"Tui! Look out!"

The dragon leapt at me. In desperation, I raised my arm to hurl my torch at it, but I was knocked from behind. Still wearing my backpack, I went down hard. The backpack slid up, giving my head a little extra shove so my nose cracked against the rocks. By the time the stars cleared, Nathan was pulling me to my feet and hauling me to Foggy Bottom's side. He hoisted me onto her back. Oliver and Ella were already there. I reached down to grab his hand and pull him up, but Foggy Bottom launched into the air, and my hand caught only emptiness.

"Nathan!" For an instant, he looked up at me, his eyes wide. Then he turned to face the scree dragon rising up behind him.

"Foggy Bottom! We have to go back!" I pounded on her side as she flapped away from the peak. "We have to get Nathan!"

"As soon as I drop you three off somewhere safe."

"It'll be too late by then!" Oliver peered back toward the peak.

"We have to go back now!"

"He can't stand alone against three scree dragons," Ella added.

"He's got Rata."

Rata? What was she going to do? "We have to go back now!" I kicked Foggy Bottom with my heels.

Foggy Bottom suddenly banked. Ella shrieked and Oliver whooped. I gritted my teeth and crouched low as she executed a swooping turn, then furled her wings and dived. The move made me suck in my breath. Blood dripped from my throbbing nose and splattered against my chest as the wind whipped around me. *Skobni*. Nothing I could do for it at the moment. I looked toward the fight below.

Somehow, Nathan had manoeuvred himself to a jumble of large rocks. The rocks gave him some cover from the dragons closing in on him, but I could see the dragons were herding him into a trap.

I saw all this, and then realised how fast we were diving. I swore and shut my eyes, hoping Foggy Bottom knew what she was doing. My stomach bottomed out as she pulled up and blasted the first scree dragon with flame. I opened my eyes as we skimmed over the first dragon's head. Foggy Bottom reached out with all four clawed feet to grab the second dragon. The jolt of the impact knocked all three of us off her back, which probably saved our lives. The scree dragon shot fire over Foggy Bottom. It didn't faze her, but it might have toasted us.

Of course, falling onto sharp rocks from the back of a large dragon isn't pleasant. By dumb luck, I landed on my back, my backpack cushioning my fall. Oliver and Ella weren't so lucky. I tore off my pack and scrambled to Oliver. He sat up. As I reached him, he turned over his hands. His palms were a mass of cuts. I swore.

"I'm okay." Oliver forced a smile. "Could have been worse. These fireproof clothes are decent padding. Only real damage is my hands." He pressed his hands against his thighs with a wince. "Check on Ella."

She hadn't moved from where she'd fallen in a crumpled heap. As I scrambled over to her, she groaned and sat up. She raised a hand to the side of her head, then pulled it away with a cry.

"Is that … blood?" Even in the dark, I could see her face go white. Her eyes rolled back in her head and she fainted.

It was blood. Lots of it. I turned to run back to my pack for the first aid kit.

An enormous dragon rose from below the ridge. I screamed and threw myself on top of Ella. I felt the wind as the dragon flapped over us, and then heard its roar. It was the green dragon, here on dragon time. I peeked up and was relieved to see its fury was aimed at the scree dragons, not at us. I picked myself up and scrambled to my pack.

"What's wrong with her?" Oliver asked as I frantically searched for the first aid kit.

"She must have cracked her head against the rocks. Bleeding pretty badly." My hands were shaking. "You gonna be okay if I look after her first?"

"I'll be fine. Do you need me to help?"

"No." I found the first aid kit and hurried back to Ella's side. Bandaging her head would be easier if Ella was conscious. "Ella. Ella? Can you hear me?" I tapped her cheek. "Ella, please speak to me."

Her eyes fluttered and opened. She frowned. "Did I faint? My head's bleeding, isn't it?" She groaned. "I hate blood." She started to move.

"No. Stay lying down." I put a restraining hand on her shoulder. "Let me bandage your head, and then you can get up." I opened the first aid kit, searching for gauze. "Do you hurt anywhere else?"

Ella moaned. "Everywhere."

I huffed and turned Ella's head so I could see where it was bleeding. "You've got to be more specific, unless you want me to bandage you up like a mummy from head to foot."

Ella was still for a moment. "Aside from the head? Right arm. Right ankle."

"Nowhere else?"

"Maybe my hip. Thigh, actually." She shifted slightly. "Ah. That's better. I was on a rock."

I sighed and pressed a gauze pad to her head. "Can you hold that there while I start wrapping?"

As she followed my instructions, a dragon roared. She twisted to look, and grimaced. "What's going on?"

Had she hit her head that hard? "We were attacked by scree dragons."

"I know that. What's happening now? How long was I out?"

"Only for a minute." I started unrolling a length of gauze around her head.

"And Nathan? Is he okay?"

"I don't know. Another green dragon just arrived. Fighting alongside Foggy Bottom." I finished wrapping her head, and then scanned the rest of her. "Arm's bleeding, too."

"No. I don't think so." Ella raised it and wiggled it around. "I think it's just bruised."

"Then what's all this blood?" I pointed to her sleeve.

"It's yours, Tui." She grimaced. "Your nose."

I reached up and gingerly probed my face. "Lovely." I grabbed another wound pad from the first aid kit and pressed it to my face. "And your ankle?" I asked.

"Hurts."

I rolled my eyes. "Can you move it?" Ella wiggled it in answer. "Good. At least it's not broken."

A great rumble shook the ground. I looked up to see a scree dragon tumbling off the side of the ridge in a shower of rocks. It bounced and rolled down the slope onto an ice field below. When it came to a rest—a black smudge on the white ice—it did not move.

Quiet descended on the mountain top. I hadn't realised quite how chaotic it had been until everything was still. I'd blocked it all out to focus on Ella. Now I glanced around. Thankfully, there was no vegetation up here. Nothing had caught fire. Nathan was standing—a good sign. I heard the rumble of Foggy Bottom's voice, but couldn't make out the words. The other green dragon, Lightning, took off down the slope toward the fallen scree dragon. I didn't know where the other dragons had gone. Escaped, presumably. Nathan patted Foggy Bottom's leg, then made his way to where Oliver, Ella and I were.

"You guys okay?" His voice was as shaky as mine.

"I think so." I shone my flashlight at him. "You're covered in blood."

He barked a laugh. "Says you."

"Fair enough."

Nathan swiped a hand across his bloody cheek. "It's a scratch, really. Doesn't even hurt."

Foggy Bottom lumbered over. "Sorry about the rough landing. Didn't really think you'd all go flying like that."

"Seatbelts. That's what we need," Oliver suggested.

Foggy Bottom lowered her head and sniffed at Ella. "Are you going to be okay?"

Ella was still on her back. She raised a hand. "I'll be okay. Horizontal is good at the moment." She grimaced and waved a hand at us. "You guys need to clean that blood up."

I smiled, trying not to laugh. "She fainted when she realised her head was bleeding."

"Sure it wasn't a concussion?" Nathan asked.

Ella scowled. "It wasn't a concussion. I just don't like blood, okay? I'll be fine."

I looked around. "Where's Rata?"

Foggy Bottom chuckled. "Oh, somewhere out there, embedded in the side of a scree dragon, I'd say."

"What?"

"You should have seen her, Tui." Nathan smiled. "She was amazing. Took on a scree dragon all by herself. She latched onto its back and started tearing at it."

"It's the kea trick," Foggy Bottom said.

"The kea trick?"

"Haven't you heard the stories about kea and sheep?"

Oliver's eyes went wide. "Oh! You mean the thing where they sit on the back of a sheep and pick out its kidneys?"

"Ew!" Ella wrinkled her nose. "That's disgusting!"

"I, personally, prefer to singe the wool off a sheep first," Foggy Bottom commented.

Ella gagged. Oliver chuckled.

"So, she's picking out some dragon's kidneys?" I asked.

"Oh, I doubt she'll go so far as to take both kidneys. She's a glutton, but I think even Rata would have difficulty with that much food."

Ella moaned. "I'm gonna be sick."

Fourteen

We couldn't stay on Mount Ward. It was too popular as a climbing destination, and Lightning knew of three climbing parties in the area who would no doubt be ascending the peak the following day. Besides, it looked like there was more rain on the way, and it would be better to be in a sheltered place, rather than here on the peak.

While we were discussing what to do, Rata returned. Foggy Bottom raised an eye ridge at her.

"All taken care of." Rata licked her face.

"I don't want to know the details," Ella said.

"Fine. Suffice it to say you won't have to worry about that fellow for a while."

"You didn't really eat out his kidneys, did you?" I asked.

"No details!" Even in the dark I could tell Ella had gone pale.

"You can tell us about it later," Oliver said in a mock whisper.

Foggy Bottom turned the conversation back to our needs. "Rata, we've been discussing where we're going from here. Our next official stop is on the coast, but I don't think we should take Ella that far tonight. Concussion or not, she had a good crack on the head. We can't stay here. Any suggestions? You know this area well."

"How about we go to my mum's territory?"

"Your mum lives here?" I'd never thought about Rata's family.

"Yeah. Not too far." She turned back to Foggy Bottom. "You could drop them off below Caroline Peak. Plenty of spots for you to hole up on the peak, and the kids could head down to Lake Hauroko from there. It's an easy slope, and there's a hut on the edge of the lake."

"If there's a hut, won't we risk being seen?" Nathan asked.

"Nah. There's no track to the hut. It's used occasionally by fishermen. They come in by boat. But there's almost never anyone there. And I can hide, if someone shows up. With Foggy Bottom on the peak, it's not a big deal."

A hut sounded great. And a short trip to a night and day of rest sounded even better.

It was a bit of a trick getting Ella onto Foggy Bottom's back. She was still a bit woozy. She claimed it was from the sight of blood, but I wondered if we should be taking her to a hospital. No one else suggested it, though, and Ella seemed determined to prove she was okay.

Still, I made her put on her climbing harness and I clipped her into a rope I tied around Foggy Bottom's middle.

"Might not be a bad idea for all of us to clip in," Nathan suggested.

"Seatbelts!" Oliver gave a thumbs-up.

We managed the short flight in good time. Clouds were rolling in as we landed beside a small lake above the tree line. Foggy Bottom flew off to the broken rock of the peak, and Rata flitted ahead of us, leading the way downstream to the hut.

It was raining lightly when we arrived at the hut. It was a sad-looking thing. Much neglected, but thankfully empty. Four bunks, a tiny wood stove, and a small table were all it offered, but it was enough. I thought we could all use a decent meal, so I offered to cook. Instant rice and a packet of Indian curry. While I cooked, Nathan picked gravel out of Oliver's palms, and then wrapped them up.

"You're next, Tui."

"What do you mean?"

"Let me clean up your face for you."

"I'm cooking."

"Oliver can stir the pot as well as you can."

I blinked back tears. Why was I about to cry? When I had control of my face, I turned to Nathan. Oliver stepped in and took charge of my spoon.

I closed my eyes as Nathan searched my face for embedded gravel. "Do you think your nose is broken?" he asked. "It looks like it bled a fair bit."

I reached up and poked at it. It hurt, but not too much. "No. Probably just bruised."

"Do you want me to clean off the blood? I need it cleaned up so I can see if there's more gravel in there."

"No. I'll do it." I stepped outside. The hut sat at the point where the stream met the lake. There wasn't much of a shore by the lake, but it was easy enough to find a spot by the stream where I could get water. The icy water made me break out in goose bumps, but it felt good on my face. I dried my face with my T-shirt. It came off red.

Back in the hut, the smell of curry made my stomach growl. Nathan found another stone embedded in my nose, and then declared me mineral-free. He frowned at my face.

"What?"

"I don't think I can really bandage that, short of wrapping your entire face in gauze."

"Do it! Do it!" Oliver cheered. "Then she and Ella can be mummies together."

I narrowed my eyes. "Oliver, if you weren't so cute, I'd punch you."

Oliver giggled, and it took effort to suppress my smile and glare at him properly.

"Time to eat, I think," Oliver announced.

It felt so good to eat. I was hungry. But more than that, I needed comfort. Warm food, friends, and a roof over our heads revived my spirits.

As I pulled out my sleeping bag an hour later, I fingered the scorch marks. I looked over at Ella, already in bed with her eyes closed, her head swathed in bandages. I glanced to Rata, curled up at Nathan's feet. My anger at them fizzled. I spread the bag out on my bunk, crawled in, and fell asleep.

It poured all day the next day. The whole idea of being at the hut was to rest, but being stuck in a tiny space with nothing to do was a bit *too* restful for me. Rata announced she would visit her mum. We encouraged her to bring her back to the hut so we could meet her.

Rata grimaced. "Are you kidding? My mum? What, so you can see her treat me like a dragonlet—lick my face and nip my ears? No thanks. Too embarrassing."

We all laughed, and Rata zipped out into the rain.

By mid-morning I was climbing the walls in boredom.

Oliver sighed. "I can't believe we didn't think to bring things to *do*."

"Well, we were mostly focused on safety when we packed," Nathan reasoned.

I laughed. "And look how well that worked out."

"Hey, none of us got burnt." Nathan had a point. He'd been blasted repeatedly by the scree dragons before

Foggy Bottom, Lightning and Rata had come to the rescue, but his clothes had protected him.

"And those fireproof clothes are tough," Oliver added. "Do you know how far we fell off Foggy Bottom last night? And all I got were scraped up hands."

I grimaced. "Yeah, I know exactly how far we fell. So does Ella's head." I gestured to Ella, asleep on her bunk. She'd been awake earlier. She'd eaten and seemed to be in reasonable shape, aside from a headache. Nathan had fished a paracetamol tablet out of the first aid kit for her, and she'd gone back to bed shortly after she'd taken it.

I envied her ability to sleep. Sitting around doing nothing was driving me crazy. I stood up. "I'm going up to visit Foggy Bottom on the peak."

"What? In this rain?"

I shrugged. "I've got rain gear. I'm going nuts sitting here. It's something to do. Anyone else want to come with me?"

"We shouldn't leave Ella alone here," Nathan said. "If she's dizzy or not feeling well when she wakes, she might need help getting to the loo or something." He and Oliver eyed one another. I could tell both of them were dying to get out.

Nathan sighed. "I'll stay." I felt bad for him, but I agreed he was the one who should stay. If Ella needed help, Oliver was simply too small.

"Yes! I'll get my rain gear on." Oliver hopped up and started flinging things out of his bag.

I moved to do the same. As I pulled on my rain pants, I thought about Nathan sitting here bored with a sleeping Ella. I made an executive decision. I knew where Ella kept the ATM card Leandro had given us. It wasn't supposed to be used for frivolous things, but keeping ourselves from going mad wasn't frivolous. I slipped the card out of her

123

bag and into my pocket. A water bottle, a sandwich and a few muesli bars completed my kit.

"We'll be a while," I said to Nathan as Oliver and I headed out.

He nodded. "Have fun."

"I'm singin' in the rain!" Oliver belted out the tune as we stepped into the downpour.

I let Oliver sing for a while as we climbed back up the hill. Then I told him my plan.

"Great idea!"

Going up was slower than coming down had been. When we emerged from the trees two hours later, I was hot and sweaty inside my rain gear.

I scanned the slopes above us, squinting into the rain. "Where do you think Foggy Bottom is?"

"Somewhere dry, I hope. How are we going to find her?"

I shrugged. I hadn't considered that. "Call her name?"

We trudged upward, calling Foggy Bottom's name every few minutes. I was beginning to think we wouldn't find her when Oliver pointed. "There!"

She emerged from the mist above, gave a heave into the air, and glided down to us.

"I didn't expect to see you so early. Where are the others? Is everything okay?"

"Yeah, we're all fine. Just bored," I said. "Nathan's looking after Ella, who is sleeping."

"We thought you might be able to take us into a town, so we can pick up some supplies."

"Hmm … I don't like flying around inhabited areas during the day."

"Storm Cloud took Nathan and me to Alexandra once. Dropped us off outside of town in the dark, but picked us up midday. It was raining, and visibility was low. Easy peasy." Oliver brimmed with confidence.

"Where do you want to go?"

"That's the problem." I shrugged. "We don't know where the nearest store is."

"What about those mobile phones of yours? Can't you find the information there?"

Oliver laughed. "Not out here. No cell phone signal."

Foggy Bottom thought for a moment. "Well, we'll have to figure it out as we go, then. Hop on." She knelt down to help us up.

Oliver and I both grinned. I wasn't really looking forward to the wet flight, but I was glad to be doing something.

Foggy Bottom glided down a long, forested valley and soared out across Lake Hauroko. For half an hour, we flew over unbroken forest. Then suddenly the trees gave way to farmland.

"If you keep going east, you should eventually hit a road," I shouted to Foggy Bottom over the wind and rain.

She nodded. "I'll find a big road and follow it to the nearest town."

As it turned out, we could see the town before we saw the road. Foggy Bottom circled around, looking for a good landing spot.

"How about there?" Oliver pointed to a gravel bar in the river bisecting the town. A forested reserve shielded the bar from town, but it was only a short walk from there to the main road.

Foggy Bottom approached from the north, gliding down the river below the tops of the trees to avoid notice. She landed neatly on the gravel bar, and we slid off her back.

"You'll wait here for us?" I asked.

"Don't be too long. I don't like being this close to town."

"We'll be back as quickly as we can."

The gravel bar was obviously a popular fishing spot. A well-beaten path led toward town. I worried Foggy Bottom would be discovered, and I hoped the rain would keep people indoors.

We emerged onto the road through what looked like school grounds. "I wonder what town we're in," Oliver mused.

"Tuatapere."

"How do you know that? Have you been here before?"

I pointed to the sign. "Tuatapere Community College."

"Ah, yes. Kinda gives it away, doesn't it?"

"Come on. Let's find a store." We splashed down the deserted sidewalk.

"Tuatapere Health and Gift?" Oliver read out the sign above a shop.

"Let's see what they've got."

The woman at the counter took one look at us and said, "First aid supplies are on the left." I paused. Then I remembered my face. I decided to ignore her.

"Have you got playing cards?" Oliver asked.

By the time we headed back to the river, we'd stopped in every promising store in the entire town. That is to say, three. We'd picked up a selection of special items that we tied up into plastic bags and stuffed into our pockets for the trip back.

The rain was tapering off, and Oliver and I jogged back to where Foggy Bottom waited for us. She wasn't happy about how long we'd taken.

"Hurry up, you two," she snapped. "It's time we were out of here."

We scrambled onto her back, and she leapt into the air. We cruised upriver for a kilometre or so, then shot straight upward into the clouds.

The rain had stopped by the time we touched down near Caroline Peak. We thanked Foggy Bottom and agreed to meet her at the same spot at dusk, provided Ella was well enough to move on. Then we trotted down the stream to the hut.

We heard Ella before we came in sight of the hut.

"I don't *care*. I'm not sitting here any longer."

We stopped and listened. I heard the murmur of Nathan's voice, but I couldn't make out the words.

"The rain's almost stopped. Look at this! They've even gotten into the powdered milk. Didn't you see them? What were you doing in here all day?"

Oliver turned to me with raised eyebrows. "*Blarghstra.*"

Rata zipped out of the undergrowth. "You might not want to go in there. Mice got into her pack. I told her I'd come out and hunt them. I don't really like mice, but it was an excuse to get out of there."

I snorted. "Well, she must feel okay; she's acting normal. Come on. Let's go rescue Nathan." We hurried to the hut.

We walked in to find Ella surveying the contents of her backpack, spread out on the table. She scowled at us as we came through the door. "Where have you two been?"

"We braved the rain and the prying eyes of the residents of Tuatapere to pick up treats." Oliver and I spilled the contents of our pockets and bags onto a bunk.

"You went to town and didn't tell us? I bet you went to a café, too, didn't you and—" She slipped her hand into the side pocket of her pack. "You took the cash card, didn't you?"

She opened her mouth, and I was certain she would launch into a tirade, but Nathan held up his hand. "Why don't you show us what you bought."

Oliver began. "Well, we *did* go to a café, but only to pick up something good for dinner. Look! Pies!" He held up four grease-stained paper bags. "They're all different. We thought we could cut them into quarters and we could all have a little of each."

"We also stopped by the grocery store." I held up a bottle of Coca-Cola and a big chocolate bar. "To go with the pies."

Ella grunted. I had chosen Coca-Cola because I knew it was her favourite.

"But the real reason we went was to get some entertainment." Oliver worked at a knot in one of our bags.

"We were supposed to use the card for necessities only."

I raised my hand. "I know, Ella. But we didn't spend much, and I think Leandro will agree preventing terminal boredom is a necessity."

Oliver held up our purchases one by one. "A deck of cards! Do you all know how to play hearts? Never mind. I can teach you if you don't. A mini Frisbee!"

"Excellent!" Nathan was smiling now.

"A multi-game travel set—includes chess, draughts, backgammon, and Parcheesi!"

"I hate chess." Ella was certainly in a mood.

"And ... Pass the Pigs!"

"Pass the Pigs?" Nathan asked.

Ella's eyes widened. "Oh, I know that game. It's awesome! You throw these little pigs like dice and get points based on how they land. It's, like, one point for a sider, five points for a trotter or a razorback, twenty if you get two trotters ..." She looked around at us, staring with our mouths open. "What? I know it sounds dumb, but it really is fun."

We ate our pies and drank the Coke. Ella insisted on a game of Pass the Pigs while we devoured the chocolate bar, and then it was time to pack up and head back up the hill. Rata zipped ahead to let Foggy Bottom know we were on our way. Ella was slow; she kept complaining of a headache. We stopped to let her take some paracetamol, and it seemed to help after a while. My legs felt the fact Oliver and I had done the climb once already. I was happy to keep the pace down for Ella.

In spite of the slow hike, we reached the tree line right on time. The clouds had cleared, and sunset gave an orange cast to the landscape. The dragons were waiting for us. We rigged up a rope harness for Foggy Bottom, put on our climbing harnesses and climbed on, clipping into the rope for safety.

"Next stop, Stewart Island." Foggy Bottom lifted into the air.

Fifteen

I was excited to go to Stewart Island. I'd never been there before, and I hoped we'd have time to explore a bit. Unfortunately, we only had one stop to make there. We zipped in, met with a few southern blue dragons who thought our plan was a good idea, and zipped out as quickly as possible.

After Stewart Island, we headed back to the mainland, travelling up the West Coast. Over the next five days, we met nothing but southern blue dragons. All of the meetings went well. We dressed in our fireproof clothing every time—we weren't about to make that mistake again—but it wasn't necessary. Seems word had gotten around to most of the southern blues, and they were happy to support us. Many of them remembered a time when the seals they prey on were so scarce they had to resort to scraping mussels off the rocks at low tide to survive. They'd seen what human legislation had done for the seals, and were happy to gain the same protection for themselves.

We lucked out on the weather. Except for a few passing showers, the sun shone every day. On the last West Coast day, we were sitting on a scrap of beach south of Martyr Homestead, where we'd rescued Nathan's dad. We were watching the sunset, waiting for darkness so we could move on to our next meeting.

So close to Martyr Homestead, I thought about the day when we'd rescued Archie, and how the dragons came to help, even the tiny gold fairy dragons who couldn't do much more than harass Drachenmorder and Sir Christopher.

"Rata?"

"Hmm?" Rata raised her head from the rock where she had been sunning.

"Why haven't we met with any gold fairy dragons yet? You said you grew up in Southland, and those gold fairies came to Martyr Homestead to help free Nathan. Why haven't we met the others?"

"There are no others." Rata's voice lacked its usual brightness.

Oliver sat up. "What do you mean?"

"The twelve of us who were at Martyr Homestead? That's all there are. The entire population."

"You mean, in all of New Zealand there are only a dozen gold fairy dragons?"

"In all of the world. We're endemic to New Zealand. Found nowhere else."

"Oh, Rata. I'm so sorry." Ella looked like she might cry.

Rata snorted. "It's not your fault, Ella. Our population plummeted long before you were born. We were pleased to learn the dragon slayers considered us extinct. It took some pressure off us."

"Did dragon slayers kill gold fairy dragons?" It seemed ridiculous; they were all but harmless.

"Well, we *did* learn that trick from the kea." Rata chuckled, and Ella made a face. "I suppose they had some cause. But dragon slayers were never our biggest problem. Mostly it was habitat loss and the pet trade."

We were all silent. What do you say to someone whose entire species is on the brink of extinction? Especially when your own species is responsible.

131

Rata shook herself. "Well, we're going to change that, aren't we? Someday these forests will teem with gold fairy dragons again."

"They will," I said. But I wasn't convinced. Twelve individuals wasn't much to start with.

"Foggy Bottom?" Nathan called to the big green dragon sitting on a rock jutting into the waves. With two effortless leaps she was at our side. "We're headed to Kahurangi National Park tonight?"

"Yes. It's a long way. It'll take us all night. Our meeting isn't until tomorrow night."

"Aren't there any dragons between us and Kahurangi? I assumed we'd stop at Mount Cook. With Mount Cook and Westland National parks right next to each other, there *must* be dragons there."

"Yes, you would think so, wouldn't you," Foggy Bottom mused. "There *should* be dragons there—scree dragons at the very least, and a green dragon or two."

"So why aren't we stopping there?"

"Because, regardless of what *should* be there, no dragons live around Mount Cook."

"Why is that?" Oliver asked.

"It is sacred. Tapu, your people would say, Tui."

I nodded. "Aoraki Mount Cook *is* tapu." I cocked my head. "It's tapu to dragons, too? Why?"

"Well, according to our lore, a great taniwha lives there."

I laughed. "Aren't taniwha dragons themselves?"

Foggy Bottom nodded. "Many are."

"So, you're saying a huge dragon lives on Mount Cook?" Oliver sat up and grinned.

Foggy Bottom shook her head. "As far as I know, no dragon lives there. It's sacred. We don't go there."

"So ... the taniwha?" I asked.

"Is a mystery," Foggy Bottom concluded. Then she scoffed. "I doubt there's anything there. Mount Cook is nothing but ice and rock. What would a dragon eat there? Even scree dragons, who can spend half the year in hibernation, would struggle."

The light was fading. We had nearly eight hours of travel ahead of us. I stood. "Shouldn't we get going?"

After so much travel, flying dragonback had lost its glamour. It was cold and often wet. The wind was fierce, and holding on was tiresome. Not to mention the sore thighs from straddling such a huge animal.

The first leg of our trip was short. We stopped off briefly at Foggy Bottom's lair near Haast. Foggy Bottom hadn't been home in a while, and she wanted to check on her hoard. She'd been happy to share it with us when we were searching for Archie, but she was still protective of it.

She landed by the lake near the top of Mount Marks and took a long drink while we clung to her spines to stay on her back. Then she lumbered to the cliff face and tucked her chin into a crack. One at a time, we clambered up her neck and across her broad head to step through the crack and into her lair.

"I love this place!" Oliver shone the beam of his torch over the glittering walls and piles of gold and jade.

I sniffed. "And it smells better than it did last time."

Rata landed on my shoulder and nipped my ear. "It wasn't entirely my fault. You're the ones who fed me bread."

"Yeah. Never again," Ella said with a shudder. "Those farts were vile."

Foggy Bottom entered the lair and sniffed. A rumbling growl emanated from her throat, and we all instinctively took a step away from her. "Somebody's been in here." She snorted smoke from her nostrils. "Men."

"What men?" Oliver asked.

Foggy Bottom rounded on him. "How should I know?" Oliver let out a squeak and pressed himself against the wall.

Foggy Bottom sniffed some more, nosing around in the piles of treasure on the floor of her lair. "Three of them." She swiped a front foot through the largest pile, scattering jade and gold. "And they've stolen from me. Some of my gold is missing." A burst of flame lit the cavern, and I dropped to the floor, along with Nathan, Ella and Oliver.

Rata launched off my shoulder and hovered overhead. "Calm down, Foggy Bottom. Maybe it's simply misplaced."

"I don't misplace treasure." Foggy Bottom directed a blast of fire at Rata. The smaller dragon dodged it, and then swooped low over my head.

"Better get out until she calms down."

I didn't need to be told twice. Rata flew back up and drew Foggy Bottom's attention away from us. I motioned to the others, and we all scurried for the exit.

We were stopped by the ten-metre drop to the ground. Nathan quickly slung off his pack and pulled out a length of climbing rope.

"Harnesses?" Ella whispered.

"I'm not waiting around that long," Nathan said. He tied the rope to a rock and tossed the free end out of the crack. "Oliver."

In a twinkling, Oliver was lowering himself down the cliff. A roar and blast of fire behind us made me wince.

Ella was next down the rope. Nathan and I fought for last place, but he prevailed. Finally he descended, too. We stood looking up at the crack.

"Good thing we never stole from her," Oliver chirped.

"Yeah," Nathan agreed.

"So, who do you think it was?" I could tell Ella had a fair idea.

I expect we were all thinking the same thing. "Ling Chang's dragon catchers."

"Has to be," Oliver agreed.

"She sure replaced her previous crew quickly."

"I expect her crews don't generally last very long." This elicited grim chuckles from the others. We listened to Foggy Bottom's rage in silence for a minute. Then Ella spoke up.

"She's going to want to go after them."

"We can't do that," Nathan said.

"Why not? They're stealing dragons and eggs, too, not only gold and jade." I didn't entirely understand Foggy Bottom's rage at the theft of her treasure, but knowing what the men's real goal probably was, I was ready to go after them myself.

"And what are we going to do when we catch them?" Nathan's eyes challenged me to think through the scenario.

"We'll call the police and have them jailed, like we did with the ones who were holding your dad."

Nathan raised his eyebrows. "What were those guys charged with?"

Realisation dawned. "Kidnapping, overstaying a visa, tax fraud, jade smuggling …" I lapsed into silence.

"Nathan's right," Oliver said. "Even if we found these guys, we couldn't do anything about it. As far as we know, they've broken no laws."

"We've got to finish this trip and get the dragons behind our plan. Then we've got to get laws in place so we can actually punish Ling Chang and her dragon

135

smugglers. Those laws are critical. Without them, there's no way to protect the dragons."

My shoulders slumped. "You sound like your dad, Nathan."

He smiled and shrugged. "Well, I *am* his son."

I sighed. "So how are we going to convince Foggy Bottom not to go on a rampage after these guys?" We all turned to Ella.

"What?"

"Well, you've proven you can talk a dragon down," Nathan reasoned.

"Yeah, all you have to do is put on your *blarghstra* act." Oliver grinned.

Ella looked at me, like she expected me to disagree.

"They're right. You *are* good at talking dragons down." I gazed up at the cave opening, where Foggy Bottom was still growling and knocking about. "Go in there with your guns blazing. Tell her we need to leave now or we won't make it to our next meeting."

"Me?"

"We'll all be right behind you," Nathan assured her.

Ella frowned. Then she closed her eyes and took a deep breath. "Okay. But maybe it would be wise to suit up first?"

An excellent idea. We all donned our fireproof gear, just in case.

With the rope in place, it was an easy climb to the lair. When we'd all reached the top and were crowded in the entrance, Ella took another breath and barged into the cave, with Nathan, Oliver and me at her heels.

"Foggy Bottom, we need to go." Ella's voice was firm, but not loud enough. Foggy Bottom continued growling. Her tail thrashed. "We need to go." Louder this time, but not loud enough. Ella stepped further into the lair, dodging Foggy Bottom's tail tip.

"Shut it!"

The dragon turned to face us, snorting smoke from her nostrils, eyes wild with anger. Ella staggered back a step before recovering herself.

"We have to go, Foggy Bottom. We need to get to Kahurangi before dawn."

"I'm going nowhere until I've turned those thieves into cinders!" She let out a gout of flame as if to demonstrate.

"No. You're taking us to Kahurangi, and you're doing it now. We don't have time for you to waste chasing these men."

"Waste? They stole my treasure!" Foggy Bottom's tail scattered jade and gold across the cavern. "A dragon does not suffer thieves to live."

Ella raised a hand. "Nor does a dragon hang out with a bunch of human kids, but that's exactly what you've been doing. And that's exactly what you're going to continue doing. We have a job to do. A far more important job than catching a few thieves."

"She's right, you know." Rata swooped down to perch on Ella's shoulder. Ella's stance relaxed slightly.

It was five against one. What could go wrong?

Foggy Bottom's pupils dilated, giving us just enough time to drop to the floor and protect our faces from her blast.

I was seriously tired of being injured by friendly dragons. The instant the flames stopped, I jumped up and strode toward Foggy Bottom. I must have looked wild, because she drew back from me as I approached.

"Don't. Ever. Breathe. Fire. On. Us. Again!" I punctuated each word with a poke at Foggy Bottom's chest. "We are here for *your* benefit. We're *allies*. Start acting like it. You're an *intelligent* creature. Start acting like it. Control your temper. You bloody near killed us all, you overgrown lizard!"

I heard a snort behind me and whirled to see Rata shaking with suppressed laughter.

"What are you laughing at?"

Gasping between giggles, Rata replied, "You're such a *blarghstra*."

"Well if that's what it takes to get through to that oversized pile of *skobni*—" I waved a hand toward Foggy Bottom and was about to go on when Ella laid a hand on my arm.

"Tui. Stop." For a moment there was complete silence. I breathed in and let it out in a huff. I heard Foggy Bottom do the same and turned to face her. She lowered her head to mine.

"Sorry."

"Sorry."

We both spoke at once.

"I didn't mean to—"

"I didn't mean to—"

I found myself smiling. Foggy Bottom let out a snort that could have been a laugh.

"Well, if the dragons have made up, shall we be on our way?" Rata asked brightly.

Sixteen

The flight was as I expected—long, cold and boring. It had the added joy of also being wet. Somewhere north of Greymouth a drenching mist began, and we flew through it for the final two and a half hours of the trip.

The sun hadn't quite risen when we touched down on Mount Domett. I gratefully slid off Foggy Bottom's back. Ella groaned as she did the same.

"I'm not sure I can walk," Oliver said, hobbling stiffly away from the dragon.

These peaks were greener than those we'd visited further south. We were well above the tree line, but the peak wasn't a mass of jagged bare rock. Low plants softened the rock and carpeted the slopes to the trees.

"Who are we meeting here?" I asked. "No scree dragons, I assume."

"No. Here we meet only Nimbus."

"A green dragon," Ella guessed. The meteorological name gave it away.

"The oldest New Zealand green dragon alive."

Oliver's eyes widened. "How old is she?"

"Seven hundred and eighty-six years."

Nathan let out a low whistle.

"She would have been here when the very first humans arrived in New Zealand," I said.

"I didn't know dragons could live that long." Oliver gave Foggy Bottom a quizzical look. "Dad always said the dragons he … um … met … were a few hundred years old at most."

"Yes. He would have mostly met younger dragons. They're the ones who most frequently get into trouble."

Oliver laughed. "Like teenagers?"

"Something like that. We live hundreds of years. But Nimbus is old, even for a dragon. Even you will notice, when you meet her." Foggy Bottom yawned. "Now, I am exhausted. I need to sleep. We meet with Nimbus late tonight. Get some rest."

After scouting the area, we scrambled down to a broad flat spot above the tree line and pitched our tents. None of us had the energy to cook. We ate cold sandwiches in silence, then collapsed into our sleeping bags.

I woke late in the afternoon feeling well-rested, but sore from so much time on Foggy Bottom's back the night before. Ella was still sleeping as I crawled stiffly out of the tent. The rain had passed, and the sun warmed me as I stretched out the kinks in my limbs.

Oliver and Nathan were still asleep, too. No surprise. It had been an exhausting night.

I was hungry, but we'd spread the food and cooking equipment among our packs. Food would have to wait until the others woke. I squinted up at the peak where we'd left Foggy Bottom. Maybe I would go up and see if she was awake.

That was odd. There was a large rocky outcrop I hadn't seen when we landed. I must have been really tired not to notice it; we would have walked right past it on our way to our campsite. Curious, I started up the hill to investigate and stretch my legs.

The ground was rocky, and I spent most of the climb looking at my feet. Nearing the top, I glanced up and sucked in my breath in surprise.

The rocky outcrop I'd noticed from below wasn't a rock.

It was a dragon.

The most enormous dragon I'd ever seen.

Nimbus made Storm Cloud look small. She easily topped thirty-five metres from head to tail. She was sprawled in the sun with her eyes closed. Her scales were rough and dull—she really did look like a rock. As I drew closer, I wondered if she were even alive. My steps slowed.

"Do not be afraid, little human." Nimbus hadn't even opened her eyes. "I have already eaten." The dragon sniffed and her nostrils twitched. "You are of the first peoples, are you not?"

First peoples? I frowned for a moment, then understood. Remembering my dragon manners, I replied, "Greetings, Your Majestic Greenness. Yes. I am Māori."

"And do you have a name, little Māori?"

"Tui Rahui. And you must be Nimbus."

"I am." The immense dragon finally opened her eyes, and I involuntarily took a step backward. The yellow eye facing me did more than just look. It engulfed me in its depths as though I were some unfortunate prehistoric insect in Baltic amber. I swallowed and focused on keeping my knees from trembling.

I am Tui Rahui. A warrior. I am Tui Rahui. A warrior. I am Tui Rahui. A ... I am Tui ... I am Tui ... I am Tui ...

Nimbus snorted and shifted her gaze, releasing me. "I see Rata was right—you have a dragon's heart. It has been long years since anyone, human or dragon, has stood my

141

gaze." I relaxed a little, and Nimbus continued. "You have come to gain my support for your plan."

"Yes, your Majestic—"

"Don't waste your time," she interrupted. "I will not support your plan."

My fear returned, and I began to wonder if coming up here had been a bad idea. I'd expected to find Foggy Bottom, not Nimbus.

"Nor will I oppose it." The dragon heaved a sigh, and I noted how listless she seemed. She still hadn't even raised her head, but spoke to me sprawled across the rocks. She turned her eye to me again, but this time I controlled my terror better.

"My time is nearly up. I belong to the past. It is no longer my place to shape the future of dragonkind. And it was never my place to shape the affairs of humans, except, of course, when dinner was involved." Her chuckle almost sent me scampering back down the hill. But her eye grew distant. "We considered eradicating your people when they arrived on these shores back in my youth. You were loud, irksome animals." She huffed. "But the elders thought you'd make a nice addition to our diet, which was fairly monotonous—moa and the occasional seal. In hard times, we ate smaller dragons—there was no Draconic Council at the time, no agreements among dragons, and we Greens were lords of the mountains. For many hundreds of years, we could have wiped you out. Some said we should, the way you burned and hunted, eating the very land." Nimbus' voice rose and I glanced around for cover, should I need it. "You were clever, and learned how to evade us. The moa dwindled, and we dragons dwindled with them." She paused and sighed. "And then the second peoples arrived, and it was too late for us."

"I'm sorry."

Nimbus snorted. "You're sorry your people survived and multiplied? Sorry you were clever and resourceful?

142

There is nothing to be sorry about in that. A true dragonheart would be proud. You triumphed over the likes of me." Nimbus gathered herself and rose to her full height, towering over me. "You drove us from our homes and stole the food from our mouths." I staggered back from her and she laughed, deep and rumbling. "I love it when they do that." Another laugh. "I told you not to fear, little human." She sank back to the ground. "A hundred years ago, I would never have let you set foot on my mountain. No dragon would have. But Foggy Bottom tells me times are changing. No longer are we ruled by elders—most of us are dead anyway—and I am too old and tired to care. All I ask is, whatever you plan, I am left to myself." She closed her eyes again.

"Thank you, Your Majestic Greenness." I looked at the magnificent, decrepit dragon before me and thought about her long life and all she had seen. I gazed out over the surrounding forest, wondering what it had been like for her before humans had arrived. "I won't bore you with our plans, but could you tell me about—"

"No."

"I was just wondering—"

"Go away."

"Since we're already here—"

Nimbus hurled herself to her feet, her eyes flashing, smoke billowing from her nostrils. "I said *leave me alone*!" The ground shook with her voice, and rocks skittered away from her thrashing tail.

I ran.

Seventeen

The others were awake when I pelted, breathless, into the campsite ten minutes later.

"Pack up. Pack up now." I leaned forward, bracing my hands on my thighs, trying to catch my breath.

"We *were* packing, but we should eat something first," Ella said.

"No. We need to go. Now. Into the bush."

"Where have you been? What's happened?" Nathan asked.

"Pack up. I'll tell you while we work." I started pulling tent stakes, and the others followed suit with no more questions. I told them about my conversation with Nimbus, and how it had ended. Glancing up at the mountain, I said, "She didn't chase me, but I'm not messing around with her. She makes Storm Cloud look small, and she's got the temper of—" I chuckled in spite of my fear, "—of a dragon." Glancing around, I saw we were all ready, packs shouldered. I frowned. "Where's Rata?"

"Foraging. In the bush." Oliver hooked a thumb toward the trees.

"Good. Let's go." I took one more look at the mountain, then hurried downhill with the others.

I pushed us far into the bush, keeping close to the stream we had camped near so we wouldn't get too lost. When we finally stopped, the questions began.

"Where is Foggy Bottom?"

"What do we do now?"

"What if Nimbus sets the bush on fire?"

This last question came from Oliver, and his face paled as he asked it. I held up my hand. "I didn't get the feeling Nimbus would come after us. She just wanted us gone. Immediately. I think if we're not within sight or hearing—"

A roar split the still air. I swore.

"That came from the peak. It was far away," Nathan assured, though at a whisper. We strained our ears, listening.

"That rumble could have been Foggy Bottom," Ella suggested.

"How could you tell?" I asked.

Another rumble, deeper, shook the trees. Oliver's eyes widened. "Nimbus?"

I nodded.

The rumbles continued, punctuated with roars and what sounded like gouts of flame. We stood frozen, trying to make sense of it.

We all jumped when Rata zipped up behind us. "Hey guys! What's going on?"

"Nimbus isn't very happy to see us." I grimaced and pointed uphill. I quickly related what had happened.

Rata sighed. "I've never met Nimbus, but I've heard stories about her." She peered up the hill as if trying to see through the trees. "I hope Foggy Bottom knows what she's doing." A shuddering thud and a roar made us all cringe. "Maybe I should go up there and check on things."

"Be careful, Rata!" Ella's eyes were wide.

Rata shrugged. "I'm pretty much impervious to her fire. I'll be fine. Be back soon." Then she zipped off.

"Maybe she's impervious to flame, but not to teeth," I said with a frown.

"Do you think we should go up there?" Oliver asked.

Nathan shook his head. "What could we do, except get hurt?"

"We could go to the edge of the bush," I suggested. "I'm guessing we're going to have to make a quick escape, and Foggy Bottom can't pick us up here under the trees."

"Are you kidding?" Ella asked. "I'm not going any closer to a pair of fighting dragons than I have to."

"Tui's probably right." Nathan squinted uphill. "We should be in the open, ready to fly."

Ella huffed, but she followed as Nathan began the trudge back up to the tree line.

"Why did you have to piss her off?" she grumbled at me.

"I didn't *mean* to."

"Well you did a pretty good job of it."

"Maybe you'd like to go up there and apologise? I'd like to see you do better than I did."

"*Maybe* I'm smart enough not to have gone up there in the first place. Did you even consider what might happen if you went up there and started talking to her?"

"I thought she was a rock!"

"Did you *look*?"

I opened my mouth to retort, but Nathan interrupted. "Shut it! What is up with you two? You're as irritable as dragons."

I gave Ella a dirty look and she returned it with interest, but neither of us said another word until we emerged from the trees.

For a moment we all simply stared. Then Oliver whispered, "Foggy Bottom looks like a baby next to Nimbus."

We cringed as Nimbus lunged at Foggy Bottom, jaws agape. "What did Rata think she could do?" Nathan asked. Foggy Bottom lurched aside, slashing Nimbus across the face with her tail.

"Look! Here she comes." Ella pointed up the slope, where a glittering form hurtled toward us.

"Good. You guys are up here," Rata panted when she arrived. "Be ready to go as soon as Foggy Bottom lands. We won't have much time." Then she zipped up the hill again.

Foggy Bottom and Nimbus circled one another on the peak. I sucked in my breath as Nimbus leapt onto Foggy Bottom's back. Foggy Bottom roared and turned to sink her teeth into Nimbus' leg. Nimbus lost her balance, and Foggy Bottom rolled out from under her and staggered away. Nimbus crouched like a cat, readying for another lunge at Foggy Bottom when it seemed she was distracted by something. She turned her head this way and that, snapping at the air.

"It must be Rata," Nathan murmured.

"She's distracting Nimbus so Foggy Bottom can get away," Oliver said.

"Here she comes. Get ready."

Foggy Bottom lifted off and swooped down the mountainside, practically skimming the ground. We stumbled backward as she skidded to an awkward landing that sent gravel flying at our faces.

"Get on!"

Nathan and Ella scrambled up. I boosted Oliver, then grabbed Nathan's hand as he reached down to help me up. My feet had barely left the ground when Foggy Bottom launched herself upward. My squeak of surprise as I scrabbled for a handhold on Foggy Bottom's spikes was drowned out by Ella's scream. Righting myself and looking back, I understood her cry. Nimbus hurtled down the slope toward us.

I felt like we were tethered to the ground. Foggy Bottom's wings beat in powerful strokes, but we seemed to rise in slow motion. All the while, Nimbus screamed toward us like a house on wings. Gravity was in her favour, and against us. We were never going to make it. The impact alone would send us all tumbling to the rocks below, never mind the claws, teeth and flame that would accompany it. I stared in horror as Nimbus closed the gap between us. She must have been moving at more than a hundred kilometres per hour. I urged Foggy Bottom to flap faster, curling my fingers around her back spikes in a desperate attempt to keep my seat.

It was seconds until impact. Ella screamed again. Nimbus roared, flame licking from her toothy maw. The instant before I squeezed my eyes shut, I saw a flash of copper at Nimbus' ear. My eyes flew open again in time to see Nimbus jerk her head violently to the right, catch her foot on a protruding boulder, and tumble to the ground in a spray of rock and flailing limbs. End over end she went until she ploughed into the trees and came to a halt in a shower of falling leaves. Foggy Bottom lifted us over the ridge and caught an updraft. She soared into the evening sky.

I could feel my knees shaking and hoped no one could see them. I took a deep breath to calm my nerves, and tried to make sense of what I'd seen below.

We didn't go far. Foggy Bottom brought us down on another peak after about five minutes.

She landed clumsily, and we slid off her back. All of us were breathing hard.

"Won't Nimbus follow us?" Oliver peered back toward Mount Domett.

Foggy Bottom snorted. "I doubt it. Grandmother is a *blarghstra*, but she's old and took quite a tumble."

"*Grandmother?*" My mouth fell open. "Nimbus is your *grandmother?*"

148

Foggy Bottom shrugged. "There aren't many of us. Most of us are related in some way."

"What grandmother would attack her own grandchild?" Ella asked.

"As I said, she's a *blarghstra*. Anyway, it was only a spat. She wasn't trying to kill me."

I scanned Foggy Bottom's hide. There was a gash on her right foreleg, a bloody rip in her flank, a constellation of oozing puncture wounds on her snout, and a chunk missing from one of her wings. "Not trying to kill you?"

"Of course, it would have gone badly for you if she'd caught us."

"Yeah." Nathan's face was still pale. "Good thing Rata was there."

I grinned. "Is *that* what I saw?"

"What?" Ella asked. "I had my eyes shut."

"Rata was clinging to Nimbus' neck," Nathan explained. "It looked to me like she bit her ear."

Now I understood what I'd seen. "And it made Nimbus jerk her head to the side and lose her concentration. She clipped a rock and, with the speed she was going, she couldn't control herself."

"It was a pretty spectacular tumble," Oliver commented.

Ella's eyes widened. "What about Rata?"

A rippling laugh answered her question as Rata zoomed into sight. She tumbled through the air and landed on my shoulder, still giggling.

"Well done, Foggy Bottom. We outfoxed the old *blarghstra*."

"Thanks for your help, but I'm not sure singing *Nimbus is a bimbus, her brains are like whim dust* was a good idea."

"*Whim dust?*" Oliver gave Rata a quizzical look.

"What else was I going to rhyme with Nimbus?" Rata laughed and nearly tumbled off my shoulder.

149

Foggy Bottom rumbled. "It didn't improve her mood."

Ella frowned at me.

"Well, it wasn't *my* fault," I said. "*I* didn't call her a *bimbus*. I was perfectly respectful to her."

Foggy Bottom laughed. "Yes, she mentioned your visit, but was too busy reciting my failings as a granddaughter to give me details. She called you a filthy little upstart rat, which implies you were pretty impressive."

I blushed. "I didn't try to make her mad."

"I'm sure you didn't. It takes very little to irritate Nimbus. So, what happened?"

I told her how I'd mistaken Nimbus for a rock and gone up to the peak to explore.

"She knew of our plan already."

"Yes, she found me there earlier, when she returned from her night's hunt. I thought I'd ease your meeting with her by warning her of what was coming." She sighed. "I think all it did was irritate her. She wasn't exactly happy about my involvement with you."

"She may have been irritated, but at least she told me she wouldn't eat me." I explained how she had looked me in the eye.

"You stood up to Nimbus' gaze?" Foggy Bottom's tone was incredulous. A deep rumbling laugh rolled off her. "I know other green dragons who can't do that. No wonder she was so tetchy. To have a human—a child no less—stand up to her would have thrown her."

I shrugged. "She seemed impressed by it."

"Oh, she would have been *very* impressed. And probably a little nervous about you."

Now it was my turn to laugh. "About *me*? She could eat twenty of me for breakfast and still have room for more."

"True. But she's old enough to have seen humans nearly drive dragons to extinction. She would be foolish not to be a bit frightened of you."

"Are *you* afraid of me?" It was a dumb question, but I couldn't help asking.

Foggy Bottom cocked her head and narrowed her eyes. "I am not afraid of you, Tui, in the same way I'm not afraid of my grandmother. Nimbus could kill me, in spite of her advanced age. I do not doubt it. She *would* kill me if the cause were good enough—if I betrayed dragonkind, or proved a danger to her. I respect that, and I don't fear her because, while she doesn't agree with what I've done, she knows I've done it for the good of dragonkind."

"So ... you're saying you think I could ... would ... kill you? But I won't?"

"Exactly." Foggy Bottom cast her gaze around, taking in all of us. "I feel the same about all of you."

I wasn't sure how to take the idea. Foggy Bottom thought we might kill her? We weren't even fully trained dragon slayers. How could we do that? A moment of reflection brought the answer. The same way we'd brought dragons to the brink of extinction—simply by being ourselves. By turning forest into farmland, hunting dragons' prey to extinction, and invading dragon habitat.

So, how did I feel about Foggy Bottom? I fingered my still-healing bruises and cuts—all inflicted by friendly dragons. I smiled.

"I suppose I feel the same way about you."

Foggy Bottom gave a little bow. "A true dragonheart." She scanned the darkening landscape. "Now, how about we get out of Nimbus' territory before she comes out for her evening hunt?"

Eighteen

We came down on a rocky headland in the Marlborough Sounds. Our next stop was on the North Island, but Foggy Bottom didn't want to cross Cook Strait until she'd rested from her fight with Nimbus.

"She might not have been trying to kill me, but she wasn't gentle. Give me a couple of hours. Then we'll cross the strait. We'll get to Cape Palliser shortly before dawn."

As it turned out, Foggy Bottom misjudged her timing. The sun was nearly over the horizon when we reached the coast. She swept low up the coast, looking for a good spot to land and spend the day out of sight.

"Look!" Oliver pointed toward the sea.

"Is that someone in the water?" Nathan's brow furrowed.

It was no place to be swimming. The waves were high, and the rocks treacherous. We swept past. "Foggy Bottom," I shouted over the wind. "Turn back!"

The dragon turned, and we came in lower. A man floundered in the water.

"He's going under!" Ella's voice was urgent. "We've got to help him!"

"Rata and I can't be seen," Foggy Bottom argued, taking care to stay out of the man's line of sight.

"But he's going to drown. We can't let him die." Ella pounded on Foggy Bottom's side. "Go down!"

Foggy Bottom rumbled.

"She's right. We have to help him," I said.

"Yeah. Go down!" Oliver added a kick to Foggy Bottom's flank.

"We'll convince him it was his imagination," Nathan said. "Now hurry, or we'll lose him!"

Foggy Bottom dived, and I sucked in my breath. "You could have warned us," I yelled over the wind. I struggled to cling to the spikes in front of me and avoid smashing into Oliver.

Predictably, Oliver whooped with glee. Rata cackled wildly from her perch on Nathan's shoulder.

Seconds before she hit the sea, Foggy Bottom pulled out of her dive, skimming the surface of the waves and deftly plucking the struggling man from the water. He craned his neck to see what had snatched him. His eyes went wide and he screamed, and then passed out.

Foggy Bottom chuckled.

She glided to the shore and gently deposited the man on the rocks, well above the waves.

"He won't be out for long," she rumbled.

"Leave us here with him. He may need our help. You two go somewhere." Nathan waved a hand up the coast. "We'll see you later."

Oliver, Nathan, Ella and I slipped off Foggy Bottom's back. The man groaned and shifted.

"Go!" I waved the dragons off.

The man groaned again, and Ella knelt down beside him. "Sir? Are you alright? Sir?" Another groan, and the man vomited buckets of seawater.

Ella leapt back, stumbling on the rocks. "Lovely." She wrinkled her nose.

The man pulled himself to his hands and knees and retched again. He blinked seawater from his eyes and looked up at us. Then he scanned his surroundings and frowned.

"Did I see—"

I figured it was best if he didn't have time to formulate his thoughts. "You were drowning."

"We rescued you," Nathan added.

The man frowned. "But something grabbed me. In the water. Something big, like …"

Ella shook her head at him. "Just us. Nothing else grabbed you. You were nearly gone. Lucky thing we happened by."

The man seemed content with this explanation for the moment. He sat heavily on the rock and scrubbed his face with his hands. I wondered how long we could keep up the ruse. We had no boat. None of us was wet. We all still had our packs on our backs. It was clear none of us had been in the water.

"Are you hurt at all?" Ella asked. "We have first aid supplies." We shrugged off our packs.

The man shook his head. "No. Just waterlogged."

"What were you doing out here, anyway?" I asked. Best to keep him talking about himself.

"Fishing. Big wave came and sucked me out."

"Where were you fishing from? Is your car somewhere nearby?" I had seen a road of sorts along the coast as we flew up. I hoped we could get him into his car and on his way quickly.

"A friend dropped me off yesterday. I—" He vomited again and began to shiver.

"Were you camping out here?" Ella asked. "Do you have dry clothing anywhere? You need to get out of these wet clothes."

The man looked up and down the shore. "I don't know where we are. I walked in from the lighthouse."

"We're a long way from the lighthouse," I said.

Nathan opened his pack and rummaged around. "Here." He wrapped a silvery emergency blanket around the man's shoulders. "Oliver, get the stove out. Ella, do you have the tea in your bag?"

"Of course. It will warm him up." Oliver jumped to work.

The man sat on the rocks shivering and frowning slightly at us. I could tell he was trying to work out what had happened. I pulled Nathan aside. "What are we going to do with him?"

"Let's get him warm. Then maybe we can send him walking back toward the lighthouse. He must have a camp somewhere along the way."

"I mean, how are we going to explain what he saw? Once he's not hypothermic, he's going to start asking questions. We can't explain what we're doing here, how we got here, or how he was rescued."

"We were hiking along the shore. We saw him in the water and pulled him out of the waves. He was nearly unconscious. He passed out when we got him to shore. We had plenty of time to change out of our wet clothes before he came to." Nathan shrugged. "I think it's the best we can do for a story."

I sighed. It was pretty flimsy.

Walking back to the man, Nathan said, "We'll get you warmed up, and then you can walk back to your campsite."

"I think I'll wait here," he said. "They'll be along soon, I would think."

"Who?"

"Search and Rescue." The man dug his hand into a pocket and produced a personal locator beacon. He smiled. "Might have been dumb enough to leave the life vest back at camp, but I always carry this."

I shared a look of dismay with the others. The last thing we wanted was to have to explain ourselves to more

155

people. There was no way we could make excuses and leave before Search and Rescue arrived. Nathan gave a tiny shrug.

Nothing for it but to carry on.

I turned to the man. "What's your name?"

"Mark. Mark Randall. Thanks for saving me." He frowned again. "I remember … What I remember is bizarre … A …"

"You were almost unconscious when we got to you," Nathan said.

"Yeah. How did you …"

"You'd floated pretty close to shore," Oliver said. I smiled to myself. Oliver had a knack with stories. "Ella saw you first. Took us a minute to figure out how to get you, but then Nathan here came up with the idea of a rope."

I saw where Oliver was going with the story and picked up his enthusiasm for it. "Nathan's a good swimmer, but the surf is rough here, so we tied the rope around his waist."

Oliver nodded. "Nathan swam out to get you, and Ella, Tui and I held on to the rope. Pulled you both in once he'd gotten you."

"Huh." The man shook his head. "Then I must have been hallucinating, because that's not what I remember."

"You passed out before we reached the shore," Nathan explained. "It's no surprise you don't remember."

"It's not that I don't remember anything. It's just …" He shook his head and gave a little laugh. "Well, I'd swear a great flying dragon picked me out of the water."

I didn't dare look at the others. Ella laughed. "Here, have a cup of tea. It will warm you up. Hypothermia does weird things to your brain." She stepped forward and handed the man a steaming mug.

He wrapped his hands around the cup and sighed. "I *am* a bit cold, I suppose."

156

"Nathan?" Ella asked. "Do you want some tea, too? You must be cold after being in the water."

"Um. Yeah ... Yeah, thanks. I am cold." He shivered a little too theatrically.

As Ella made another cup of tea, a sound began to swell in the distance.

"Helicopter." Oliver pointed to a growing speck in the sky. The chopper flew low, obviously scanning the water.

"That's my ride." The man set down his tea, shrugged off the emergency blanket, and tried to stand. He staggered a bit. "Oh! Might have hurt my ankle. Didn't feel it before." Regaining his balance, he waved his arms at the helicopter, which slowed and hovered briefly. A woman in the window gave us a thumbs-up, and then the helicopter veered off down the coast. It landed several hundred metres away on a stretch of gravelly beach.

Nathan turned to the man. "Can you walk?"

He put weight on his left foot and winced. "Maybe."

A pair hopped out of the helicopter and began striding toward us. Nathan positioned himself on the man's left side. "Lean on me. We'll at least get you off these rocks."

I ran ahead of them. When I reached the two Search and Rescue staff, I turned to walk with them, explaining our version of events as we went.

Thankfully, they seemed to accept my story. There wasn't time for them to ask any questions before we met Nathan and the man.

They took charge, wrapping the man in a fleecy blanket and splinting his ankle, which was purple and swollen. When they had dealt with his injury, one of the rescue personnel—a burly bloke—helped the man hobble toward the helicopter. The woman stayed behind. She looked us over, her gaze lingering on my face. I self-consciously fingered the still-healing cuts and bruises.

"He's lucky you kids were here and were quick-thinking." She frowned. "What're you doing here, anyway?"

"Tramping." Oliver grinned at the woman.

"Aren't you a little young to be out here by yourselves?"

"Ella's seventeen." Oliver pointed at Ella, then whispered conspiratorially to the woman, "I know, she looks about fourteen. Don't tell her. She's sensitive about it."

Ella gave Oliver a nasty look I thought was only partly put on.

The helicopter started up, and the woman glanced toward it. "You sure you're okay out here? You look a little worse for wear." Her eyes flicked to my face.

I forced a smile. "We're fine."

She didn't look convinced, but her partner had the man situated in the helicopter and waved her over. "Well, then. Be safe. Thanks for your quick thinking."

We let out a collective sigh of relief as the woman turned and jogged toward the helicopter.

"Come on," I said. "Let's find Foggy Bottom and get out of here."

Shouldering our packs, we headed up the coast, away from the helicopter still idling on the beach. We clambered over an outcrop of jumbled rocks. Dropping down the other side, I was surprised to find Foggy Bottom and Rata awaiting us.

"I thought you'd go farther away."

"There was no need. We easily hid here, and Rata could keep an eye on you."

"You were watching? But they could have seen you," Nathan said.

Rata scoffed. "They weren't even looking in this direction. Foggy Bottom could have been sitting on top of the rocks and they wouldn't have noticed."

"Was the man okay?" Foggy Bottom asked.

"Yeah. He was cold. And I think he sprained his ankle, but he'd already called Search and Rescue," Ella said.

"So our rescue wasn't necessary?"

I grimaced. "I wouldn't say that. I think he would have drowned before Search and Rescue arrived. He was—"

Everyone's eyes widened. We all ducked as the helicopter burst over the rocks, skimming low over the coast. It turned in a wide arc over us. I looked up to see a face in the window, peering at us with a frown. Then the chopper headed back down the coast.

As the sound of the helicopter faded, we all stared at one another.

Skobni.

Nineteen

Our travels in the North Island were relatively uneventful. There were few dragons there compared with the South Island, so we did a lot of flying and not much talking to dragons. Our last stop was one I'd been looking forward to—Waimangu Valley, near Rotorua. I'd always wanted to visit the hot pools around Rotorua, and that's exactly where we were going. The North Island fire lizards lived in the hot pools.

Unfortunately, the area was a popular tourist destination—swarming with people from dawn to dusk. We had to slip in late at night and slip out again before dawn. We flew in over Mount Tarawera—so different from the mountains of the South Island—so obviously a volcano, with its long fissured crater. Maybe it was my imagination, but I swear I felt heat coming off it as we skimmed overhead.

We swooped over Lake Rotomahana and into Waimangu Valley, landing neatly beside Frying Pan Lake.

"Awesome!" Oliver breathed as we slipped off Foggy Bottom's back. In the moonlight, the still water of the lake steamed gently. A spire of rock on the opposite shore also spouted steam, like a chimney to the earth below. From somewhere came the hiss and burble of boiling water.

"Ew!" Ella wrinkled her nose. "Who farted?"

"Wasn't me," Rata chirped as she flitted to a tree overhanging the water.

"That's the sulphur in the hot pools," Foggy Bottom explained.

I bent down and quickly dipped my fingers into the water. "Oh! It's hot!"

"No kidding," Ella said. "It's steaming."

I straightened up. "And dragons live in there?"

"They do," Foggy Bottom said. "The trick is going to be drawing them out to talk to us."

Rata snorted. "Good luck on that one."

"We have to try. Even if they do nothing but listen."

"They're more likely to simply ignore us."

"Nevertheless, I'll call them." Foggy Bottom let out a low boom—so low-pitched I felt it more than heard it. It wasn't loud but I could almost see it rippling out through the water, as though she'd dropped a stone. We fell silent, ears straining and eyes scanning the still water.

Foggy Bottom boomed again. We waited.

"Where are they?" Oliver whispered.

"It will take some time," Foggy Bottom explained. Another boom rippled the water.

Then, behind us, we heard the unmistakable hiss of a sword being unsheathed. We all whipped around. Foggy Bottom snarled.

The man stood with his sword raised, surprise written on his face. He looked vaguely familiar, but I couldn't quite place him. He was a dragon slayer, no doubt about it.

Without a word, Nathan, Ella, Oliver and I stepped between the dragons and the dragon slayer, staring him down like a line-up of the Avengers.

No one spoke as we sized each other up. After weeks of living with dragons, I hardly knew what to say to a dragon slayer.

Ella recovered first. "Will Walker."

I looked at her with a frown. Then it dawned on me. The man resembled Will, a fellow student; Will was from Rotorua, nearby.

The dragon slayer relaxed his stance fractionally. "You know Will?"

"We were in the same class for a while. You look like him."

"I'm his uncle." His eyes darted between Foggy Bottom and us. "Who are you? What are you doing here?"

"We could ask the same of you, dragon slayer." Foggy Bottom's voice dripped with menace.

Nathan laid a hand on Foggy Bottom's leg. "Steady. We don't need a fight."

"He's the one with the sword drawn."

Nathan turned to the man and crossed his arms over his chest. "We're happy to explain who we are and why we're here. But we won't do it while you threaten us."

"It's not you my sword threatens." He glared at Foggy Bottom.

I stepped forward, and Rata flitted to my shoulder. I gave her a flash of a smile, glad for her presence. "If you threaten Foggy Bottom, you threaten us all. We're together." I glanced around at them. "A team."

The man's sword sagged and his jaw dropped. "It's a … it's a gold fairy dragon! But they're extinct!"

I couldn't help it. Along with everyone else, I laughed. We had seen the same reaction so many times.

Rata giggled. "I love it when they get that look."

The tension eased. I looked pointedly at the man's sword and he sheathed it. I stepped forward, my hand extended. "Tui Rahui." We shook hands while the man gaped at Rata.

"I'm Rata. Nice to meet you …"

"John. Sir John Bridgeman." He nodded at Rata, a bit uncomfortably.

Nathan, Ella and Oliver all introduced themselves. The man glanced at Foggy Bottom, and she eyed him menacingly. Ella rolled her eyes and jabbed her. Foggy Bottom snorted and then introduced herself.

The man swallowed nervously, then answered, "Greetings, Your Majestic Greenness."

At least he knew his manners.

"So, what are you all doing here ... together?" he asked.

Nathan stepped forward. "We are a delegation from the Alexandra Institute and the Draconic Council."

The man frowned. I could tell this would take a lot of explaining. He wouldn't recognise the new name for the school and probably didn't even know what the Draconic Council was.

We launched into the same speeches we used on the dragons to explain our purpose and plans. The man was as sceptical as any scree dragon at first. His eyebrows kept rising higher and higher until I thought they might fly right off the top of his head.

"Why is this the first I've heard of these plans?"

"While we have been talking with dragons, my dad has been contacting dragon slayers. If you haven't heard from him yet, you will soon."

"Your dad? Archie McMannis? Isn't he dead?"

We had been so busy since our rescue of Archie, I'd forgotten it had only been a month.

So we told the story of how we rescued Nathan's dad. With Oliver's talent for dramatic storytelling, John's eyes grew wide. Again, his eyebrows looked like they might take flight.

John shook his head when we'd finished our tale. "Huh. Well, I'll be interested to hear what Sir Archie has to say about all this at the New Zealand Dragon Slayers annual meeting next month." His gaze flicked uneasily to

Foggy Bottom. "He'll have to do a lot of talking to convince me it's the right move."

Like lightning, John drew his sword and lunged past me. Taken aback, I simply watched as his blade swung through the air toward something I couldn't see. Foggy Bottom reacted more quickly. By the time John's sword was at the top of its arc, she was in motion, stepping into the path of the blade.

"No!" Ella's scream broke my daze. I leapt at John, body slamming him and sending us both sprawling. His sword clattered to the ground.

As I picked myself up, Nathan, Ella and Oliver were jumping into the fray, pinning John to the ground where he lay. I strode to his sword and picked it up.

"What was that all about?" I asked.

"Fire lizard!"

And then I saw it, virtually at my feet and so well camouflaged it was almost invisible. The fire lizard was about the size and shape of a large crocodile, but had the neck fringe and back spines of a dragon. It growled and grunted at me, and I frowned. It sounded like Draconic, but I couldn't understand a word.

I looked up at Foggy Bottom. Before I could even ask, she answered my question. "Yes, it's a dialect unique to fire lizards."

"Can you understand it? What did it say?"

"Well, I won't tell you precisely, but basically he said, 'Go away. You're making too much noise and bothering me.' But ... hm ... with a lot more swearing." Then Foggy Bottom turned to the fire lizard and said something I couldn't make out. Swivelling back to us, she explained, "I've apologised and explained we ... well, all of us except John ... have come to talk to the fire lizards."

More grunting from the fire lizard.

"Ah, he says he heard our plans when we told the dragon slayer. He thinks they're stupid and we should go away. And … um … some more swearing."

Oliver giggled.

Nathan looked up from where he sat on John's legs. "Can you ask him to please tell the other fire lizards about the plan? And tell him we're hoping for their support and participation."

Foggy Bottom snorted. "I'll tell him, but don't expect much." She grunted and growled at the fire lizard, but before she'd finished what she had to say, the lizard snarled and lunged at her, snapping at her legs. Foggy Bottom stood calmly as the fire lizard attempted to gnaw her foot off. Then she shook her leg and the fire lizard let go, splashing back into the water with a growl. "It's probably time for us to go," she suggested.

"And definitely time to let *me* go." John struggled out from under Nathan, Oliver and Ella. He stood and held his hand out to me. "My sword?"

I slipped the sword behind my back. "You came here to kill fire lizards, didn't you?"

"It's my job. Now hand me my sword please."

"Only if you agree not to kill any more dragons."

He snorted. "I'm a dragon slayer. I'm *supposed* to kill dragons. Now give me my sword." He took a step toward me, and I backed toward the water.

"Not any more, you're not. There won't be any more dragon killing in New Zealand. Didn't you hear what we said?"

"Like I have to obey a thirteen-year-old girl. Give. Me. My. Sword."

The way he said *thirteen-year-old girl* made my blood boil. "Remember, this thirteen-year-old girl has been sent on this mission by Archie McMannis, Patriarch of the Fraternal Order of Dragon Slayers International. He'll back me up."

"So will I." Nathan stepped to my side, arms crossed.

"Me too." Oliver grinned as he joined me.

"And me." Ella took her place by my side.

"And me." Foggy Bottom's voice boomed with authority, and she wrapped her tail protectively around us.

"Don't forget me," Rata chirped. She growled, let out a burst of flame, and then giggled. I struggled to keep a straight face.

John cast a nervous glance at Foggy Bottom. Between gritted teeth, he said again, "Give me my sword! You have no idea what you're doing. Dragons are dangerous!"

Oliver laughed. "As if we didn't know already."

"They're also endangered species, and they should have the same protections as other endangered species," declared Nathan.

I smiled. "The Draconic Council, the Alexandra Institute, Foggy Bottom, Rata, us—" I waved my hand at my companions, "—we're a team. And we look after our own." I turned and flung John's sword far out over Frying Pan Lake. It spun end over end, flashing in the moonlight, and hit the water with a splash. I turned to my companions. "Time to go."

John stood with his mouth hanging open as we mounted Foggy Bottom and launched into the dark sky.

Out of sight and earshot, Rata burst into giggles. "Tui, you were brilliant! The look on his face!"

I smiled. It had felt good, tossing John's sword into the lake.

"You've just made an enemy, though," Ella warned.

Foggy Bottom rumbled what might have been a laugh. "But she may have made more than one friend."

"What? The fire lizards?" I had a hard time imagining that aggressive creature as a friend.

"Exactly."

"But the only one who showed up hated us."

"Yes, he did. Fire lizards hate everyone, even themselves. But there were more than one of them in the lake. You might not have seen them, but I caught their eyes poking above the water. They were watching and listening. What you did, Tui, won't have gone unnoticed."

Three uneventful nights of travel brought us back to the Alexandra Institute. We spiralled down to the school around midnight and were surprised to see lights still on in the headmaster's chalet.

We slipped off Foggy Bottom's back, wished her a safe flight home, and she lifted off into the night. Rata yawned. "I could sleep for a week!"

"Go on then," I said with a smile. "Off to bed with you."

Rata lifted off and flitted toward the cosy lair Magnus had built her next to the staff chalets—a chalet-shaped birdhouse on a pole.

"I can't wait to sleep in a bed," Ella groaned.

"We should check in with my dad first." Nathan waved a hand toward the headmaster's chalet. "He must be waiting up for us."

"We shouldn't have texted him from over Nelson," Oliver said. "Then we could have gone right to bed."

Ella sighed. "Yeah, we could have let him know in the morning."

"Come on. It won't take long." We all followed Nathan down the hill.

Twenty

As we neared the chalet, the sound of music wafted out. And the smell of food. I shared a smile with Oliver.

"Christmas!" His eyes shone. "I forgot all about it!"

Our exhaustion was forgotten as we stepped into the chalet to find it bursting with people. All the school staff, plus a bunch of people I didn't know. A glittering Christmas tree stood in the corner of the reception area, and the reception counter was lined with platters of food.

"Nathan!" Archie strode across the room with a smile to give Nathan a bear hug.

"Oh! And there's my Oliver!" Oliver's mum practically tackled him. "Merry Christmas, love."

"Mum?" Ella's voice quavered as she rushed to her mother's side.

I focused on the floor and clenched my fists. I would *not* cry. I would *not* cry.

"Tui." I looked up at Archie. "Anaru wanted to be here, but he couldn't get off work."

I nodded and swallowed the lump in my throat.

"Come on. Have something to eat. There are fizzy drinks in the kitchen, if you're thirsty." With a hand on my shoulder, he guided me into the room.

He left me at the spread of food—cookies, little pies, asparagus rolls, sandwiches stacked in towering pyramids. I filled a plate, but I didn't feel like eating.

"Tui!" Magnus waved me over to a couch. "Sit down. Tell me about your trip."

I started to tell him about the scree dragons we'd met, and that reminded him of one of his first dragon slaying missions. Always the storyteller, he launched into a dramatic account of the mission, which I didn't really hear. I stared at my plate and ate my food without tasting it.

"Excuse me." I stood. "I need to get a drink."

I wended my way through the crowd, trying not to notice Ella with her arm draped over her mother's shoulder, and Oliver having his hair ruffled by his mum as she recounted some tale from his childhood. No doubt it was a story about Oliver doing something cheeky.

I grabbed a drink from the kitchen and carried on out the back door, which had been propped open to let in the cool night air. I stepped down onto the grass and sighed.

I wanted to cry. Instead I laughed. "Merry Christmas, Tui. Here's a reminder you're an orphan." Saying it out loud—*you're an orphan*—was a bad idea. Tears rolled down my cheeks and I felt like I couldn't breathe. I gave an angry growl and hurled my drink into the darkness, listening to it splash and clatter into the rocky tussocks beyond the lawn.

"Tui."

I jumped and whirled. I hadn't heard anyone come out behind me.

"Roz."

"Sorry I startled you." Roz smiled.

"So, you got the job?" I asked.

"Yes. I'll be teaching starting in January. I've already moved into my chalet."

We stood awkwardly for a moment.

"Tui." She opened her mouth as if to continue, then hesitated.

169

"Look, I'm exhausted. I was headed back to the Lodge."

"May I walk with you?"

I shrugged. "Sure. I guess."

As we strolled toward the Lodge, she began to talk. "My husband Ned was killed on the twenty-second of December. Makes Christmas difficult." She was silent for a minute, and I wondered if I was supposed to respond. Then she went on. "We never had kids. I knew Ned could die, and I knew if he did, our children would have to replace him. I wasn't willing to be a dragon slayer's mother, to watch my children mourn the loss of their father, and then maybe bury my children, too."

I had never thought of it that way, from the perspective of the parent. "Did you want to have kids?"

Roz gave a little laugh. "More than anything. That's why I couldn't bear to have them become dragon slayers. Better to be childless than to have my children taken from me like that." We walked a few steps in silence. "And I suppose it was my way of contributing to ending dragon slaying. If there were no children to train, there could be no dragon slayers."

I laughed. "And now you're teaching dragon slayers' children."

"Ah! But not to become dragon slayers."

Another laugh. "Doesn't mean we won't be killed by dragons. You haven't heard yet what happened on our little trip."

"I know at least some of what went on. Archie kept the staff informed." She sighed. "I can't say I like the fact he's put you up to this."

"Archie didn't put us up to it. We chose this."

"I know. And for me it makes all the difference." She sighed. "Look, Tui. I know you're hurting. I can't say I know how you feel—anyone who tells you that is lying, unless they've also lost both parents. But I wanted you to

170

know I'm here if you … if you need someone to talk to, or …" It was clear she was struggling. "I mean, has anyone even talked to you about puberty and your period and all that stuff?"

I was glad it was dark, because I felt my face go red with embarrassment. I hardly knew Roz, and she was talking to me about … that stuff? We reached the door of the Lodge.

"Thanks Roz," I said. "I'll … I'll talk to you if I need to. Good night." Then I opened the door and went in.

Later, as I lay in bed, I considered what she'd said. She had guessed right—no one had ever talked to me about puberty, the birds and the bees. We'd had a little bit in school, so I knew about the changes my body would go through, but I certainly didn't know what to do when my period started or anything. I expected Ella knew. She was far more … grown up … than I was.

I was too tired to think about it now, but as I drifted off to sleep I felt a little better, knowing Roz was going to be one of our teachers.

Ella and I woke in the morning to Oliver's excited voice as he burst into the dorm.

"Tui! Ella! We're going to the beach!"

"Don't you guys knock?" Ella asked, sitting up and rubbing her eyes.

Nathan had the good sense to look sorry, but Oliver was too excited. "Come on! The sooner we have breakfast, the sooner we get to go. Leandro's taking us in the *helicopter*!"

"But don't we have work to do? What about the dragons? We don't even know what's been going on here while we were away. What if that reporter's been back?"

Archie stepped into the room. "For the moment, everything is under control. You kids need a break. We can't do anything until Rata and Foggy Bottom meet again with the Council for their final decision. It will take at least two days, probably more. Pack for two nights."

Ella's face fell. "Camping again?"

Archie chuckled. "I booked you a bach. Have fun and try not to give Leandro too much trouble." He ruffled Nathan's hair, and Nathan turned beet red.

Archie left, and I jumped out of bed with a grin. "The price of having your dad back." I ruffled Nathan's hair, and he swatted my hand away.

Oliver shook his head. "Come on! Let's go!"

We returned from our vacation sunburnt, sandy, and ready to get back to work. Leandro had been the perfect chaperone—that is to say, he paid for everything and let us do pretty much whatever we wanted. We spent all three days kayaking, swimming and snorkelling, ate vast quantities of junk food, and stayed up late playing board games at night. Even Ella didn't find much to complain about.

As we flew back to school, Leandro circled low over the hills.

Oliver sat by the window. We all wore communication headsets, but Leandro had warned us not to chatter and distract him, so when Oliver saw something on the slopes below, he tapped my arm and pointed.

Following his direction, I looked down and saw a blue car tucked among the tussocks about a kilometre from school.

"Leandro, I think we have unwanted company," I said.

"Huh?" Leandro's voice crackled a little over the communications channel.

"Blue car below. Looks like that reporter's."

Leandro circled back. "I see." He hovered over the car for a moment. "I'm going to do a couple of low sweeps between here and the school. I want everyone to keep their eyes open—see if we can see the woman herself."

We made three passes, but saw no sign of her. Leandro's voice crackled in my ears again. "I've alerted the school. Let's get back. Time to test those tracking skills you learned in Dan's classes last year."

Nathan grinned at me. "Tui will find her," he said.

I grinned back. Tracking had been my best class.

By the time we scrambled down the hill from the helicopter landing pad, Archie, Magnus and Dan were waiting for us outside Archie's chalet. We tossed our bags onto the porch and joined the adults.

Archie handed out walkie-talkies. "We'll go out in pairs. Keep in touch. If you find her, or signs of her, let everyone know. Marshall's going through the CCTV footage—he'll alert us if he finds anything."

"Rata is likely to be back this evening," Dan added. "We've got to get the reporter out of here before she returns."

I thought of the dragon books in the library, the dragon posters on classroom walls, and all the incriminating paperwork in offices and dorm rooms. "And we need to make sure she doesn't get into any buildings."

Archie nodded. "Many of them have been locked all day, but it doesn't mean she couldn't have forced her way in."

We fanned out in all directions. Oliver and I took the area around the Lodge.

"Should we start at the stream?" Oliver asked. "She could have cut across to it from her car. She used it last time she came."

I pursed my lips, thinking. "After the pig incident, I'd think she'd stay away from the stream."

"Unless she knows we tricked her."

I sighed. "You're right, but she's not going to learn anything down at the stream. Let's start at the building— make sure she hasn't gotten in."

Oliver nodded, and we began a slow circuit of the Lodge, scanning the ground and the building for any sign of the reporter.

We'd made it to the back of the Lodge with no sign of Katie, when we heard the whir of wingbeats. Oliver looked at me with wide eyes. An instant later, Rata popped over the top of the building and landed on my shoulder.

"Hi guys!" she chirped.

"Shh!" I clamped a hand over her muzzle. She snorted, and I jerked my hand back from the hot blast. "The reporter is here somewhere. You've got to hide!" I whispered, shaking my stinging hand.

A yelp behind us made us turn.

"Too late," Oliver muttered.

Katie Garner stood at the corner of the building, her eyes wide, and a triumphant grin on her face. She took a step closer. "So it *is* true! You *are* hiding dragons here." She fumbled in her purse and pulled out a phone.

"No!" I lunged toward her, but Oliver held me back.

"This?" he said calmly, pointing to Rata. "This isn't a dragon."

"Hm?" Rata said, straightening up.

"Shh!" I warned, not knowing what Oliver was up to.

"Not a dragon?" Katie said, her eyebrows rising.

Oliver scoffed. "Of course not!" Then he grinned. "Do you really think it looks live? I've been working on

174

the robotics for *ages*." He pulled out his phone and tapped at it a few times. "I've made my own app, see? I can make it lower its head ..." he tapped a few times on the phone and stared hard at Rata; she hesitated a moment, then lowered her head, "... and then raise its head." Rata obediently raised her head. "Flap its wings." Rata flapped. "Twitch its tail." Rata twitched. If I hadn't been so scared, I would have burst out laughing. I glanced at Katie. She frowned.

"I can even make it breathe fire," Oliver said, with a few more taps of his fingers. Rata breathed a gout of flame in Katie's direction, and she flinched back. Then her eyes narrowed.

"I heard a voice. It wasn't either of yours."

Oliver sighed. "Yeah, I've been working on that, too, but so far, all it can say is, 'Hi guys!'" He tapped on the phone, and Rata cocked her head and said, "Hi guys!" I had to turn my head and hide a laugh in a cough.

Katie took a step closer. "And you've done this robotics work yourself?" She reached for her phone again, but I raised a hand.

"No photos. We're worried about someone stealing his idea. You know, intellectual property and all. This has massive potential. Can you imagine what people would pay for a robot that looks and acts like a miniature dragon?"

Katie put her phone away. "Is this what you've been hiding up here? Just a ... a toy robot?"

Oliver looked offended. "It's not just a *toy*. The apps we're developing—"

I slapped Oliver on the arm. "Hey! Don't give away all our secrets." After not telling her anything the last two times we'd caught her at the school, we couldn't be too free with our lies. I narrowed my eyes and crossed my arms, trying not to move too much so Rata didn't have to adjust her balance on my shoulder. "And *you* aren't supposed to be here, sneaking around."

Katie took a step back and straightened her shoulders. "You *kids* can't tell me what I can do. I'm a reporter. It's my *job* to sneak around and find things out." She scoffed. "But if I'd known all you were doing was making *toys*, I wouldn't have bothered to come back."

Oliver smiled. "Did I mention it can fly, too?" He tapped his phone and Rata lifted off my shoulder and dived at Katie, flame leaping from her jaws.

Twenty-one

"You did *what?*" Ella asked around the table in Archie's office fifteen minutes later. Rata, Oliver and I had hounded Katie away from school. A quick call on the walkie-talkie had brought Magnus to our side, and he had followed the reporter to make sure she left, while we had returned.

"And she believed you?" Archie asked.

Nathan, Ella and I laughed, and Nathan said, "Oliver can make any adult believe anything he wants."

Oliver sighed. "Except my mum."

"And you're sure she didn't get any photographs?" Dan asked.

I grimaced. "I don't think so. She did have her phone out for a minute, but I think we kept her from taking any photos."

"And I think I singed her butt, too!" Rata chirped. "A *toy*? Hah!"

Leandro sighed and gave a chuckle. "Well, whatever damage has been done is done."

Nathan turned to Rata. "What's the news from the Council?"

"Oh! Everything's a go. They've agreed to working with Parliament and you guys on legislation, and then once our status and protections are in place, a public announcement."

"Yes!" I pumped a fist in the air.

"So, I guess we need to talk to some MPs?" Ella asked. "How do we get a bill through Parliament?"

"How about we go to Wellington!" Oliver suggested.

Nathan smiled and nodded. "Yeah, we could make a presentation to Parliament."

Archie cleared his throat. "*You four* will be busy with classes."

"Aw!" We cried out in unison.

"We have a job to do," Nathan argued. "We can't stop now."

Archie put up a hand. "That's what Leandro and Dan are for."

"What?" I sighed and slumped in my seat. "So we have to go to classes while you do all the fun, important stuff?"

Dan chuckled. "If you'd rather make dozens of phone calls and arrange meetings with stuffy politicians, you're welcome to do it."

"Besides, they'd never agree to meet with a bunch of kids," Archie added.

"We're the negotiating team; we're not just kids," I said.

Ella slapped a hand on the table. "And we started this. You can't cut us out now."

Leandro raised a hand. "We're not cutting you out. We'll need you at every meeting." He turned to Oliver with a smile. "Especially Oliver, with his powers of persuasion. But Archie's right—setting up these meetings has got to be done by an adult. And in the meantime, you are required by law to be in school."

I sighed. The adults were right, but it still felt like we had been demoted.

"How long will it take you to set up a meeting?" Ella asked.

"A week or two?" Dan shrugged. "I don't know."

Ella nodded curtly. "It needs to be done within a week. We can't trust the reporter not to leak something."

Leandro chuckled, and Dan gave her a salute. "Yes, ma'm."

The next morning, Magnus came to the dining hall while we were eating breakfast.

"The other students arrive tomorrow. I'll be whipping this building into shape today, but I can't do that with all your stuff scattered everywhere. Soon as you're done here you've got work to do. Anything lying around after lunch gets tossed."

We all sighed. It was true. We'd sort of taken over the entire Lodge in the absence of other students. We spent the morning tidying, and then doing odd jobs for Magnus.

The staff all showed up for lunch, and we filled a table. Though I had a hard time imagining simply going back to normal classes, I was kind of excited for the other students to come back. I gingerly touched my battered face. It would be nice to have a few days to heal, too.

"You gave everyone the choice whether to return or not?" I asked Archie. Dragon slayers' children had never been able to choose whether or not we became dragon slayers. We were simply taken for the job, with no say in what happened.

Archie nodded.

"How many are coming back?"

"Nearly all. We lost the King brothers."

Nathan snorted and swallowed a mouthful of food. "No surprise. They were clearly too good to be here with us rabble." His dad gave him a reproachful glare. "Well, it's true. They said it themselves. Repeatedly."

"Are there any new kids coming in?" Oliver asked.

Archie shook his head. "We still haven't gotten final accreditation from the Ministry of Education as an official secondary school. As soon as we have that, we'll open admissions to current dragon slayers' children. We can't open admissions to the public until dragons have gone public."

Ella set down her glass. "So Tui and I are still going to be the only two girls."

"I'm afraid so," Archie replied. "Sorry. We'll remedy it as soon as we can."

I shrugged. "Hey, at least we still have our room all to ourselves."

"You mean we don't get our own chalets? I thought we were staff now." Oliver's eyes twinkled with mischief.

"Nice try," Archie said. "But, no. You're also students." His voice was stern, but his mouth twitched upward at the corners.

"We'll be able to spread out, though, won't we?" Nathan reasoned. "With fewer students than last year?"

Archie nodded. "Seven fewer this year, so you'll have more space."

"Is Joshua coming back?" Ella asked.

"He didn't want to. He feels terrible about telling Drachenmorder about you last year, forcing you to leave the school and all."

"He was being beaten up!" The others nodded at my words. We'd all forgiven Joshua.

Archie raised his hand. "I sat down with his mother and explained what had happened. I explained to both of them you didn't hold it against him."

"So why won't he come back?" Oliver asked.

I rolled my eyes. "Hunter was using him as a punching bag." I looked at Archie. "Hunter's coming back, isn't he?"

180

Archie nodded and sighed. "I can't blame Josh for not wanting to return. But both his mother and I think it's best if he doesn't run away from this conflict." His eyes narrowed. "Hunter will *not* beat up anyone this year."

I smiled, and it must have been clear on my face what I was thinking, because Archie added, "And none of you will beat up Hunter, either. Understand?"

I sighed. "Well, I promise not to hit him if he promises not to hit me. But if he throws the first punch, I'm not responsible for my actions."

That earned me a glare and a fork jabbed in my direction. "You are *always* responsible for your actions, Tui. A punch does not have to be met with a punch."

"Humph." I slumped in my seat.

"That goes for all of you." Archie waved his fork around. "Drachenmorder turned a blind eye to it, but I won't tolerate any bullying, any violence. If Hunter gives anyone any trouble, they should come to me or one of the other staff. I don't want any fistfights."

The others nodded. I simply shrugged. If Hunter hurt me, I would hurt him back. That was that. The only thing I could promise was to try to avoid being hurt.

By dinner time the next day, the Lodge was bustling with students. They lounged in the atrium, played pool, and threw Frisbees and rugby balls on the lawn. It felt good to have the place full again. Even after weeks alone there, it had still felt as though the four of us were rattling around like peas in a bucket.

Unfortunately, everyone knew last year we'd rescued Nathan's dad, the new headmaster. They all knew we'd spent the summer break doing something related to the school and dragons. Many students gave us a wide berth, as though they weren't quite sure how to approach us.

Sitting by ourselves at a table in the dining hall, Ella muttered, "Is it just me, or do you feel like we have the plague?"

Oliver giggled.

"Oh! We have company now." I pointed toward the open window, where Rata swooped in. A collective gasp went up from the other students, and Rata zipped across the dining hall to land on the back of the chair next to me.

"Hey guys! How's it going?" All eyes were on Rata, and she knew it. She ruffled her scales and preened, glittering like a disco ball in the evening sunshine.

"Show-off," I muttered to her. She stuck out her tongue at me, and I laughed. Then Miss Brumby came out from the kitchen carrying a small plate arrayed with artistically arranged food. She set the plate before Rata and gave the dragon a friendly pat on the head.

"Don't puff yourself up too much, you might explode," she warned Rata with a smile.

Rata snorted and dived into her food.

A minute later, Will appeared at our table.

"Will!" Nathan waved him to the seat across from Rata. Will briefly greeted us all, but his eyes quickly snapped back to Rata.

"Will, this is Rata," I said. "Rata, Will Walker. He was in our class most of last year, until he graduated into the Level Two class."

Rata raised her head, a piece of lettuce still stuck between her teeth. "Nice to meet you, Will." Her eyes narrowed. "You're John Bridgeman's nephew."

Will blinked and his brow furrowed. "Um, yeah. You know my uncle John?"

Rata snorted. A wisp of smoke curled upward from her left nostril. I shared a panicked glance with Ella.

Ella leaned in. "We all met him briefly this summer. So how was your break?"

Will didn't answer. He seemed star-struck, staring at Rata with wide eyes. Then he shook himself and said, "Nice to meet you, Rata. Are you a ... a ..."

We all finished his sentence in unison. "A gold fairy dragon? But they're extinct!"

The tension broke, and we all laughed. Rata snorted bits of roast grasshopper. Will went red.

Ella recovered herself first. "It's okay, Will. Everyone who meets Rata for the first time is a bit dumbfounded." Slowly the red receded from Will's face and neck.

"Rata is the Draconic Council representative here," I explained. "She lives here now."

"What? In the dormitory?"

Rata snorted. "With you rabble? Nah. I've got my very own chalet. I'm staff, after all."

Will's eyes widened. Ella rolled her eyes. "It's not a *real* chalet. You'll see it later—Magnus made it. It looks like a ..." she glanced at Rata, "...like a bird house."

Rata scoffed, and the burst of flame that escaped her mouth made Will lean back. "Bird house! Pah! It's a *lair*."

"If you say so," Ella replied with a smile. Then she turned to Will. "So how was your break?"

"It was okay. Looks like it was better than yours."

I looked up to find him scrutinising my face, still scraped and bruised. I shrugged and shared a glance with Nathan, Oliver and Ella. "Our break was ..." I smiled. "It was good."

"Come on, Tui. It was awesome!" Oliver grinned.

Will frowned. "So, why do you look like you spent it with Hunter Godfry, then?"

I laughed and we began to regale him with the tale of our adventure. As we talked, I noticed the dining hall had gone unusually quiet. It wasn't only Will listening. It

183

made me a little uncomfortable, but Oliver seemed to enjoy the attention. He didn't embellish the story—not much, anyway—but he chose only the most exciting details to tell, and made it sound like our mission with Foggy Bottom and Rata had been an unending string of remarkable adventures, untroubled by rain, mud, aching bruises and long cold flights on dragonback.

Everyone had heard the story in the dining hall, but the four of us were besieged most of the evening by fellow students wanting to hear more. Rata stayed with us, perched on Nathan's shoulder, and she drew a steady stream of admirers.

I was comfortably sunk into a couch, feet up on a low table, listening to Oliver chatter, when Will plopped down beside me.

"Hey."

"Hi Will," Ella said, leaning forward from her seat on my other side.

I nodded at Will and scooted over to give him a little more room.

"You ready for classes tomorrow?" Ella asked. "Have you met Roz yet? The new teacher?"

"Um. Yeah." He shrugged. "She seems okay. Didn't really talk to her much."

"We met her when she interviewed." Ella nodded vaguely toward me, Oliver and Nathan. "I think she's great. She's teaching English and maths. I'm excited to have a female teacher. I guess she hasn't taught for a while—worked for the Department of Conservation before this."

"Mmm." Will turned his attention to me. "So how *did* you get those injuries?"

I sighed and rolled my eyes. "Dragons are dangerous."

"But you were with … um … friendly dragons."

"You heard Oliver." I waved my hand in his direction. "You know what happened."

"Yeah, but he didn't tell me how you were hurt."

"We were all injured."

"Yeah, but you … um … well, yours are …"

"The ugliest?"

Will's face reddened and he opened his mouth.

Ella cut off whatever he intended to say. "Excuse me. I'm tired. I'm going to bed."

I dropped my feet off the table to let her pass. "Good night," I said. She didn't respond.

A moment of silence passed, and then Will spoke up again. "So, are you going to tell me?"

"Look, I don't want to talk about my injuries. They're nothing." I couldn't wait until I'd healed and people stopped asking about my face.

"Sorry … I …"

"Excuse me." I stood. I'd spotted Josh on the other side of the room, sitting by himself, folding a paper airplane. "I need to go talk to Josh."

"Oh. See you later then."

Josh glanced up as I neared. His eyes dropped back to his airplane, and he continued folding, pressing each crease with deliberate care.

"Hi Josh."

He made another fold and ran a finger along the crease. "Didn't think you'd want to talk to me."

"Why did you think that?"

Josh snorted and didn't answer.

Okay, it had been a dumb question. "Can I sit down?"

A shrug was all the answer I got. I sat down across the table from him. "None of us blame you. For telling Drachenmorder. We all know Hunter beat you up."

"I betrayed you."

"Hunter used you as a punching bag, and was egged on by his uncle the headmaster."

"He hit Oliver and Nathan, too, and they didn't spout our plans to Drachenmorder."

"He hit them, yes, but he *targeted* you."

"Because he knew I was weak. He knew I'd break under pressure. He knew I was pathetic." Josh folded furiously now, pounding the creases into place.

I reached out and snatched the plane away from him, forcing him to look at me. "Josh. Stop."

His eyes widened. "Tui! What happened to your face?"

I took a deep breath and bit back the snarky retort on the tip of my tongue. "Didn't you hear our story in the dining hall?"

Josh shook his head. "I … I didn't eat dinner. I couldn't face everyone." He dropped his gaze.

"Josh, we really don't blame you. And it all turned out fine in the end."

Josh's eyes flicked back to my face. "Doesn't look that way."

I laughed and fingered my cuts and bruises. "These are from the dragons. They've got nothing to do with Drachenmorder or Hunter." I told him briefly of our successful quest to rescue Archie, and the job he gave us over the summer. When I finished he shook his head and smiled weakly.

"It's probably a good thing I didn't end up going with you all. I'd have freaked out when dragons started attacking."

"Oh, we freaked out plenty, too. It sounds exciting when Oliver tells the tale, but it scared the you-know-what out of us at the time." I gave him a smile. "Don't beat yourself up, Josh."

He stared at his hands on the table. "I really wanted to be part of the Dragon Defence League. I wanted to be part of Nathan's team."

"And you are. We all are, now. The whole school is part of the Dragon Defence League."

He shrugged and didn't look up.

I sighed. "Well, I'm glad you came back. Ella, Nathan and Oliver are, too. We asked Archie yesterday, and we were all prepared to go to your house and drag you here when we heard you didn't want to come."

He looked up.

I nodded. "It's true." Okay, maybe it was a bit of an exaggeration. We probably wouldn't have dragged him back, but we *did* ask, and we *did* want him to come back.

I stood and smiled. "It's good to see you, Josh." He gave a tentative smile. "But I'm exhausted." I stroked my bruised face. "And I clearly need my beauty sleep."

Finally, I got the laugh I'd been hoping for. And a genuine smile to go with it.

"See you tomorrow," I said.

"See you tomorrow, Tui."

Twenty-two

It seemed an age had passed since the last time we'd entered the classrooms. Everything had changed, and nothing had changed. The idea of going to class and not working on our mission when we knew time was so short put me on edge. I felt like we were wasting time in class.

We started the week with Draconic. Our class was the same as it had always been—me, Nathan, Ella, Oliver, Josh and Will. The only one who surprised me was Will.

"Aren't you in the next class up?" I asked as Will stepped into the classroom. "You passed your six-month exams already."

Will shrugged. "Dunno. This is what was on my schedule."

Leandro turned from the whiteboard where he'd been writing something. "Will is in the right place."

"But these are noobs." Will waved his hand at us. "I'm beyond their level."

Leandro smiled. "Ah! You *were* beyond their level when you passed your six-month exams. But they have spent the past two months in the company of dragons. I think you'll find their Draconic has improved." He chuckled. "In fact, don't be surprised if they know more Draconic than you do."

"I'll bet we know more swear words!" Oliver grinned.

Leandro's good eye crinkled and his stern words held the hint of laughter. "That you do. But we're going to refrain from swearing in Draconic in this class. Your bad words won't be of any use in an exam."

"We'll teach you the swear words after class," Oliver whispered to Will, sotto voce. We all chuckled, and Will found a seat between me and Nathan.

When we had all settled, Leandro addressed us. "You are all familiar with the school's change of focus. This means a change in curriculum. In the past, the Draconic I taught focused largely on the limited vocabulary you would need as dragon slayers. We didn't worry much about subtleties of meaning, because your encounters with dragons were to be purely confrontational. With the Alexandra Institute's new mission, you need a more advanced grasp of the language. With that in mind, I have asked a native speaker to co-teach this class with me."

I heard a familiar flutter of wings and turned to see Rata swoop into the room. I smiled as she circled our heads once, then landed on the back of a chair next to Leandro.

"That's a ... that's a ..." Josh's jaw hung open, and his eyes were wide.

Rata giggled, then introduced herself in Draconic. "*Skrgleyīn. Ni toma Rata czt Klemta Fragnich.*" She looked at Josh. "*Ni dila tsitsi likneti.*"

Josh frowned. "You're a ... a small sparkler? From Mount Tall Cracks?"

"Well done, Josh," Leandro said. "You've got the literal translation correct." He turned to Rata, and she translated.

"What I said was, *Good morning. My name is Rata of Mount Somers. I am a gold fairy dragon.*"

Josh's eyes grew wide again. "A gold fairy dragon! But they're extinct!" His face went red as we all burst out laughing. Rata giggled so hard she tumbled off her perch onto the floor.

Ella recovered first. She turned to Josh and apologised. "Everyone says that when they meet Rata. Everyone. It's become a bit of a joke."

Josh gave a weak smile, and the red faded somewhat from his face.

"Shall we carry on with the lesson, then?" asked Leandro.

"I'm never going to be able to catch up to you guys," Josh moaned as we stepped out of the classroom an hour later.

"You and me both," Will agreed. "I can't believe how much you four have picked up in the last couple of months."

Nathan shrugged. "We didn't have much choice."

"It was either that, or …"

"… or die." Ella finished my sentence for me.

I nodded. "Yeah, that's about it."

The other classroom doors opened and students spilled into the hallway, chattering and mingling.

Roz stepped into the hall and clapped her hands. "Okay everyone. On to your next classes."

Most of my Draconic class filed into Roz's classroom for a double period with her—English and maths. I wasn't exactly looking forward to it. Will smiled and waved goodbye as he went on to Social Studies with Archie. Leo Wilson joined us in Roz's room. I didn't know Leo very well. He had arrived at the school about eight months ahead of me, so we'd never been in the same class before. But he was young—maybe eleven. It was no surprise he was in our class for the academic subjects. He entered the room, looked around at us and frowned. He slouched into the one remaining desk, next to Oliver, who smiled and greeted him.

Roz introduced herself, though we had all met her already. Then she got down to business.

"First thing we need to do is find out where each of you sits academically. Since you haven't had English and maths for up to a year, we can't go by your scores from your old schools. So today I'll be testing you."

All six of us slumped in our seats. Josh and Ella groaned.

Roz smiled. "Okay everyone, we need two teams of three. One on the left, one on the right. Slide your desks together so you're facing your team members.

Teams? For testing? Our confused looks only made Roz smile more broadly. She clapped her hands. "Come on. Split up, or I'll do it for you."

I made eye contact with Ella. We were the two oldest in the class. If we were going to compete in academic subjects, I wanted her on my team. She nodded, and we began to push our desks together. I turned to try to grab Oliver for our team. He was the youngest, but I had no illusions about the fact he was smarter than everyone else in the room put together. But he and Nathan had already pushed their desks together, and before I could say anything to woo Oliver away, Ella spoke up.

"Josh, come over here to our team."

I sighed inwardly. Of course Ella would invite him to our team, for the same reason I went and talked to him yesterday when I saw him alone in the atrium. It was the right thing to do. Still, Josh wouldn't have been my first, or even second pick for our team. Not if we wanted to win.

In spite of my thoughts, I flashed Josh a smile and waved him over. He grinned and joined us, butting his desk up against ours.

"Great," said Roz once we were re-seated. "Now. I hate exams every bit as much as you do. Eventually, we'll have to do all the e-asTTle tests for the Ministry of Education. But for now, I thought we'd do our testing in a more entertaining way. This will give me an idea of what you still need to learn, and we can trickle those Ministry tests in through the year."

The game we played was like a television game show. It pitted individual members of each team against one another to answer questions. The first correct answer gained a point for the team. The questions were a wild mix of English and maths questions, so you never knew what you might have to answer when it was your turn in the hot seat. Relieved to be spared a boring Ministry test, we all got into the game.

"Buzzers!" Oliver cried. "We need buzzers."

Roz smiled. "I have just the thing." She pulled out two squeaky toys—the kind you might give to a dog—a rubber chicken and a hamburger.

"I want the chicken!" Oliver stood and stretched his hand out.

Roz threw the chicken to him across the room. Then she tossed the hamburger to my group. It bounced off Josh's face as he tried to catch it. Leo chuckled, and Josh blushed and bent to pick it up.

The competition was fierce. The teams were well-matched, and neither could edge far ahead of the other. Josh surprised me. He wasn't fast with his answers, and whoever he played against usually answered first, but if the first person got it wrong, Josh invariably gave the correct answer and gained a point for our team.

We were tied at forty-six points.

"Five minutes left," Roz warned. I glanced at the clock. I couldn't believe nearly two hours had passed already.

"Okay team," I said. We can do this. We can beat them." I nodded to Josh. "Your turn."

He was pitted against Leo, who swaggered to the front of the room swinging the rubber chicken in circles like a poi.

"We're gonna bring you down," Leo said, jabbing a finger into Josh's chest. They stood next to one another facing us.

"What is twenty percent of eighty?" Roz asked.

Within two seconds, Leo squeezed the rubber chicken. "Eighteen," he said with a smirk.

"Incorrect. Josh?"

Josh thought for a moment. "Sixteen."

"That's a point for Josh's team." Roz turned to make another tick mark on the board. Josh grinned.

Leo stomped back to his seat and hurled the rubber chicken onto the desk with a frown.

Having correctly answered the question, Josh stayed at the front of the room, and Oliver came to stand next to him. He grinned at Josh, and Josh smiled back, but he was clearly disappointed. Josh didn't stand a chance against Oliver.

"Give me an example of a metaphor," Roz said.

Oliver grinned and squeezed the rubber chicken. "That's a piece of cake!"

I couldn't help but smile. But my smile soured as Leo pumped his fists in the air. "Yeah!" He pointed at my team. "We're gonna smash you!"

Ella raised an eyebrow as if to say, *Who cares?*

I stood, patting Josh on the arm as I passed him on my way to stand next to Oliver. I jostled him playfully. "You're going to let us win this one, right?"

He grinned. "Fat chance."

"Oliver! Oliver! Oliver!" Leo began chanting. He bumped Nathan on the shoulder, encouraging him to join in. Nathan frowned and shook his head.

Roz clapped her hands. "Last question. Whoever gets this one wins."

Josh and Ella gave me a thumbs-up.

"What is five times seven times twenty."

I had barely gotten to thirty five when Oliver squeezed the chicken and blurted out the answer.

"Seven hundred!"

"Well done, Oliver." Roz clapped politely.

Leo jumped up, fists in the air. "Yes! Hahaha! We beat you guys. Beaten by an eight-year-old!"

My hands tightened on the squeaky hamburger I held, making it yelp. I didn't mind being bested by Oliver—his brains had saved our butts more than once over the past couple of months. But to have Leo rub my face in it? I raised my arm to hurl the hamburger at his head.

A vice-like grip on my wrist stopped me, and the hamburger dropped at my feet. Roz met my eyes and shook her head.

"That's enough, Leo," she said sternly. Leo sat. "Class is dismissed. Please return your desks to their proper spots. Leo, stay here for a moment." She let go of my wrist, but still held my gaze. Under her breath, she said, "Rata calls you Dragonheart. Try not to be dragon-tempered as well."

"He started it." I hooked a thumb toward Leo, who still sat at his desk.

Roz held up a placating hand. "I know, but it takes two to have a fight."

"But—"

Roz cut me off again. "No excuses. You are responsible for your own behaviour—no one else."

I glared at her for a moment, then gathered my things and left.

Nathan, Oliver and Ella were waiting for me in the atrium. Oliver frowned.

"You aren't mad at me are you?"

I realised I was still scowling. I huffed a laugh and forced my face to relax into a smile. "No, Oliver. There's no one else I'd rather be beaten by."

"Leo was seriously out of line," Ella said. She looked at Nathan and Oliver. "Is he always like that?"

Nathan and Oliver shared a bunkroom with Leo, and Nathan sometimes played rugby with him.

"Well, he can be …" Oliver frowned as he searched for the right word.

"Annoying?" Nathan suggested. Oliver nodded his agreement, and Nathan added, "But he's usually not that bad. He's definitely competitive. Doesn't like losing."

"Well, he's a rude winner, too," I grumbled. "Come on. Let's get lunch. I'm starving."

Twenty-three

Classes were fine. Even English and maths weren't too boring. But Nathan, Oliver, Ella and I wanted to be working with the dragons, not wasting time in class.

One day after Draconic, we cornered Leandro.

"What's going on with the dragon negotiations?" Nathan asked.

"We said we'd give you a week, and it's been six days already," Ella said.

"I've been meaning to bring you kids up to date." Leandro picked up his laptop. "Walk with me to my office. I'll tell you." Crunching along the gravel drive to his chalet, he began. "Rata and I met with representatives from the Department of Conservation last week."

"What? You met with DOC without us?" Ella sounded as offended as I was.

"It was a preliminary meeting. No need for you four to be there."

"But—"

Leandro cut me off. "You four had classes to attend."

"We don't mind missing class," Oliver offered.

Leandro chuckled. "I'm sure you don't, which is a good thing, because we're trying to arrange a meeting with some key DOC staff and MPs for next week to draft a dragon conservation bill."

"And we're going to go to that meeting?" Nathan asked.

Leandro nodded, and we all shared a smile. "We'll be bringing the officials here, so Rata and Foggy Bottom can attend as well. I expect you kids will miss a day or two of classes."

Ella frowned. "I thought we'd go to Wellington to meet them."

Leandro smiled and mounted the steps to his chalet. "Sorry, no trip to Wellington. The dragons are adamant we keep their existence secret until protective legislation is in place, and I agree with them. They also insist upon being at the meeting, which I also think is critical." He shrugged. "This is the only place we can manage both those things."

"So, when is the meeting?" I asked.

"We're aiming for next Wednesday and Thursday— we're just waiting to see if key folks can show. I'll let you know as soon as I have a firm date." He put his hand on the door handle.

"And what should we do to prepare?" Nathan asked.

"Attend classes."

"But shouldn't we be—" Oliver began.

Leandro raised a hand. "You are fully prepared for this meeting. You've spent months in the company of dragons—more time than any other humans alive. You've convinced *dragons* to go along with this plan. MPs will be simple."

I frowned. I wasn't sure it would be so easy. "The lawmakers are going to want to ensure the safety of the public, the Department of Conservation is going to want to do research and captive breeding, someone is sure to bring up the potential for a bump in tourism, particularly if we had a few captive dragons—"

"We can't put them in a zoo!" Nathan said.

I raised a hand. "I'm just pointing out that this isn't as simple as talking to dragons."

Everyone looked at me for a moment, and then burst out laughing.

Ella nodded. "Tui's right, you know. We'll need solid arguments in order to negotiate this legislation to the benefit of everyone."

"We'll also need your understanding of dragons to keep certain tempers from flaring … literally," added Leandro.

We all nodded. We couldn't afford Foggy Bottom flying into a rage and torching anyone while negotiating the protection of dragons.

"Now, off you go. I know you have homework to do. I expect you four to hand in flawless essays." He waved us off his porch and disappeared into his chalet.

I raised my eyebrows. "Homework?"

"With the meeting coming up?" Ella said.

Nathan sighed. "I was kind of hoping to spend a couple of hours not worrying about homework *or* dragons."

"It *is* Friday afternoon," Oliver argued.

Ella frowned and then sighed. "I suppose you're right."

"Shall we take a break until dinner?" I asked. "Then maybe we can work on stuff for the meeting in the evening."

We grabbed a Frisbee and headed to the back lawn. We weren't the only students there. There was a rugby game on by the time we stepped out the back door. I could tell Nathan wanted to join in, but Frisbee had been his suggestion so he couldn't very well go play rugby instead.

He shouted encouragement to Charlie Anderson, who barrelled down the pitch with the ball as we passed. We all winced as Hunter caught up with him and smashed him to the ground.

"What was that about Hunter not hurting anyone this year?" I muttered under my breath.

"Charlie can take care of himself," Nathan said. "Besides, it's rugby."

I snorted. "If you say so. I thought you guys were supposed to play touch."

Nathan shrugged, and I rolled my eyes at him.

We threw the Frisbee until Miss Brumby's dinner bell rang out across the field.

"Friday pizza!" Oliver made a beeline for the Lodge. The rest of us followed more slowly. Ella stopped to tie her shoe.

Nathan and I continued to toss the Frisbee back and forth as we made our way inside. One of his throws went wild and I backed up to catch it, running straight into Hunter.

I let out an involuntary grunt as I ricocheted to the ground.

"Watch where you're going!" Hunter stepped past me, kicking me sharply in the side as he went.

"You *glavnig metzi flenka*!" I jumped to my feet and tackled Hunter from behind. He staggered, but didn't go down like I'd hoped. Instead, I clung to his back, my left arm wrapped around his neck, and my right pulling back to punch him in the kidneys.

Before I could land my punch he bent at the waist, hurling me over his shoulder. I landed on my back on the grass and rolled away just in time to avoid another kick.

"Filthy b—"

"Stop!" Nathan sprinted toward us, and Hunter looked up. The distraction was enough for me to regain my feet.

A sneer spread across Hunter's face. "Don't tell me what to do."

I kicked him in the back of the knee, making him stagger and turn his attention back to me. He roared and lunged at me. His fist clipped my chin and sent me spinning. Before I could recover, he viciously grabbed my hair, wrenching my head back until I could barely keep my balance.

"How about we add some more bruises to your face? Can't get any uglier."

"Let her go!" Nathan stood, his fists raised like a boxer.

"Or you'll do what?"

I got my legs back under me and hooked one of Hunter's ankles with a foot, trying to tug him off balance. His leg was solid as a tree trunk. He shook me by the hair, and I cried out. I reached up and grabbed his arm in both hands, digging my nails in as hard as I could and raking them along the flesh.

I almost smiled when he yelled and let go of me like he'd been burnt.

Nathan grabbed my arm and pulled me toward the Lodge at a run. At least, he tried. Seeing red, I fought his grip, eager to beat Hunter to a pulp, and foolishly thinking I could.

We might have made it to the Lodge if I hadn't slowed us down. Instead, Hunter caught up with us. He hit me at full tilt, flattening me to the ground and knocking the wind out of me. Then he grabbed my hair again and lifted my head, only to slam my face into the ground over and over again. Every slam exploded in a constellation of starry pain. I tried to wriggle out from under him, get my arms free, do anything to make him stop, but I was immobilised by his bulk.

Then I heard a familiar metallic sound. Hunter froze, with my head raised. He let go of my hair, and my face hit the ground one last time. I whimpered.

"Hunter Godfry." Roz's voice was calm. "The other staff warned me to keep a good eye on you."

Roz? I turned my head to look out of the corner of my eye. Roz stood holding a sword against Hunter's neck. Holding it like she was quite comfortable with the weapon. In spite of the pain in my nose, I smiled.

"Get off her." There was no refusing the request. Hunter gingerly rose, hands in the air and eyes wide.

I groaned and rolled onto my back. Roz's eyes flicked to me, then up to where Nathan stood. "Take her to Dan, please."

I might have made it to my feet on my own, but I didn't argue when Nathan bent to help me up. I clutched the hem of my shirt to my bleeding nose. Neither of us spoke until we reached Dan's chalet. We climbed the steps and Nathan knocked on the door.

Dan sighed when he opened the door and saw us. "Why is it I'm always patching you up, Tui?" He stepped back. "Come in. Have a seat in the kitchen. The light's best there."

I smiled ruefully as Nathan eased me into a chair in Dan's kitchen. "At least it's not dragons this time."

"Yes, but I'm guessing you didn't simply trip on the stairs."

I shook my head.

"It was Hunter," Nathan offered.

Dan sighed again. "Naturally. Tell me what happened while I get you cleaned up."

"Nathan and I were throwing a Frisbee on the way in to dinner. I backed up to catch it and ran into Hunter."

Nathan snorted. "You didn't run into him. He moved to intercept you."

I turned sharply to look at him, wincing as my nose twinged. "What?"

He nodded. "He wanted you to run into him."

"A convenient excuse to beat me up."

Dan bent over me, a wet cloth in his hand. "Hold still. I can't even see where you're hurt through the dirt."

"Ow!" I cried as he swiped the cloth over my face.

He didn't apologise, but he pressed more gently after that.

"This will probably hurt. Try to hold still," he pressed his fingers against my nose, prodding firmly. It did hurt, and I bit back a curse.

When he pulled his hands away, he sighed. "Well, I don't think it's broken. That's positive. But we do need to deal with all these abrasions." He pulled out a bottle of antiseptic and began swabbing my face. "So, you did nothing to incite Hunter's attack except accidentally running into him?"

"If he walked into me, then I didn't even accidentally run into him," I snapped.

"But afterwards. Who threw the first punch?" Dan raised his eyebrows at me. I suppose I couldn't blame him. I *had* punched a hole in the dormitory wall, after all. And I had punched Hunter last year, when he was harassing Josh.

Again, Nathan came to my defence. "Hunter did. Tui was thrown to the ground when … when they ran into each other, and then he kicked her. After that …" He trailed off.

"After that, I kind of attacked him," I admitted.

Dan stifled a chuckle. "You *kind of* attacked him?"

"What was I supposed to do? Lie down and let him kick me?"

Dan raised a hand. "I'm not passing judgement, Tui. I'm merely gathering information." He straightened and frowned at me. "Bruises and scrapes, that's all. You were

202

lucky. Hunter could have done some serious damage." He turned from me and opened the freezer. "I can't do much for you, but some ice on that nose will keep the swelling and the pain down a bit." He wrapped a blue ice pack in a tea towel and handed it to me. I pressed it gingerly to my face.

A knock sounded on Dan's door and he went to answer it. He came back a moment later to shoo Nathan and me out the back door. "I see you did more than *kind of* attack Hunter. Those are some spectacular scratches." I suppressed a smile. "Go on. I need to patch him up. Get out before he comes in. Go get dinner. I'm sure Archie will be talking to you both later."

Nathan and I were walking back toward the Lodge when Roz caught up with us.

"Tui, wait."

We stopped and turned. Roz strode up, her sheathed sword tucked under her arm. I spoke before she even reached us.

"Thanks for that." I gestured toward her sword. "It surprised me, though, you not being a dragon slayer."

Roz smiled a little. "My husband and I practised together." She laughed. "Never thought I'd actually use it."

"Probably the only thing that would have stopped him," I said grimly.

Roz nodded. "That's how I read the situation. I hope Archie agrees when we talk to him later. I can't imagine any school where it's okay to threaten a student with a sword." She sighed. "I expect to be in more trouble than you and Hunter are, actually."

"Well, thanks anyway."

"I'll put in a good word for you with Dad," Nathan added.

"Hunter says you tackled him on the way to dinner."

I laughed. "Only after he knocked me down and kicked me."

"Tui ran backwards to catch a Frisbee. Hunter purposely stepped into her way."

"I see. And then he kicked you?"

I nodded. "While I was on the ground. When he walked away, I jumped on his back."

"He kicked you and walked away? Why didn't you simply let him go?"

"What? And let him get away with it? He knocked me down and kicked me—he deserved everything I gave him. More than I gave him. Someone needs to stand up to him and his bullying."

Roz cut me off. "There are other ways to stand up to him, Tui. Fighting back is exactly what he wants you to do. He's twice your size and knows it. You fight back, and you give him an excuse to beat you up. You don't need to resort to violence. You can tell a staff member."

"So you can threaten him with a sword? Because that's not violent at all." Sarcasm dripped from my voice. I knew I shouldn't talk to a teacher like that, but I was fuming. I clenched my fists. If they thought I would lie down and let Hunter beat me, they could think again. I quickened my pace and strode ahead of Roz and Nathan, taking the steps to the porch two at a time, and slamming the door shut behind me.

The smell of pizza and the sound of laughter wafted from the dining hall. I stalked past the door and made my way upstairs to my dorm room.

Twenty-four

Both Hunter and I were punished for fighting. I thought it was unfair, since he had started it. But Archie said the same thing Roz had said to me when I tried to throw the rubber hamburger at Leo—I had to control my own actions and take responsibility for them. He told me I should think about that as I worked off my punishment in the shearing shed with Marshall.

Yeah, right. All I could think about as I skirted fleeces to the sound of hundreds of bleating sheep was how disgusting sheep poo was when mixed with wool.

At least the fresh injuries didn't elicit questions—everyone knew what had happened.

A few days later, Will caught me alone on the porch, enjoying the spectacle of Rata preening herself in the evening sun.

"She's a bit of a show-off, isn't she?" he asked as he sat down beside me.

"I heard that," Rata warned.

I chuckled. "And you can't deny it's true."

Rata flitted to my shoulder and nipped me playfully on the ear. "And no one can resist my charm."

This got a laugh from both Will and me. "I suppose you're about to go practise your charm on the staff. Isn't there a staff meeting this evening?"

"Have to look my professional best," she chirped. "See you later." She flitted off toward the headmaster's chalet.

Will and I sat in silence, watching Rata's scales glitter in the sun. Just as I started to wonder why he'd come out, he spoke.

"Look, I wanted to tell you if Hunter is harassing you …" He trailed off.

"You'll beat him up for me?" I asked, not looking at him. I barked a laugh. "It's not worth getting in trouble for. Besides, no offence intended, but I don't think the two of us together would stand a chance against him. The guy's built like an Angus bull."

"Why did he attack you, anyway?"

"No idea." Then I smiled a little. "Well, it might have something to do with the time I humiliated him in front of everyone …"

Will chuckled. "That was truly brilliant."

"Thanks. I thought so, too. Of course, I got lucky that day. I think Hunter was too shocked to retaliate."

"Maybe you're even now?"

"Unlikely."

Will stood. "Well, the offer still stands. If you want some help with him, let me know."

I looked up at him. "Thanks, Will."

Going back inside, Will passed Ella coming out.

"What was he doing out here?" she asked as she sat down next to me.

I shrugged. "Offered to beat Hunter up for me."

Ella frowned.

"Yeah. That's about what I reckoned. He doesn't stand a chance against Hunter. Did you win?"

"Huh?"

"The game of pool you were playing with Nathan? Did you win?"

Ella scoffed. "Of course I did. Nathan only plays so he can goof off. Hey, Dan caught up with me and Nathan while we were playing. Says the four of us are supposed to show up to the second hour of the staff meeting." I raised my eyebrows and Ella answered my unspoken question. "The meeting with DOC and the MPs is confirmed for Wednesday and Thursday. They want to touch base with us so we all know what we're supposed to do."

I smiled. "Finally."

Ella nodded. "It'll be good to be *doing* something again."

I woke Wednesday feeling nervous. The idea of meeting with a bunch of MPs frightened me as much as meeting with a bunch of dragons. More so, perhaps, because I had never done it before.

Ella and I met Nathan and Oliver in the dining hall at breakfast. We were wearing our best. No T-shirts, shorts or hoodies. I felt myself go red under the stares of the other students as we crossed the room in our skirts, dress shoes clicking on the floor like drum beats.

"You shine up well," Ella said, nodding to the boys.

Nathan blushed and shrugged. Oliver grinned. "I even combed my hair. Take note; you won't see it again soon."

I smiled and ruffled his carefully combed hair as I sat down next to him. "Wouldn't want you looking *too* good."

We ate quickly and then escaped from the stares of the other students to walk to Archie's chalet, where we were holding the meeting.

We helped Archie carry tables to his front porch to create one large table we could all sit around. The other staff trickled over, and Archie went out to greet the arriving MPs.

Nathan, Ella, Oliver and I sat together near one end of the table. Rata ignored the perch set up for her in favour of Nathan's shoulder. Her presence calmed me a little.

Seven MPs and two officials from DOC attended the meeting. Every one of them stopped and stared, mouths agape as they stepped onto the porch and saw Rata. She played her part, greeting each of them politely and snaking her sinuous neck to make her burnished scales glitter in the sunlight.

I leaned toward her and whispered, "You're such a peacock, Rata." She responded with a playful nip on my ear, which made one of the MPs gasp. I struggled to suppress a giggle.

"Wait until Foggy Bottom arrives," Nathan whispered with a grin.

We didn't have to wait long. "Incoming," Oliver warned.

This was our cue. Nathan, Ella, Oliver and I stood and stepped off the porch as Foggy Bottom circled downward.

Chairs scraped behind us as the visiting officials stood. Several gasped. One swore. I glanced back to see them all pressed up against the wall of the building, eyes wide.

We walked out to greet Foggy Bottom as she touched down on the gravel drive. While the officials watched, we greeted Foggy Bottom formally, first in Draconic, then in English.

"Greetings, Your Majestic Greenness," I said with a smile. Foggy Bottom leaned close and sniffed loudly. The greetings were purely for show. We hoped to show the officials the appropriate way to greet a newly-met dragon, and to show them Foggy Bottom was harmless.

Oliver couldn't suppress his glee at seeing Foggy Bottom. After the formal greeting, he leapt forward and hugged Foggy Bottom's leg. This elicited another round of gasps from the porch, and I bit my lip to keep from smiling.

"They're a little nervous," Ella whispered.

Foggy Bottom chuckled. "Wait until I join the meeting."

I gave her a hard look. "Don't frighten them on purpose. You know we need to show them how reasonable and intelligent you are."

Foggy Bottom snorted. The door of the chalet slammed as one of the MPs ducked inside. "Just a little flame?" She winked at me.

"No!" we all hissed.

"Oh, all right." She looked toward the porch. "Well, have we given enough reassurance?"

"Wait until Dad waves us over," Nathan said.

It took a few minutes for everyone to sit back down, and then Archie raised his arm to call us back. We walked to the porch, Foggy Bottom keeping pace with us. As we resumed our seats, Foggy Bottom lowered her head and poked her nose onto the porch. Several of the officials went pale.

"Greetings, Your Majestic Greenness," Archie said. "Welcome to the meeting." He introduced Foggy Bottom and then all the officials at the table. Most nodded mutely, too stunned to speak. But the Deputy Director-General of Biodiversity from DOC, Joe Hart, managed a breathless greeting. His face had gone from terrified to fascinated. Foggy Bottom acknowledged him with a nod of the head and a polite, "Pleased to meet you."

The first part of the meeting was formal and boring. Archie explained the need for the meeting, and then Foggy Bottom outlined our plan for the protection of dragons and their habitat, and the recognition of dragons as New Zealand citizens.

Then things got interesting.

Joe Hart started it, with a comment about population monitoring and captive breeding.

"There will be no captive breeding of dragons." Foggy Bottom's voice shook the porch. "We are not livestock."

Joe blanched. "I was just saying … you know … captive breeding has worked well to help increase the populations of other wildlife—"

"Would you create a captive breeding programme for redheads because there aren't many of them?" Wisps of smoke curled from Foggy Bottom's nostrils.

"Well, no, but—"

"Dragons are not brainless songbirds, to be manipulated as you humans see fit. We don't come to you as lesser beings—as wildlife—needing your wise council or superior intellect to help us increase our numbers." The way she said *wise* and *superior* implied she felt humans were neither wise nor superior. "We come to you as partners. We come to you to demand in law the respect we rightfully deserve as fellow citizens of these islands."

"Of course." Joe's voice shook slightly. "We'll draw up a management plan together."

"There will be no *management plan*."

Joe leaned back and swallowed visibly. An MP spoke up. "I don't see why this is such a big deal. We don't need any new legislation. All native wildlife is protected under the Wildlife Management Act."

"We are not *wildlife*!"

The invited officials all shrank in their seats. I put a hand on Foggy Bottom's muzzle and muttered, "Calm down. We knew this would be their starting position."

Nathan spoke up. "I think what we're working toward today is an agreement more on the lines of the

Treaty of Waitangi, not a conservation plan." He raised his eyebrows at Archie, who smiled and nodded, encouraging Nathan to continue. "Dragons aren't animals, in the way you want to think of them."

"And what would a child know of that?" asked a sharp-faced MP who looked like she'd give anything to be elsewhere.

Anger blossomed in my chest, but Nathan responded calmly. "Tui, Oliver, Ella and I have spent most of the past two months travelling with Foggy Bottom and Rata. We have visited dragons all over New Zealand to discuss the formation of an agreement with humans—a treaty. We have addressed the Draconic Council, the dragon's governing body, which Foggy Bottom and Rata represent today. We have worked with the Council to rescue my father—" he gestured toward Archie, "—from wildlife smugglers who kidnapped him for his knowledge of dragons."

Archie stepped in. "They may be children, but they know more about dragons than anyone else alive."

"And they would have us protect these … beings …? Look at what two months with dragons has done to them." The MP who spoke this time gave Archie a dark look.

It was true. We all looked a little rough around the edges, but I could tell by the way he scrutinised my face that he referred to me. I spoke up, trying to suppress my anger and sound reasonable.

"It's true. Dragons are dangerous creatures. They are enormous. They have sharp teeth and claws. They breathe fire." And here I couldn't hide my embarrassment. "But a boy gave me this lovely face, not a dragon."

Eyebrows rose around the table. Leandro smiled. Rata chuckled and flitted to my shoulder. "Kids these days." She gave a dramatic sigh. Archie disguised his laugh as a cough, and then brought the conversation back on track. He passed around wads of stapled paper.

"This is a document the staff of the Alexandra Institute and members of the Draconic Council have drafted. It is a place for us to start our negotiation. There are certain non-negotiable points. These are marked on the document. Other points are up for discussion. What I hope to leave with by the end of our meeting is an unambiguous treaty we can present to the whole of Parliament." He made eye contact with the MPs around the table. "I'm counting on you to bring up issues you know your colleagues will. Help us find loopholes and close them. Make it watertight."

"And what if we don't agree to making a treaty with the dragons?" asked a broad-shouldered MP at the far end of the table.

"Then prepare to be disappointed," I said. "Dragons live in New Zealand. They have been here since before human arrival. The only reason you haven't known about it is because of the dragons' skill at concealment, and the corps of dragon slayers who have kept them at bay."

"So, why not continue as we have for the past hundreds of years?" The man leaned back in his chair and smiled. "It's been working for me."

Foggy Bottom snorted, and I touched her face again, though I could barely control my own irritation.

Archie cleared his throat. "I am technically a dragon slayer. In fact, I am Patriarch of the Fraternal Order of Dragon Slayers International. I have already set in motion the steps to disband New Zealand's dragon slayers. I have cancelled all dragon slaying missions in New Zealand. If we don't come to an agreement with the dragons, there will be no one here to protect you."

I wondered if it was a good idea to threaten violence. Then I laughed at myself. It was exactly what I would have done. I sighed. If it came to outright violence, humans would eventually win, but it wouldn't be pretty.

212

"Would dragons really attack humans if we don't come to an agreement?" I whispered to Rata.

She gave me a look that reminded me, even though Rata seemed frivolous and happy-go-lucky, she was a dragon. I swallowed nervously. Rata's look softened, and she murmured in my ear. "We're here because we want a solution that doesn't involve killing. It's up to us to make sure we get one."

Twenty-five

Nathan, Ella, Oliver and I staggered out of the meeting shortly before six on Thursday evening, minds numb after two days' wrestling with the details of formal policy documents. We farewelled Foggy Bottom and Rata, who both flew off for a Draconic Council meeting, and then headed to the dining hall for dinner. The visiting officials streamed out in their fancy vehicles, raising dust from the drive.

"I think I'd rather face an angry dragon than sit in a two-day meeting like that again," Oliver said. We all nodded and laughed.

"At least we came to an agreement in the end," Ella said.

"Yeah. Do you think it'll make it through Parliament?" I had my doubts. Even with Rata and Foggy Bottom there, proving their own existence and showing their more civilised nature, it hadn't been easy to convince all seven MPs at the meeting. It would be even more difficult in Wellington with no dragons to back us up.

"Let's hope so," Nathan said.

When we reached the Lodge, the sound of voices from the dining hall told us dinner was already in progress. The hall fell silent as we appeared in the doorway. The other students knew we'd been in a meeting for two days—a meeting with a whole bunch of government officials, all the teachers, and an enormous green dragon.

"Hey everyone!" Oliver waved. "Did you miss me?"

Scattered laughter broke out. Then Will spoke up. "So what happened?"

"Yeah, how'd the meeting go?" Josh asked.

Before any of us had a chance to respond, Archie appeared in the doorway. "Let these four eat first. They've had a full two days. I'll tell you all about it in the atrium afterwards."

Gratefully, we collected our food and sat down to eat.

In the atrium later, all the students sprawled in armchairs and sofas listening to Archie. I wasn't paying a lot of attention—I knew what he had to say. I doodled idly on a scrap of notebook paper while Oliver watched and made snide comments about my drawings.

When Archie's voice suddenly faltered, I glanced up. His face was ashen. I turned to follow his gaze out the window. I'd barely registered the dragons when Archie shouted, "Get down!"

The entire Lodge shook as three scree dragons roared over the building breathing fire. A few students screamed as they dived to the floor.

"Looks like our friends have come to find us," Ella muttered.

When the dragons had passed, Archie sprang into action. "Everybody up! Follow me. Quickly!" He strode toward the dining hall. Students straggled after him, faces pale.

"Where are we going?" someone asked.

"Emergency bunker. Under the dining hall."

"Emergency bunker?" Oliver raised his eyebrows. "Wow! I didn't know there was an emergency bunker! Cool!"

I rolled my eyes and pushed him in front of me as we made our way with the other students. I glanced at the ceiling, expecting to see flames.

Then there was a loud thud on the roof, and everyone cowered. "Come on!" Archie hurried us along.

Panicked students started running for the dining hall. I tried to stay calm, but was shoved to the floor by a large body hurtling through the crowd. Hunter. I scowled at his retreating back, considering tackling him.

"Leave him," Nathan warned as he bent to help me up. "We've got a bigger fight to deal with."

A moment later, my irritation with Hunter was blasted from my mind by the sound of shattering glass. A dragon's tail had smashed the huge windows at the front of the atrium. I threw my arms over my head and felt them sliced by a rain of glass knives falling around us. But glass was the least of our worries. The dragon's tail was followed by a second dragon, who shot a gout of flame through the broken window as it soared past. Nathan and I dived behind a couch to escape the blast. When the dragon had passed, we jumped up. The couch was smouldering and half a dozen other items of furniture around the room were in flames.

"Nathan!" We both turned to see Oliver darting across the room with two fire extinguishers under his arms. He threw one to Nathan, and they got to work putting out the fires.

"Incoming!" Ella screamed. We dived for cover again as a dragon crashed head first through the glass wall into the atrium. Wood and glass splintered and flew everywhere. The dragon skidded to a halt near the back wall, sending chairs and couches tumbling like kicked toys. It turned and roared. Flame shot toward the ceiling.

"Help! Help me!"

The dragon took a step toward Hunter's terrified voice. Hunter was pinned under a beam that had fallen when the dragon crashed through the wall. His eyes were focused on the beam as he frantically pushed at it, seemingly unaware his screams were attracting the dragon's attention.

"Well, well, well." The dragon sounded pleased with himself. "A little squealing pig. I *was* getting a bit peckish." The dragon prowled closer, and Hunter grew still, staring white-faced at the towering animal.

"Hmm … let's see. Shall we have you raw, or cooked?"

"Don't eat me!" Hunter's voice was little more than a squeak.

"And why not? You look so tasty. So juicy." He took a step closer. "And if you don't want to be eaten, why do you hang around? Why don't you run and hide like the other *metzi flenka* filth in this place?" The dragon snorted a laugh. "And you call yourselves dragon slayers. Pathetic."

"No! No. We're not dragon slayers. We're—"

"Cooked, I think. You're too noisy to eat raw."

Hunter squeaked and his eyes went wide as the dragon took a deep breath, drawing it out for effect.

Then Ella jumped up and hurled a broken chair leg at the dragon. "Stay away from him, you *glavnig skobni*!"

The dragon flinched and turned toward Ella.

Ella continued. "We are *not* dragon slayers, and you know it. You're a disgrace! The Draconic Council is working toward an agreement with humans that will benefit all dragons, and you're trying to sabotage it? What do you think you're going to get out of this? Huh? Another hundred years of skulking around trying to hide until you're wiped out by habitat loss and wildlife smugglers? What good does that do anyone?"

The dragon's tail lashed. "Don't you try to tell me what's best for dragons, you little *skobni*. You think you're so tough. Think your pathetic *blarghstra* act will make me turn tail? Ha! Think again." The dragon lunged, and Ella dived behind an upturned table.

I scanned the room wildly for some sort of weapon. A piece of wood, broken glass, anything. My eyes lit on a decorative sword hung on the wall. I raced over and snatched it from its mounting. Brandishing the sword and roaring an inarticulate battle cry, I charged to the middle of the room. I really didn't expect to do any damage to the dragon, but I hoped to distract him from Ella.

The distraction worked. Better than I'd hoped it would. "Hmmm! This one has a claw." The dragon snaked his head toward me and twitched the tip of his tail. "Let's play, little girl."

Play? I was toast. Or maybe not. "Okay. But no fire. Just my claw against yours."

The dragon chuckled and swung his head side to side, as if trying to get the full measure of me. "A feisty one, this. And why should I agree to your terms?"

I gave what I hoped was a feral grin. "Because it'll be more fun." Then, for good measure, I stuck my tongue out at him and rolled my eyes like a Māori warrior.

A great belly laugh shook the room. I saw Nathan and Oliver out of the corner of my eye, darting under cover of the noise to where Hunter lay trapped. "Deal. Claw against claw. No fire, no teeth." Then it struck.

I scrambled backward, tripping over an armchair. It was lucky I did—the dragon's front claws hit the chair instead of me, slamming it into the wall. I scrambled to my feet and swung the sword. It connected with the dragon's leg and did nothing but bounce off. What had I expected from a wild swing with a decorative sword? Still, it was all I had. I tried to remember the four cuts of tameshigiri Sir Christopher had taught us last year, and came up completely blank. Then another swipe from the dragon's paw forced me to duck behind a table, driving away all thoughts beyond simple survival.

A swipe with the left paw hit me and I tumbled to the floor. Another from the right tossed me the other direction. Neither left a scratch on me, and I knew the dragon was simply toying with me.

"Leave her alone!" Ella stood behind the dragon, a shard of glass in her hand. The dragon didn't even look her way, but swept his tail across the floor, knocking Ella sprawling. Anger boiled up in me, and when the dragon came at me with another swipe, I set my feet and slashed at his foot with my sword.

The dragon roared and staggered back a step. To my amazement, I saw I'd nearly severed one of his toes. Blood poured from the toe, and it hung by a ragged flap of flesh. The dragon seemed equally astonished by my luck. His eyes went wide and he sucked in a gasping breath. Then he focused back on me. His eyes narrowed and he lunged at me with no-nonsense speed.

I scrambled out of his way, tripping over jumbled furniture. A coffee table hurtled toward me, crashing into my knees. The table's impact flipped me onto my back, knocking the wind out of me. I gasped for air as the dragon raised his foot to sink his claws into me. In the nick of time, I regained my wits and my breath. I tucked the sword in close to my body and rolled out of the way. The dragon's foot came down with a crash where I had just been.

I rolled underneath a couch and lay still. The dragon snorted, took a few steps, and then spoke. "Hiding, are you? Afraid, little mouse? Why don't you come out and play?" He laughed. "Don't think you can hide. I'll find you. A little hunt will simply whet my appetite."

As the dragon spoke, I shimmied along the floor. The tumbled furniture made a maze of tunnels at floor level. I hoped to get far enough from the dragon to regain my feet and prepare before he came at me again.

I knocked my knee against a chair, and it scraped loudly on the floor.

The dragon came closer. "Ah! I can hear the mouse squeaking. Where have you gone, little mouse?"

I shimmied further, and then came to a couch lying on its side, blocking my progress.

"Let's see if you're under here," the dragon said. I heard a piece of furniture skitter across the floor. "How about under here?" Another crash. "Hmm ... little mouse is good at hiding, but I will tear this room apart to find you." He laughed. "I like this game."

Another piece of furniture flew, and the chair behind me shifted. I had to get out of this spot. Maybe if I crept along the couch I could find a way around it.

A massive crash and clatter behind me sent me rolling against the couch, covering my head with my arm.

"Ah!" The dragon's voice came from overhead. "Here's my little mouse. Caught in a trap."

I lifted my head and looked around. Furniture hemmed me in on all sides. I glanced up. The dragon's leering eye gazed down at me with predatory glee. Then his front feet appeared on the edge of the couch, claws sinking deep into the cushioning.

"Claw only," said the dragon. "I stick to our bargain, though it would be fun to smoke you out." He reached a paw into my cramped space. I scrambled as far as I could under the edge of a chair and watched as his claws raked inches from my face. The foot retreated, and as it did, I saw something that gave me hope.

This dragon wasn't a *he*; it was a *she*. I swallowed my fear and pulled myself into a crouch.

"Come and get me, you *blarghstra*!" I gripped the sword with both hands. As the dragon reached in for another swipe at me, I stood, thrusting upward with my sword to the bare patch over her fire stomach. The bare patch where she'd plucked her scales to incubate her eggs.

220

The dragon's blow hit me in the legs, knocking me off my feet. I let go of the sword, leaving it deep in the dragon's side, and fell against the sharp edge of a table. The table and I both went skittering across the floor.

A wounded dragon is worse than a room full of tigers. That's what Magnus had said. I believed him. The dragon roared and spouted flame. It thrashed around the room, scattering chairs and crushing tables. I scrambled on all fours, desperately trying to stay out of its way and get to the dining hall. A quick glance told me Nathan and Oliver had freed Hunter. I didn't see Ella, and I hoped she'd gotten out, too.

I'd just made it to the doorway when Leandro and Dan charged into the atrium, with Ella trailing behind. The dragon made one feeble lunge at them and then collapsed on top of the pool table, crushing it with a huge bang.

In the silence that followed, I drew myself to my feet. I took a step away from the doorway and wobbled. I looked down at my left leg, noting for the first time the long gash from knee to ankle. I noticed the dragon blood that had run down my arms. Then I blinked at the dragon sprawled across the pool table. I burst into tears.

Twenty-six

Dan tried to ask me questions as he patched me up, but I could only sob, "I killed her." So instead, he told me what had happened while I was engaged with the dragon in the Lodge.

"There were three dragons. One of them came to the staff chalets. Leandro and I dispatched that one pretty quickly." He swiped the gash on my leg with an alcohol wipe, and I winced. "It was two against one. Really the dragon didn't stand a chance."

I smiled a little at that, in spite of myself. Two against one? Leandro had only one eye, and Dan's right arm and leg were prosthetics. Neither one was deemed capable of killing a dragon anymore.

I sniffed. "And the other dragon?"

Dan shrugged and began bandaging my leg. "It attacked the stables. Marshall happened to be there. He did his best with it."

"Did he kill it?"

Dan laughed. "Marshall's an unpleasant man, but he was never cut out to be a dragon slayer. He'd have been as upset about it as you are, if he'd killed it." He stood. "Let's see those cuts on your arms."

I held out my arms. "So what did he do?"

222

"He captured it. Man's a dab hand at the lasso. Managed to truss it up nicely, but forgot to account for its fire."

I raised my eyebrows.

Dan nodded. "He used rope. The dragon burned it off its legs and tail. The rope on the neck held for a while, but …" He shrugged. "The dragon didn't stick around. As soon as it was free, it flew off."

Dan finished inspecting my arms. "Most of the blood is from the dragon. The glass cuts look like they've all stopped bleeding. I could bandage them, but …"

I shook my head. "They'll be fine." I sniffed and rubbed at a spot of blood on my hand.

Dan crouched down in front of my chair and said, "So, would you like to tell me what happened in the atrium?"

Ella, Nathan and Oliver burst into Dan's office. "Where is she? Is she okay?"

Dan stood and stepped away from where I sat. All three of my friends hurled themselves at me and hugged me. My tears started again. "You made it out," I choked between sobs.

"You killed the dragon!" There was awe in Oliver's voice, but I watched his face fall as I burst out in a fresh gale of tears.

Dan cleared his throat. "Let's give Tui a minute. Did you get Hunter off?"

"Yeah. Leandro said he'll be fine, but he wanted to stabilise the broken leg before putting him in the helicopter," Nathan said.

"We would have been here earlier, but …" Ella glanced at the others. They nodded. "He wasn't very cooperative. He kept trying to get away from Leandro."

I looked up with a frown. "Why would he do that?"

"He wanted to come see you," Oliver said.

"He wanted to make sure you were okay," Nathan added.

It didn't help my tears. Dan shuffled restlessly for a minute, and then suggested we go to the kitchen.

"I think I've got some lemonade, and maybe a bottle or two of ginger beer."

He had a packet of vanilla creme cookies, too, and the distraction of drinking and eating helped me pull myself together.

I knew they were all waiting to hear my story. I was thankful they didn't push me. After a few minutes, I began. The others chimed in, telling how Nathan and Oliver had lifted the beam off Hunter's leg. They'd stumbled out the door with Hunter sagging between them, and then sent Ella running to the chalets to get a teacher.

When I came to the part where I stabbed the dragon, Oliver perked up. "Exactly like in the story Magnus told us!"

I nodded. "That story saved my life."

"That, and your quick thinking," said Dan, shaking his head. "A first-year student should not be able to take down a full-grown female scree dragon in close quarters."

At the reminder, I frowned. "Is there any way we can find out where her lair is? It's too late in the season for eggs, but she must have babies in the nest, if she still has her brood patch. They'll die when she doesn't return."

Dan sighed. "I'm not sure, Tui. You know how secretive scree dragons are. I expect Rata will be able to identify the dead dragons when she gets back tomorrow, but even then, we may not be able to find out where she lived."

Oliver's eyes went wide. "They attacked this evening because they knew other dragons would be in a Council meeting tonight."

Dan nodded. "Yes. No dragons available to come to our aid." Then he stood, collecting our glasses and setting them in the sink. "We should probably get to the Lodge. There's an awful lot of cleaning up to do."

"Yeah, how does one remove a fifteen-metre-long dragon from a room?" Nathan asked.

Oliver giggled. "Very carefully."

More practically, Marshall had hitched the dragon to a tractor and, with all the students guiding the body, eased it through the double doors of the Lodge. When we entered, the last bit of the tail was snaking down the porch steps as Marshall hauled it away.

The students bustled around in the atrium, righting furniture that was still whole, and hauling out broken fragments of furniture that had been crushed. Whispers ran through the room as we entered. All eyes turned to me. Someone started clapping, and the others followed suit. I felt myself go red.

"How do they know already?" I muttered.

Ella shrugged. "I kinda told them. When I went to give the all clear to everyone in the shelter."

I blinked. I couldn't handle being applauded for killing a dragon. We were supposed to be *protecting* dragons. I turned and stalked out the door before anyone could see me cry.

I walked past the staff chalets. The light was dim now, and the western sky glowed a deep orange. I climbed the hill behind the stables and sat down on a rock at the top. I faced the mountains and let the tears fall. I'd orphaned a baby dragon, maybe more than one. I supposed it should have felt good—revenge for being orphaned myself by dragons—but it didn't. All I could think of was a baby dragon waiting in the nest for its mum to come home, and finally realising she wasn't going to ever return. Did dragons get the same crushing feeling, like I did when I finally understood my parents were gone? I had at least had other people to take care of me, but that dragon's babies were all alone. And it was my fault. I buried my face in my hands and sobbed.

It was nearly full dark before I heard steps in the grass behind me.

Roz came up and sat silently on the ground next to me. After a few minutes, she spoke, quietly, as though she didn't want to disturb the sleeping hill. "It's a good spot to think, up here."

I didn't answer. My tears had dried, and I felt washed out. I didn't want to talk.

"I didn't know the school was built to be dragon-resistant," she mused.

"Mm?"

"All the materials are treated with fire-retardants. Otherwise the buildings would have all gone up in flames."

It made sense, I suppose. I grunted.

Roz picked up a stone and tossed it from hand to hand. "Ned used to come home shattered after each mission. Not because of the fear or danger he'd been in." She tossed the rock down the hill. "He didn't like killing dragons. Said they were too human. Called them people."

I turned to look at her then, and she met my eyes.

"I had to remind him he'd saved a town, or a family, or all the people who would wander past that dragon's lair on their holiday."

I sighed and looked away.

"You didn't kill a dragon this evening; you saved the lives of twenty-six students."

I plucked a rough blade of tussock and began ripping it into tiny pieces. "Why does it feel like killing then?"

Roz laughed. "That's what Ned always said, too." She put a hand on my shoulder. "What you did today was brave." Another laugh. "Stupid and dangerous too. But it was the right thing to do."

Roz stood and brushed her pants off. "Lights-out is in fifteen minutes, but if you need half an hour, it's fine. I'm on duty. Just let me know when you come in."

I waited until she was gone, then slowly made my way down the hill and into the Lodge.

"Tui!" Ella stood, followed by Nathan and Oliver. They all watched as I walked across the strangely empty atrium.

"Isn't it past bedtime?" I asked.

"Roz let us stay up. To wait for you," Nathan replied.

I felt the prickling of tears again. I looked down and ran my fingers over a scorch mark on the back of the couch in front of me. I took a deep breath. "Well, I'm here now. I think I need some sleep."

The teachers held classes as usual on Friday. Oliver was disappointed, but I was happy to have a routine to keep me busy and keep me from paying attention to the stares and whispers that followed me around.

In maths class, Leo was even more irritating than usual. As I stepped into the room, he bragged loudly to Josh about how he would have killed the dragon if he'd been in the atrium when it crashed through the windows. I clenched my fists and said nothing.

Roz appeared in the doorway a moment later. She frowned. "Shut it, Leo. Hot air won't kill a dragon." She strode to the front of the room and began the lesson. I flashed her a quick smile, and she winked.

At lunch I was sitting with my usual crowd when Hunter, limping along on crutches, entered the dining hall. Ella tapped me on the arm and pointed. Conversation petered out, and a hush fell over the room. Hunter's eyes scanned the students, and then locked on me. The scowl on his face brought Will, sitting beside me, to his feet, fists clenched. I rose quickly and put a hand on his arm.

"No." I stepped around Will and walked across the dining hall until I stood in front of Hunter, just out of arm's reach.

Hunter's gazed flicked to the rest of the students, watching silently. Then he jerked his head toward the door. He turned and I followed him out into the atrium, closing the door behind me. A few steps into the room, he turned back to me, but would no longer meet my eyes. He shuffled nervously, hopping a little as he tried to maintain his balance on the crutches.

He looked smaller than before. I took pity on him.

"How's the leg?" I asked.

He shrugged. "Broken in two places."

I waited through another awkward silence for Hunter to say whatever it was he'd brought me out for.

With his eyes still on the floor, Hunter gave a sigh. "I'm sorry."

I didn't respond. After a moment, Hunter looked up. "I'm sorry about your face, about what I did to you and Josh and Nathan last year, about—" he leaned on his crutches and waved his hands around, "—everything."

I still said nothing. Hunter's eyes dropped back to the floor. I didn't know if I could forgive him. I hadn't considered ever forgiving him.

He continued. "I ... I know it's not an excuse, but ... Uncle Claus was all the family I had left. I wanted him to approve. To be proud of me. I wanted to be as fierce as he was." He laughed. "I have a habit of getting into fights anyway, so when he told me to rough you guys up ..." He shrugged. "It's not an excuse, I know."

Another silence filled the air between us.

"And then when ... when Uncle Claus was killed ..."

I swallowed. "You blamed me, Nathan, Ella and Oliver for it." I didn't feel bad about Drachenmorder's death. I might have tried to stop Storm Cloud from killing him if I could have but, as all dragon slayers know, if you live by the sword, you're likely to die by the claw. Drachenmorder had lived by the high-powered hunting rifle, but the effect had been the same.

Hunter nodded. "It was stupid, I know. He died a dragon slayer's death."

Drachenmorder didn't deserve the title dragon slayer. I was about to blurt it out when Hunter continued, almost in a whisper.

"He was horrible. I loved him, but I hated him." He sniffed, then blinked at me. "Anyway, thank you for saving my life and killing the dragon. I'm sorry I beat you up."

He shouldered his way past me and disappeared into the dining hall. I stood, stunned and blinking back my own tears, and then slowly followed.

Twenty-seven

Leandro cancelled our afternoon class to hold an emergency meeting with Nathan, Ella, Oliver and me. He wouldn't tell us what was wrong until we arrived at his office. We sat down, and Leandro slapped a newspaper onto the table in front of us.

Ella sucked in a breath. Nathan whistled. I swore.

"Oh no!" Oliver picked up the paper. The headline that had captured our attention read *Massive Lizard Rescues Fisherman, Vanishes*. Oliver read it aloud.

Mark Randall, 37, of Wellington, was swept out to sea while fishing along the coast near Cape Palliser on 21 December. It might have gone badly for him, but he was rescued by what he claims was a giant, flying lizard, accompanied by four children.

"I was hypothermic, so I guess I could have imagined it, but I remember being in the water, hearing a sound, and looking up at this huge ... dragon ... swooping down on me. It plucked me right out of the water with giant claws."

Randall says he lost consciousness, and when he came to, the creature was gone. He was lying on the shore, and four children were tending to him.

"They said they'd been tramping. Said they'd swum out to rescue me. But when I thought about it later, none of them were wet."

The Search and Rescue crew who arrived later confirmed there were four children at the scene. The children all appeared to be minors, and were unaccompanied by an adult. Concerned for the children's safety, the crew flew over the area after rescuing Mr. Randall. The children were crouched among rocks some distance down the coast.

Randall claims he saw the huge lizard with the children when they flew over.

Jane Reid, one of the Search and Rescue crew wasn't so certain.

"There was definitely something strange about the rocks where the kids were sitting, but I didn't see a lizard. Mr. Randall was understandably upset and disoriented by his ordeal. The mind can play all sorts of tricks on us under those circumstances."

A party of locals hiked out to the site of Mr. Randall's rescue the following week, but found nothing unusual.

"Well, they won't find anything there," Ella reasoned. "Foggy Bottom says there are no dragons in that area. Blue dragons visit occasionally, but there are no lairs."

"Still, I think we need to move more quickly." Leandro drummed the table with his fingers, as if to emphasise the need for speed. "There are now two staff from the Department of Conservation and seven MPs who know of the existence of dragons. They understand the need for secrecy, but they're all in Wellington. Parliament is crawling with reporters, and conversations are easily overheard. And with this out there now, along with our friend Katie Garner ..."

"How fast can we get our treaty through Parliament?" Nathan asked.

"If it were a simple issue, we might manage it in two weeks."

"But this isn't a simple issue, is it?" It wasn't really a question. I knew the issue was incredibly complex, and we weren't going to get our bill through in two weeks.

Leandro laughed. He sounded tired. "Dragons haven't even been formally described by science. You were at the meeting yesterday—the officials who came played along only because Foggy Bottom was breathing down their necks. The government will never agree to give rights to creatures that don't officially exist."

"This could take years, couldn't it?" Oliver said.

Leandro nodded. "And in the meantime, we're going to have to reveal the existence of dragons, regardless of what Archie and Storm Cloud decided in the past."

"But dragons are only safe because no one knows they're here," I said. "They'll be slaughtered once their existence is known."

Leandro held up a finger. "Regardless of whether they've been described by science or not, they *are* protected under the Wildlife Act."

"But they're not wildlife!"

Leandro sighed. "You and I understand that. But by everyone else's standards, they are wild animals. Let's take advantage of that."

"Yeah, like the Wildlife Act will actually protect them." I threw up my hands and slumped in my seat. "It doesn't stop the wildlife smugglers."

"And if people do start going after dragons, it's going to get ugly really fast," Nathan added. "Dragons aren't going to simply let themselves be killed, or let their eggs be stolen. People are going to die. It'll make a treaty even less likely to go through Parliament."

We sat silent for a minute. Then an idea popped into my head. I slapped the table and sat up straight. "That's what the Dragon Defence League is for. To protect dragons."

"The DDL? Our group?" Oliver asked.

Nathan looked confused. "We're already doing what we can."

"I'm not talking about our group, but something new. The Dragon Defence League could be made of former dragon slayers. They're trained for the conditions, they can communicate with the dragons, and they understand what's at stake. They can physically guard the dragons."

"You want dragon slayers to guard dragons?" Ella's brow furrowed.

Oliver raised his eyebrows. "What will the dragons have to say about that?"

"What will the dragons have to say about what?" Rata asked as she zipped in through the open window. "What have I missed? This place reeks of dragon fire."

I was glad Rata had arrived. We needed at least one dragon present for this discussion. We filled Rata in on what had happened while she'd been at the Draconic Council meeting. We read her the newspaper article and outlined our worries about the plan we'd been pursuing.

She listened without comment, and I couldn't tell by her body language what she was thinking.

"Hm. Those are the same concerns we discussed last night at the Draconic Council meeting. Foggy Bottom and I weren't happy with the meeting with your officials this week. Not that we didn't come up with a reasonable document by the end of the day Thursday, but we could see as well as you that no one would agree to it without an actual dragon bullying them into it. The truth is, we've been too secretive. In an effort to protect ourselves, we've made it impossible for your government even to believe in our existence, let alone agree to negotiate with us. So I expect you have a plan?"

I explained the idea of the Dragon Defence League. Rata snorted derisively, but listened to the end.

She sighed. "You're probably right. I've been talking to the other students, and almost all of them have mentioned their dragon slayer parents had mixed feelings about killing dragons. It's true, dragon slayers know better than anyone else who we are. And they have the skills to protect us while we get to know the rest of the population." She grimaced. "It's going to rankle the larger dragons to be protected by humans."

"If dragons could protect themselves without killing people, it might be different," I said.

Rata sighed again. "I know. Even Foggy Bottom struggles with the idea of talking out her problems rather than blasting fire at them." She shrugged. "It's not an issue among dragons—fire isn't a big deal—but you humans are unfortunately flammable."

Oliver snorted. "Don't I know it."

"So, do you think we can get agreement from the Council to go public and set up the DDL for dragon protection until a treaty can be negotiated?" Ella asked.

Rata looked around at all of us. "If you four act as our ambassadors, yes. I think we can get agreement from the Council."

"How soon can you get it?" asked Leandro. "I don't think we have much time before this blows up, and I'd rather make the announcement ourselves than be blindsided by it."

"I'll to go Storm Cloud immediately." With that, Rata zipped back out the window.

"She's changed." Ella looked thoughtful. "Rata. She's ... I don't know ... She's gone all responsible and ... grown-up."

Leandro smiled. "I might say the same about you four."

Twenty-eight

When Rata returned early the following morning, she brought Foggy Bottom with her. We were waiting for her, pacing as we searched the sky from the top of the hill behind the stables.

"Incoming." Oliver smiled as the glittering form of Rata came looping over the tussocks.

We waved to her, and she swooped over to greet us, landing neatly on a rock. "Look at this! My own welcoming committee."

We all smiled. "We wanted to know the Council's answer as soon as possible," I said.

"Well I only have half the answer. Foggy Bottom's got the other half. She'll be here soon. She was right behind me, but stopped off to catch some dinner on the way here."

"Foggy Bottom's coming?" Oliver asked. "Flying during the day?"

Rata nodded. "She'll be careful not to be seen. And it may not matter now if she is. Storm Cloud insisted we talk to all the members of the Council about the change of plans. I visited half last night, and Foggy Bottom went to the others."

"Who did you visit? And what did they say?" I asked.

Rata grimaced. "No one is particularly excited about the idea."

All of our shoulders slumped. Nathan spoke up. "But people are going to find out about you whether we like it or not."

"We understand that. Everyone I spoke to eventually agreed it was the best course of action, but there are a few conditions."

"Like what?"

"How about we go down to the headmaster's office," I suggested "Archie, Dan and Leandro will want to hear this, too. And Archie *did* ask to see us as soon as Rata arrived."

Everyone rose, and Rata hopped to my shoulder. On the way down, I asked Rata, "Do you think the dragons Foggy Bottom is meeting with will agree, too?"

"I expect so. I had the difficult ones—the scree dragons. For a while, I didn't think I'd talk Jade into it."

"What convinced her?" Nathan asked.

"I told her about the attack on the school. I pointed out, if rogue dragons were going to continue to attack people, there would be no hiding. We could either take control of the situation or let it spiral out of control. And if it got out of control, more dragons would die."

I swallowed and slowed my steps, letting the others get ahead of me. "Rata? Who were the three dragons who attacked the school?"

"Rocky survived. Dan and Leandro took out Greywacke."

I took a deep breath. "And me?"

"You killed Gneiss."

I blinked, feeling tears prickle my eyes. "Rata, she had babies. Do you know where she lived? Those babies are orphans now. Do you think the other scree dragons will take them in and raise them?"

Rata snorted. "Not likely. Scree dragons aren't known for compassion. They're even less social than most dragons. I can't imagine any scree dragon caring what happens to some other dragon's babies."

"What about other dragons? Would someone else take them in?"

"Other species? Not a chance."

I stopped walking and looked at Rata. "So we're going to let those babies die? We can't do that! Someone has to find them and take care of them."

Rata shook her head. "It's not the way dragons work, Tui."

"Well, it's the way *I* work. Those dragons are orphans and it's my fault. I can't leave them out there to die." I balled my hands into fists and blinked furiously to keep from crying.

Rata sighed. "I'll see if I can find out where they are. But don't get your hopes up, okay?"

I began walking again, trying to swallow the lump in my throat. "Why are dragons so violent?"

Rata shook her head. "I've been wondering that myself lately." Then she laughed. "I'd never questioned it before. I don't think any of us really did. It's just what dragons do. We breathe fire. We settle things with bite and claw. We worry about our own hides, not anyone else's." We stepped out onto the drive in front of Archie's chalet in silence. "Jade accused me of becoming 'humanised'. She meant it as an insult. I don't really see it that way."

I smiled. "So I'm dragon-hearted, and you're human-hearted?"

Rata chuckled. "Something like that."

Nathan pulled open the door to the headmaster's office without knocking. Archie looked up from his desk and smiled. "Ah! She's back." He stood. "Leandro and Dan are in the kitchen. More room in there."

"We'll need more room than that," Ella said. "Foggy Bottom's coming."

"Well, then we'd better meet on the front porch. I'll go tell the others." Archie had just turned toward the kitchen when a scream tore through the air from the front of the chalet.

We all bolted for the door. We rushed onto the porch and were drawn up short by the scene on the drive in front of us: Katie Garner sprawled unconscious on the ground in front of Foggy Bottom. The dragon sniffed at her, chuckling deep in her throat. When she noticed us, she raised her head.

"I love it when they do that." She gave another chuckle, and then cocked her head. "She doesn't smell right. She's not one of yours?"

Dan and Leandro joined us as we stepped off the porch and surrounded Katie. Dan crouched to check her pulse.

"No, she's not supposed to be here." Archie sighed. "And now we really *do* have a problem."

Dan and Leandro carried Katie inside and laid her down on the couch in the waiting area of Archie's office. Rata stayed outside with Foggy Bottom, and they both moved out of sight.

"Do you think we can convince her she didn't just see a thirty-metre-long dragon?" Nathan asked.

I laughed. "I doubt it."

Dan raised Katie's legs on a pair of cushions, and she soon revived. Her eyes flew open and darted around at us all peering down at her. She bolted upright.

"Calm down, Ms Garner," said Archie.

"That was a ... a ... a *dragon*!"

"See, told you," I whispered to Nathan.

"Ms Garner, what you've seen is alarming to you, no doubt," Archie began.

"Alarming? Of course it was alarming! I knew you were hiding something!" She glared at me and Oliver. "And it wasn't robotic toys."

"We need you to be quiet about this," I said. "Lives depend upon it."

"Quiet? You must be kidding! That was a *dragon*! A real—" she sucked in a hitching breath, "—live—"

"You're right," Nathan said. "Foggy Bottom is a dragon."

Katie turned wide eyes on Nathan. "It has a name?"

"And a home and a family," I said.

"The Alexandra Institute protects dragons," Ella said.

Katie scoffed. "That ... *beast* ... didn't look like it needed protecting. It could have killed me!"

I nodded. "Yes. But she didn't."

"Are you threatening me?" Katie stood abruptly. "You can't keep me here. My employer knows where I've gone today. If I don't come back, the police will be crawling on your doorstep within hours."

"We have no intention of keeping you here," Archie assured. "But we would ask your cooperation in keeping the existence of dragons a secret for the time being."

Katie squared her shoulders. "As an investigative journalist, I have a duty to society to reveal matters of importance. And if these ... *things* ... are roaming around out here, I think people should know about it. What were you thinking, bringing these animals here? Where did you get them, anyway?"

I sighed. "We didn't bring them here. And they're not *animals*. They're from New Zealand. They've been here longer than we have. This is their home."

"We're working on legislation to protect them, and we'll be making an official announcement of their presence soon, but we need to ... maintain control of the press surrounding dragons, for their safety," Nathan explained.

"Maintain control?" Katie laughed. "That animal out there wasn't in control when it practically landed on top of me."

I clenched my fists. Pretty soon *I* wouldn't be in control. "I'm sure Foggy Bottom wouldn't have landed on top of you. She's—"

"And what kind of a name is that? Foggy Bottom?"

Oliver piped up. "New Zealand green dragons are named after meteorological phenomenon. Now if you want awful names, the southern blue dragons—"

"There are more of them?"

"We would be happy to invite you to the press conference when we introduce New Zealand dragons to the world."

Katie snorted. "Your press conference, huh? You may have nothing to announce." She stood and turned toward the door.

I stepped in front of her, my arms crossed. "You can't tell anyone."

"Out of my way. I'm a reporter. It's what I do—tell everyone." She waved a hand at me. "Out of my way! You can't keep me here."

Archie nodded. I frowned, but stepped away.

Oliver laid a hand on Katie's arm and gave her his best puppy dog look. "Please don't tell."

Katie shrugged off his hand and flashed us a smug grin. "Are you kidding? This story will make my career!" Then she strode out the door.

Skobni.

We regrouped on the porch with Rata and Foggy Bottom.

"Well. Now what?" Leandro asked.

We sat in silence for a moment. I could see my own thoughts flashing across everyone else's faces. "We need to break this story before she does."

Nathan nodded. "We need to make sure accurate information and the conservation message go out right from the beginning."

"Foggy Bottom terrified Katie." Ella grimaced. "And the MPs who came to the meeting. If Katie talks to any of them, they're not necessarily going to say nice things about dragons."

"And she knows nothing," added Oliver. "She's never going to paint an accurate picture of dragons."

"It'll be nothing but fearmongering," agreed Archie.

There was another silence. I noticed the newspaper sitting on the table. Facing up was the headline Leandro had shown us yesterday. *Massive Lizard Rescues Fisherman.* "So let's tell them the truth." I picked up the paper. "Foggy Bottom *did* rescue that fisherman. Four kids *were* travelling with her." I looked up to see the idea taking root in the others' minds.

"We could reunite the fisherman with his rescuers. *All* of them." Ella's eyes sparkled.

"And do it publicly," Nathan added.

"Dragons are saving people, now people need to save dragons," Oliver suggested with a grin.

"I'm not sure I'd go that far," Rata cautioned. "Three dragons *did* try to burn down the school two days ago."

Oliver shrugged. "It's all about marketing."

Archie nodded. "He's right. It's about giving a good first impression. Tui, you may be on to something here. If we can contact the fisherman and arrange an event …"

Ella's eyes narrowed. "We'll have to do it right away. Katie Garner could get her story out in a few days. We want ours to hit the news first."

"Well, what are we waiting for?" said Rata. "Time to throw a dragon party!"

We divvied up the work. There was plenty for everyone to do—we were organising a major event, bringing in people from all over the country, in the space of two days.

Archie tracked down the fisherman we'd rescued and arranged for him to come to the Institute. Leandro wrote a press release and invitation and sent it out to every news outlet in the country, along with the promise of all-expenses-paid trips for any media attending the event. Nathan, Ella, Oliver, Rata and I prepared the speeches. Archie and Leandro insisted we do much of the talking, saying we were the best ambassadors.

"'Cause we're the cutest, right?" Oliver offered with a cheeky smile.

All the Institute's staff and students worked on preparing the grounds and buildings for an onslaught of visitors and scrutiny. Miss Brumby spent long hours in the kitchen, making biscuits and slices, little savoury pies and other refreshments for the human visitors, and preparing great slabs of venison and mutton to be grilled on the day for the draconic visitors.

Foggy Bottom insisted there be a strong dragon contingent at the meeting, and an even stronger defensive force out of sight, but nearby, to ward off any attack by more rogue dragons.

"We should have representatives from all the dragon species," she suggested.

Rata shook her head. "The scree dragons on the Council agreed to the plan *only* if their existence remained secret until we had secured a formal treaty. And you know the fire lizards will refuse to come."

Foggy Bottom's sigh was almost a growl. "Well, I'll collect who I can, then."

Tuesday morning dawned breezy and clear. Students and staff alike were up early, buzzing with nervous energy. A truck from Parties R Us arrived after breakfast to set up a huge marquee on the lawn behind the Lodge. The contractor who had fixed the broken windows in the atrium took down the last of the scaffolding. Miss Brumby enlisted the students in setting up tables for refreshments.

Nathan, Ella, Oliver and I met with the staff and Rata and Foggy Bottom mid-morning.

"Are the dragons in place?" Archie looked to Foggy Bottom.

"Yes. We have a dozen dragons stationed around the area to head off any trouble. Night Stalker will represent the Fiordland fringed dragons, and Bluette will represent the southern blues."

"Is Storm Cloud coming?"

Foggy Bottom paused for a moment. "He is heading up the guard contingent. I ... discouraged him from making an appearance." She shrugged. "He can be intimidating."

Oliver giggled. "And you're not?"

"Hm. Well. I like to think I'm ... friendly."

I couldn't contain my laugh. "You are ..."

"... when you're not being a *blarghstra*," Ella finished with a smile.

Foggy Bottom huffed and looked Ella up and down. "Well, I could say the same for you, young lady."

This earned a laugh all around.

Archie pulled us back to task. "Leandro, how many people can we expect today?"

Leandro smiled. "At least a hundred, maybe as many as a hundred and fifty. We've got members of Parliament, Department of Conservation staff, all the major news outlets, and a few regional councillors."

Archie nodded. "Good. Dan, are you all set to shuttle visitors from the airport?"

Dan nodded and patted his pocket. "I've talked to everyone who needs a lift. I've got the list of their flights here, and I've gotten the okay to land at Garden City Helicopters. I'll collect them in three trips. I actually need to leave in a few minutes."

Archie gave a small salute. "Roz, have the classrooms been set up?"

"All done. The second-year students made posters about the school's history and about the current curriculum. They'll be on hand in the classrooms to answer questions."

Archie turned to Miss Brumby. "I don't need to ask if you're ready. We've been smelling your preparations for days."

Miss Brumby beamed. "I've asked the first-year students to help keep the tables full, collect empty glasses and whatnot. Is that okay?"

"Perfect. Magnus?"

"The grounds are spotless. I've brought in some extra rubbish bins for the back lawn, and all the gates and sheds are locked to avoid any accidents with machinery or anything on the farm side of things."

"Marshall? What's the parking situation?"

"I've opened the north paddock and put up signs to direct people where to go."

"Excellent. And you kids?" Archie raised his eyebrows. We shared a nervous glance, and Nathan nodded at me.

I swallowed. "I think we're ready. You'll open and welcome everyone, right?" Archie nodded, and I continued. "And then we'll introduce ourselves. I'll explain our role as ambassadors, and the work we did over the summer with Rata and Foggy Bottom. Then Oliver …"

"I'll tell them our side of rescuing the fisherman, Mark Randall. I'll introduce him and let him say a few words. Then we'll pass it over to Rata." He nodded to the dragon.

"I'll explain how this event led us to decide to reveal ourselves to humans in the hope of forging a relationship with your species. I'll introduce the other dragons and let them tell a little about themselves."

"Then we'll hand it back to you for a closing," I finished.

Archie nodded his approval. "Right now the message should be in the disclosure of dragons' existence, and the fact they are intelligent beings. Let's not say anything about a treaty right now. Let people get used to the idea of your existence first, before we challenge their ideas about governance and wildlife."

Foggy Bottom grunted. It was clear the idea of being considered wildlife rankled. I didn't blame her. But I also knew Archie was right. We had to bring people step-by-step to an understanding of dragons.

Twenty-nine

Two hours before we were supposed to welcome the media and reveal the existence of dragons to the world, Foggy Bottom swooped over the shearing shed and landed beside the marquee, where Nathan, Ella, Oliver and I were practising our speeches.

She ducked her head into the tent. "We found them."

"Found who?" asked Nathan.

"Gneiss' babies."

I grinned. "Yes! Did you get them? Who's taking care of them?"

Foggy Bottom raised her eye ridges. "We know where they are. No one has collected them. Rata said *you* were going to take care of them, Tui."

My smile vanished. "Me? Take care of baby dragons? But I don't know how."

"Baby dragons? Here at school?" Ella's eyes lit up.

Oliver grinned. "That would be awesome!"

"Magnus could build them a little chalet like Rata's," suggested Nathan. Then he frowned. "Or maybe scree dragons wouldn't like a chalet. Maybe a rock pile?"

"If you want to rescue them, we should go now," said Foggy Bottom.

"But we have the event—" I began.

Nathan pushed me gently. "Go on. Go get the dragons."

Ella nodded. "If you're not back in time, we'll manage without you."

"Yeah. Rescuing those babies is more important," Oliver agreed.

I smiled and blinked back tears. Then I raced to Foggy Bottom's side. Nathan boosted me onto her back, and my friends grinned up at me.

"I'll be back as quickly as I can."

As Foggy Bottom crouched to spring into the air, Leandro came jogging out of the Lodge. "Wait!" he called. When he reached us, he handed me two pillowcases. I wrinkled my brow in a question.

Leandro smiled. "For bringing them back. The pillowcases will hold them gently and keep them calm. And—" he drew a small plastic bag out of his pocket, "—from Miss Brumby."

I smiled. Miss Brumby had filled it with tasty roasted grasshoppers. I took it and stuffed it into my own pocket.

"Now go." Leandro nodded and Foggy Bottom launched into the air.

A thousand thoughts raced through my head as we flew. It had been a couple of days since—I grimaced—since I'd killed Gneiss. Would the babies still be okay when we got there? There should be two, if scree dragons were like others and laid two eggs at a time. How would I care for two dragon babies? What if they died anyway? I was completely unprepared for this.

We spiralled down to a sharp ridge above a scree slope. I'd been so absorbed in my thoughts I had no idea where we were. Foggy Bottom landed, and I slid off her back.

"The nest is down there somewhere." Foggy Bottom nodded down the slope.

"Down there?" The slope fell away at such a steep angle, it gave me vertigo. The angular fist-sized rocks shifted underfoot. How was I going to get down the slope without tumbling to my death? Why hadn't I thought to bring climbing gear? And where was the nest? The slope seemed vast and uniform. I took a deep breath. "Any suggestions for where to look first? What does a scree dragon nest look like, anyway?"

Foggy Bottom scanned the slope. "It'll be a shallow depression—just a scrape. Look for a level spot."

"Level?" I couldn't imagine any level spot existing on such a steep slope. "You've got better eyesight than I do. Can you see anything?"

Foggy Bottom was silent for a minute as we both strained for any sign of a nest. Then Foggy Bottom spoke. "There, halfway down and smack in the centre."

I sucked in my breath. *Skobni.* How was I going to get down there? Even if I made it there alive, I'd probably bring down half the slope on top of the nest before I reached it. Rope. Why didn't I bring rope?

Then I smiled. "How good is your flying, Foggy Bottom?"

Foggy Bottom snorted.

"Can you fly me down there?"

"I can fly you down there. No problem. But there's nowhere to land. You'll have to hop off from the air."

I took a deep breath. "Okay."

"And the dragons will hide when they see me fly over."

"They will?" I frowned. "Where?"

"They'll dive right into the scree," Foggy Bottom explained. "It's a dragon eat dragon world out there, Tui. Scree dragon babies are tasty snacks for green dragons."

I turned horrified eyes on Foggy Bottom. "You wouldn't!"

Foggy Bottom grinned, showing her huge teeth, and I took a step back. "Wouldn't I?" Then she chuckled. "No. You're right. I wouldn't. But it doesn't mean other green dragons wouldn't take advantage of unprotected nestlings."

"So, if they hide …" I frowned.

"You'll have to wait patiently for them to come back up. If you dig after them, they'll only go deeper. Even the babies can move quickly through scree."

"Let's get down there, then." I clambered onto Foggy Bottom's back and she launched herself off the ridge. She skimmed along the surface down the slope. I couldn't see the nest around Foggy Bottom's bulk, but she coached me through the jump.

"Three, two, one, jump!"

I slid off her back, feet first onto the slope. I hit the rocks and fell flat on my back as the scree began to shift under me. Rocks slid away from my feet and tumbled down the slope ahead of me. I looked down and nearly panicked. What had I been thinking? My heart pounded as I imagined tumbling all the way to the bottom. I slid about two metres, and then the rocks stabilised. I took a shaky breath and looked around.

The nest lay a few metres downhill and to the right from where I stopped sliding. I could see no dragons in it. Had they already been eaten by another dragon? Had the babies tumbled out of the nest? As I watched, a few rocks shifted suspiciously in the centre of the nest. I smiled. At least one was still there and still alive.

Gingerly, I tried to stand. Rock slid from under me and I fell back with a grunt as I slipped another metre down the slope. Okay. No standing. I was almost parallel with the nest now, so I slowly rolled like a log across the slope to the edge of the nest. I pulled myself into a sitting position and waited.

Nothing moved.

I shifted slightly, easing the pain from a particularly sharp rock under my left leg.

I kept my eyes glued to the nest.

I waited ten minutes, and still nothing. A rattling above me made me look up. A trickle of rocks slithered toward me. As they picked up speed, some began to bounce. I swore and ducked my head, bracing for the impact. A minute later I looked up again. The sound had died. The rocks had stopped moving. I took a deep breath and turned my gaze back to the nest.

And there they were.

Two cat-sized scree dragons, grey and pebbly-looking.

"Meep!" One of them chirped and blinked at me. "Meep!"

I smiled. "Hello you."

The dragons dived back into the scree. *Skobni.*

I pulled the little bag of grasshoppers out of my pocket, shook a few onto my hand, and waited.

A moment later, a scaly head popped back up. "Meep!"

I laid my hand flat near the edge of the nest.

"Meep!" The dragon's eyes went wide and he cocked his head. "Meep!" He lunged at my hand.

It took all my self-control to hold still. The dragon attacked the grasshoppers, swallowing without even chewing them.

I smiled. "Slow down, mate."

The dragon looked up at me. "Meep!"

I reached out my other hand to scratch his head. He lunged at my hand and bit it.

"Ow!" I jerked my hand back, shaking the dragon off. He scurried back into the rocks. "Okay. I deserved that," I muttered to myself. I examined my hand. Blood welled up from half a dozen tooth marks. I sighed and shook a few more grasshoppers out of the bag.

I laid the insects out on the rocks and opened a pillowcase, ready to receive a dragon. By the time I was ready, two little heads had poked out from the rocks again.

"Come on. I've got grasshoppers." I nudged one of the bugs.

The dragon on the right clambered up and scrambled over to slurp up grasshoppers. I quickly snatched him up and shoved him into a pillowcase. He squealed and bit me, but I managed not to let go. Once I had him safely knotted into the pillowcase, he calmed down and lay still.

The other dragon had, of course, hidden again. I sighed. This was going to take forever.

I laid out more grasshoppers.

It took longer for the second dragon to reappear. I glanced up. Foggy Bottom circled overhead. Watching my progress, no doubt. It occurred to me we hadn't decided on a signal for me to tell her I was ready to be picked up. Oh well. We'd figure it out. I turned my attention back to the nest.

The second dragon finally peeked out from the rocks.

"Grasshopper," I sang, dangling a bug by the leg.

The poor dragons must have been starving. He lunged at the grasshopper, and I barely snatched my hand away in time to avoid his snapping jaws. I tapped my fingers on the rocks next to another grasshopper. Maybe I could lure this one directly into the pillowcase and avoid being bitten again. As the dragon ate the second insect, I laid out a line of grasshoppers, the last one deep inside the pillowcase I held open. It was my last insect. If this failed, I had no more lures. I held my breath and waited. The dragon snatched up bug after bug. He hesitated before stepping into the pillowcase. I held as still as I could, willing him to go in.

The instant he snaked inside I whipped the pillowcase off the ground, tumbling the dragon into the bottom.

"Gotcha!" The dragon squeaked, and I added, "Sorry, mate." I knotted the top of the pillowcase, and then a sound made my head snap up.

The rumble began near the top of the slope, and for a moment I couldn't place the sound. Then I realised the entire slope above me was in motion. This wasn't a little trickle of rocks like before; this was a river, a flood. It picked up speed, heading straight toward me. *Skobni.* I looked to the sky.

"Foggy Bottom!" I snatched up the pillowcases and tried to stand, only to fall as the scree beneath me started to move. The rumbling grew, and rocks began to skip and bounce around me. I clutched the dragons to my chest, trying to shield them from flying rocks. There was no point in attempting to stand. I pointed my feet downhill and simply tried to stay on top of the shifting stones.

"Foggy Bottom!" I picked up speed. Rocks shifted and boiled under me. One, bouncing down the slope, whacked me in the back of the head, and I hunched over as another pelted my back. I looked down. The whole mass of stone was moving now, sending me and the baby dragons hurtling downhill.

"Foggy Bot—" A huge set of talons wrapped around my torso and plucked me from the slope. I squeezed my eyes shut, listening to the deafening roar of the rocks below. I gripped the pillowcases with both hands.

A minute later, I lay panting on the ridge above. Foggy Bottom gave me a moment to collect myself, and then urged me to move. "Shall we go?" she asked. "If we hurry, we could still be back in time for the dragon unveiling. I'd hate to miss it."

Still shaking, I smiled up at Foggy Bottom. "Yeah. Let's go."

I nestled the baby dragons in front of me, holding them with one hand while I clung to Foggy Bottom's back with the other.

"Meep!" called one of the babies.

I laid a hand on its head through the pillowcase. "It's okay. We're headed home."

All the way back to school, I smiled through tears leaking out of my blinking eyes. I had two baby dragons to care for now. I was a dragon mum. I couldn't wait to introduce the babies to my brother Anaru. I was still an orphan—nothing would change that—but now I had a family again.

Thirty

My palms were sweaty as I stood on the low stage in the marquee, a step behind Archie.

Archie stood at the podium, looking out at almost a hundred and fifty human visitors packed into the tent. He nodded to the people, and then to the dragons arrayed outside. "Tēnā koutou. *Skrgleyīt*. Greetings. Welcome to the Alexandra Institute."

I barely listened, going over my own speech in my head as he outlined the mission and vision of the Alexandra Institute. When he turned the microphone over to me, I stood frozen at the podium for a minute. I scanned the crowd of expectant faces. I recognised the officials who had come to the meeting; was it just four days ago they'd been here? I saw Katie Garner scribbling in her notebook, a scowl on her face. No doubt she was wishing she could have broken this story herself.

Katie looked up, and every eye was fixed on me. My left knee started shaking. I cleared my throat and cringed when the sound was amplified by the microphone. I swallowed and rubbed my damp hands on my pants.

I had faced angry dragons. I'd stared down Nimbus. I'd killed a dragon with nothing but a dull sword and my wits. I'd rescued a pair of baby dragons from a shifting scree slope. But here I was paralysed by this crowd. I swallowed again.

A soft rustle sounded behind me, and Rata's familiar weight landed on my shoulder. I turned to look at her, and she pressed her muzzle against my nose.

"Go on, Dragonheart. You can do it."

Yes. I was Dragonheart. Dragon saver. Dragons were my friends, my whānau. I smiled, straightened my shoulders, and began.

Glossary

Draconic

Draconic is a difficult language for humans to learn. *Understanding* Draconic is no more difficult than understanding any human language, but *speaking* it is another matter. The guttural sounds and strange inflections are challenging for the human body to produce. Dragons have no written language (imagine trying to hold a pen with talons and no opposable thumb), so the Draconic words in this book are written phonetically. Below is a glossary of Draconic words that appear in *The Dragon Slayer's Daughter*.

Please note, because so many Draconic words are curses or insults, it can be a rather dangerous language for humans to speak. Please do not use these words without proper training. If you wish to learn Draconic, contact the Alexandra Institute for information on their course, Conversational Draconic.

blarghstra—a bossy, overbearing female dragon; used as an insult
blinch (masc.)/**blinchne** (fem.)—pleasant, fine
czt—of, from
dila—to be (used for all present tense forms, singular and plural: am, is, are)

drunig—today
flenka—eater; one who eats
fragnich—crack, fissure
glavnig—weak; used as an insult
īn—morning
īt—afternoon
klemta—tall
Klemta Fragnich—Mount Somers, New Zealand; literally means tall cracks; refers to the rhyolite bluffs characteristic of the mountain
likneti—one who sparkles, shiny thing
metzi—dirt
metzi flenka—human; literally means dirt eater
ni—my, mine
skobni—faeces, poo, usually refers to faecal material still inside the intestine; used as an insult; *very offensive*; not recommended for use by humans
skrgley—enjoyable, pleasant
skrgleyīn—good morning
skrgleyit—tasty; good for eating; delicious
skrgleyīt—good afternoon (note the similarity to skrgleyit—pronunciation is important in Draconic; if you're not careful a greeting can turn into an invitation for lunch)
toma—name
tsitsi—small
tsitsi likneti—gold fairy dragon; literally means small sparkler
vilknit—weather
zhe—the

Te Reo Māori

New Zealand has three official languages: English, te reo Māori, and New Zealand Sign Language. Most of the Māori words that appear in The Dragon Slayer's Daughter are familiar to New Zealanders, but may be unknown to other readers. These words are listed below.

kaipatu—killer, slayer
kaipatu tarākona—dragon slayer
māia—bravery, courage, confidence
Pakeha—non-Māori, usually refers to those of European origin
poi—ball on the end of a string; twirled rhythmically, often in pairs, in traditional songs
taniwha—monster, dangerous creature, often lives in water, sometimes acts as a guardian, sometimes harmful
tapu—sacred
tarākona—dragon
tēnā koutou—greetings to more than three people
whānau—extended family

#####

About the Author

Over the course of my career, I have been pleased to call myself an educator, entomologist, heritage interpreter, and an agroforestry extension agent, among other things. Through it all, I have written stories and poetry for my own pleasure. I published my first writing as a child in the 1970s, and used to confound my science teachers with poetry, scribbled at the end of essay questions. Now, after completing several novels, I'm pleased to be able to call myself an author.

My first love was the natural world, and it plays a large part in most of my stories. I currently live in New Zealand and enjoy spending time in the mountains.

Have I encountered dragons, you ask?

Well, you'll just have to visit and discover for yourself.

Discover more of my stories by visiting my website at
https://robinneweiss.com

Acknowledgements

Thank you to all my early readers and reviewers: Ian, Lochlan, Liadan, Angela, Rich, Lauren, Luke, and Mark. Particular thanks must go to Rich, for braving book two of a series without having read book one, and providing the sort of insight only a fresh pair of eyes can.

Thank you also to my te reo consultant, Regan, who told me how to say 'dragon slayer' in te reo Māori (oddly, that term doesn't show up in the Māori/English dictionaries).

Thanks also goes to Belinda for her thorough copy editing, and to Brendon for once again producing an awesome cover for me.

And thank you to everyone who kept asking when the next Dragon Slayer book would come out. This one is for you.

Printed in Great Britain
by Amazon